Mystery
at
Seagrave
Hall

BOOKS BY CLARE CHASE

Murder on the Marshes
Death on the River
Death Comes to Call
Murder in the Fens
Mystery on Hidden Lane
Mystery at Apple Tree Cottage

students. Eve had managed to sneak in at the back of the school hall to listen. The teenagers had been just as noisy and restless as usual when they'd entered the room, but the diver had them spellbound in seconds. The nonchalant way she'd talked about her life-threatening exploits had stunned even the most cocksure youths into silence. It was a rare treat. But it was the diver's philosophy on life that had hit home for Eve, so soon after her husband had walked out on her. Nye's talk of independence and the value of ploughing your own furrow made Eve feel strong. The lecture had left her full of questions. What made the diver so resilient? And how had her life unfolded, leading her into such a niche and dangerous profession?

The fete might be a chance to find out more, but for now, Eve needed to focus on practicalities. She was at the hall because of her current salary-boosting second job. She worked part-time for the village teashop, Monty's, which was providing cakes for the fete. Viv, her close friend and Monty's owner, had employed her for her organisational skills and level-headed approach. Without them, things sometimes went awry…

The Seagraves had ruled that everyone should set their stalls up the day before the fete, which pleased Eve. It was a battle to get Viv to prepare an hour in advance, let alone anything more. For once, she hadn't been the one reading the riot act.

They were in the process of sorting out their pitch. Eve headed off to fetch a folding table from an outhouse. She was struggling back with it, suppressing a shudder at the feeling of sticky chipped Formica under her fingers, when she heard a text come in. She set the table down for a moment on the gravel, balancing it on its edge, then held it steady with one hand while she pulled her phone out of her jeans pocket with her other. Her twins were young adults now, but she still had the urge to look straight away. Just in case.

The screen glowed. Ian, their father and her ex-husband. What did he want? She shifted the phone awkwardly so she could key in her passcode.

Just wanted to let you know I might be hard to reach for a couple of weeks. Sonia and I are off on a cruise of the Mediterranean and you of all people know how patchy mobile coverage can be. I know you've experienced it, up there in the sticks!

A second text came in while she was still reading the first.

You should get a break sometime. I'm sure it would do you good.

He'd included a link to a singles vacation website before signing off.

She pressed the button to shut the screen down. *What?* He'd never taken her on a cruise. And she didn't need him to tell her where he was, like she was a child who couldn't cope on her own.

She tried to shove her mobile back into her pocket but missed, and it fell to the ground. She was just attempting to reach it, still grappling with the large folded table, when Verity Nye appeared, picked it up and returned it to her, enabling her to right herself.

'Thank you so much!'

Verity smiled. 'No problem.' Her shrewd gaze focused on Eve's face. 'Are you okay?'

Eve must have looked more annoyed than she'd realised. She took a deep breath. 'Fine, fine! This is all great.' She nodded at the stalls. 'Just an annoying text from my ex.' Heck, where had that come from? It was the first time Eve had actually spoken to Verity. She never normally confided in strangers, but seeing her talk at the school had created a link, while the accident with the mobile made the situation informal. And then there was her adrenaline-fuelled drive to offload…

'Ah!' Verity laughed, and raised her eyes to heaven. 'He's oversharing?'

She was perceptive. 'He wanted to let me know he's taking his new girlfriend on a cruise. He even included a link to a singles vacation website, in case I was feeling left out.'

'Oh my! Well, at least his message proves you're better off without him.'

Eve laughed now and felt her shoulders relax as she finally managed to get her phone back inside her pocket. 'You said it.'

Verity looked up, towards where her fiancé, Rupert Seagrave, was standing. 'If you want to find yourself an upgrade, I'm sure there's someone out there waiting for you who's way more deserving than cruise-guy. But none of us *needs* anyone else. We're all happiest when we're in control of our lives, even if that happens to be alongside another person.'

'I believe you!' Before she knew it, Eve had told Verity Nye about listening to her talk at her old school, and how her rallying cry in favour of independence had come just at the right time.

Verity's smile was instant and natural. 'I'm glad it resonated with you. It's a harsh lesson I learned young, but it's been incredibly freeing.' She paused, and her brow furrowed as she moved her weight onto one hip. After another moment, she leaned a little closer to Eve. 'Do you know the Seagrave family?'

'Not really, I'm afraid.'

'Ah well, not to worry.' Verity shook her head slowly. 'I was after a fresh perspective. They don't get along amongst themselves, but oh boy, there's a closing of ranks in certain quarters when someone they hate more comes along. Talk about knives out!' But then she laughed. 'I don't think they realise how strong I am.'

The situation sounded uncomfortable; Eve assumed there must be opposition to Verity and Rupert's marriage, and she wondered why. A simple personality clash, or something more complicated?

She stumbled back to Monty's pitch, glancing over the busy grounds. A moment later, she was unfolding the rickety table on the patch of grass she and Viv had been allocated. She confessed to her friend about opening up to Verity.

'Blimey,' Viv said. 'Not a bit like you. I'm sure you took way longer than that to fill *me* in on Ian.'

Eve frowned. 'I told you quite quickly.'

'Not within a sentence or two of us meeting.'

'No. Well, it was odd. She was easy to talk to. You are too, though, of course,' she said in response to Viv's look.

'Sounds as though she was a bit preachy. Preachier than I would have been.'

'It didn't come across that way. Sorry to disappoint.' Eve hid a smile.

'Do you think the independence thing is part of her mantra, and she was repeating it to herself before she ties the knot with Rupert?'

'Maybe. She was looking in his direction.' It made Eve wonder about the background. Was Rupert her ideal partner? One who let her go her own way? Or was he trying to have more influence on Verity's life than she wanted? Eve put herself in Rupert's shoes: it couldn't be easy, watching Verity travel halfway round the world to risk her life. Their wedding was only a couple of weeks off; if either of them was going to have a wobble, now was the time. And if the family were being difficult that would add to the strain.

Eve looked up and saw the cave diver had paused to speak with the chief executive of Wide Blue Yonder. She couldn't hear their words, but Verity was shaking her head vehemently, after which she jabbed her finger towards the side door to the hall. The charity manager put her hands on her hips, and Verity stopped abruptly and leaned in, putting a hand on her shoulder. They exchanged a few more words, and the other woman seemed to relax. But when

Verity turned away, and strode across the lawn, the manager stared after her for a long time.

'I think I've caught your people-watching compulsion,' said Viv, who was wrestling with a second table they'd fetched from the outhouse earlier. 'But it's partly because I find it impossible to take my eyes off Ms Nye. It's a relief to see she puts some people's backs up, otherwise she'd be that bit too perfect, what with her job and her looks.'

'Maybe she's an acquired taste.' Eve had liked her for being upfront. 'She's quick to put her point of view. I guess she has to be assertive and decisive in her profession.' She couldn't imagine wanting to go cave diving. From what she'd read, the mortality rate sounded way too high and she'd get claustrophobic anyway. Then, if things went wrong, you had to act calmly and quickly if you wanted to survive. Eve was measured, but she liked to have time to plan, not to have events thrust upon her.

'She's so stunningly attractive,' Viv said, still looking in the direction Verity had gone. 'I rather resent that anyone should have quite so much going for them. I presume she and Rupert will inherit this place.' She glanced up at the hall. 'He must have had everything on a plate too.'

'Verity's not from a privileged background.' Eve had researched her after her talk at the school, then dug further when she knew their paths were likely to cross again. 'And even people born into money can face challenges.' Thoughts of the Seagrave family dynamics filled her head again.

Viv gave a deliberate sigh. 'If you say so. I know, I know – get the facts first, make judgements later.' She grinned. 'But guessing and making sweeping statements is so much more fun.' She peered at the equipment they'd been given. 'This is going to be a laugh. Two tables of entirely different heights, both wobbly and – quite honestly – disgusting.' Her bobbed hair (sea green this season) swung forward as she bent to examine a mark which looked like solidified jam, featuring the odd bit of fossilised mould.

'Don't worry. I've brought what we need.' Eve reached for a box next to her bag and took out cloths, scourers and an antibacterial cleaner.

'You're a marvel, you know that? A weird one, obviously, but still a marvel. Did you predict that the Seagraves' kit would be a health hazard?'

'I guessed they might have equipment that's only used once a year.' Eve liked to be prepared. She spent a lot of time anticipating stuff and she couldn't help getting a tiny buzz out of Viv's wide-eyed look of appreciation.

As she worked on her sticky table, she surveyed her surroundings.

Viv was looking up at the cedar tree above them, its dark cooling branches stretched out over their heads. The canopy gave some welcome relief from the heat of the day and made their space fragrant – a mix of the resin and wood that reminded Eve of the sharp pencils she'd treasured when she was in school. She still liked them now: the satisfyingly precise dark marks they made on a brand-new pad of paper.

'I'm glad we managed to nab this patch of shade,' Viv said, pulling her out of her thoughts.

'I'm not sure everyone is so pleased.' Eve nodded at Saxford's village storekeeper, who had just tripped past in teetering high-heeled shoes. She'd tutted as she'd scooped up the crystal ball she'd left by the side of her emerald green tent, which was now in full sun.

'She's got no reason to complain!' Viv said. 'She's got the protection of her canvas, and our cakes will get a lot stickier than her tarot cards. You know, I don't think two tables are going to be enough.'

'I'll nip back to the outhouse and see if I can find a third.'

'Want me to do it?'

'It's fine.' Eve enjoyed weaving through the villagers making their preparations, dipping in and out of a series of cameos.

She was just on her way back from the outhouse again, moving awkwardly with the final table, which was larger than the first two, when she passed the main marquee. She heard Verity Nye's voice coming from inside.

'You should stop following her around; you're making it too obvious.'

'It's necessary. To protect our interests.' A man's voice, deep, urgent and low.

'Oh for heaven's sake!' Verity's voice rang out, louder suddenly.

The next few words were inaudible, but then the man's voice came clear again.

'Verity, let's talk.' His tone had changed. It was almost pleading. 'We can still make this work!'

Eve heard the adventurer sigh – a mix of fury and upset. 'We've said all there is to say. Of course we can't "make this work". How can you not see that? It's over.'

Eve couldn't hear his words in response but his tone was angry.

She lugged the table awkwardly past. She could hear movement inside now. One of them must be about to exit the tent. The edge of the folded table knocked painfully against her shin as she tried to pick up speed.

She kept her back to the marquee's entrance for a moment but then risked glancing over her shoulder. Verity had appeared in the doorway. She looked upset and angry. Behind her was the medic from her expedition team – Eve recognised him from Verity's presentation slides and her own more recent research. Pete Smith – that was his name. Blond and tanned, tall and handsome. He followed Verity to the entrance of the marquee, staring after her, his jaw taut, eyes narrow. The pair were to be the stars of the event the following day, showing off the equipment for their next cave dive in China, giving talks and presenting prizes.

Their words echoed in Eve's head. Who had Pete been following around? And what about the last part of their conversation? Were he and Verity lovers? If so, it sounded as though Pete was having trouble letting go – and that Verity had only just called time on the affair, ahead of her marriage. Eve felt a stab of disappointment in the woman. She'd struck her as the sort to play fair.

CHAPTER TWO

Eve sighed as she returned to Monty's pitch on the lawn behind Seagrave Hall. It was always fascinating to see the secrets people kept, but Verity Nye's conversation with her medic had left her feeling conflicted. She'd felt an immediate connection with the woman when they'd finally spoken; something had told her they might be on the same wavelength. But now, she wasn't so sure.

Other villagers were hard at work all around her. The vicar had rigged up a splat-the-rat game from some old piping and was now in the process of balancing coconuts on high stands, ready for players to try to knock them off with cricket balls the following day.

One of Eve's neighbours was setting out a junk gamelan on a large purple rug. She was a potter by trade, but Eve knew she was fond of music too. The wavering sound of her violin often wafted out onto Haunted Lane on the summer breeze. She'd laid out a series of terracotta plant pots and a selection of metal lids in size order and was now roping lengths of tubing in place. This last arrangement looked like a supersize xylophone made from drainpipes. After a moment she sat back on her haunches to check her work, then picked up a pair of wooden sticks and tentatively began to hit the various items in front of her. It was surprisingly melodious but that didn't stop her blushing when she looked up and caught Eve watching her. The vicar was glancing over too. Eve could tell he wanted a go. She doubted he'd resist for long.

Movement caught her eye. 'Did I just see a customer going into the fortune-telling tent?' That seemed a bit keen, given the fete itself didn't start until the following day.

'I overheard some of the key players being invited in,' Viv said, lowering her voice. 'The pretext was the need to practise before tomorrow, but I suspect fear of missing out was the real driver.'

With the best will in the world, it sounded likely. Some of the people with free time that day were celebrities, like Verity, who'd appeared on TV. Based on past performance, Moira the storekeeper would want to lure them in so that she could tell everyone in the village she'd spoken with them.

'Besides,' Viv said, 'you know how it is with fortune telling. People pretend not to believe in it, but really, deep down, everyone's just a little bit susceptible.'

Eve folded her arms. 'I'm not.'

'Really? Not even if life was a bit rough and you were after a hint that there was something better just around the corner?' Viv caught her look. 'Ah. No. Well, all right then. Everyone apart from you. I should have known. Don't you ever find being one hundred per cent rational takes the fun out of life?'

'No.'

The sound of the vicar putting the junk gamelan to the test interrupted their conversation. In a moment, he was singing too – a reverberating baritone that brought Moira out of her tent momentarily, her lips pursed. At some point she'd changed into her costume: an alarmingly tight multi-layered red dress with a lace-up bodice. Eve peered in to see who she'd got with her.

'I think it's Rupert's cousin,' Viv hissed. 'Cora Seagrave. She lives on the estate. The Seagraves adopted her when her parents were killed in a plane crash.'

A moment later, Eve's second neighbour from Haunted Lane appeared with her camera. Photography was her profession and she'd been asked to record the event, from the preparation through to the closing speeches the following day.

'This is a photo opportunity not to be missed,' she said, grinning. Her thick plait of grey hair fell forward over her shoulder as she aimed her lens at the potter and the vicar, who were both intent on playing the gamelan now. The former still had a slightly self-conscious air, the latter, not so much.

Eve turned her attention back to the three tables at her and Viv's disposal. Matching tablecloths from Monty's would make them look smarter. They were deep sea green, tying in with Viv's current hair colour. The two women pinned the linen in place, added miniature bunting along the front of the tables, then decorated the legs with coordinating ribbons.

'We can put them in size order,' said Viv, 'and then lay the cakes out by type tomorrow. Maybe it'll look as though the whole thing was planned.'

'Sounds good.' Eve was writing a list. 'The citrus cakes, followed by the berries, and then onto the coffee and chocolate?' She'd made sure they'd only have cakes with sticky chocolate centres, despite some protests from Viv. Anything with chocolate on top would be a disaster in the heat.

Once they'd finished, they went to help the gang from the Cross Keys pub finish erecting their stall to the side of the hall. As they approached, Eve saw one of the two brothers who ran the place sample some beer from the keg. He caught Eve's eye and grinned broadly.

'Just checking it's settled.'

At that moment, his wife arrived, a fiery look in her eye, and he shoved his half-empty glass behind a box full of crisps.

Eve went to help them lug food into the house, ready to store until the following day's barbecue. As they trudged to and fro in companionable silence, she heard Verity again, out on the back lawn.

'Oh, nonsense! I'll get it!' She was laughing, but Eve could hear a note of exasperation in her voice.

She was talking to a blonde woman Eve recognised as the Seagraves' estate manager.

'Wouldn't you like a hand? It's pretty unwieldy.'

'I *think* I can cope,' Verity said. 'There's nothing like swimming in strong currents for upper-body strength.' But then she smiled. 'Thanks all the same.'

The blonde woman turned away. Eve didn't like people fussing either, though she would have hidden her irritation better. Maybe that just made her two-faced.

Once Eve had helped the pub gang, she wandered back towards her and Viv's stall, past Mrs Walker, who was down to run the tombola. Her three-year-old son had clambered up onto a stool. Teetering precariously, he pulled out a toy from the bottom of the display she'd carefully set up, causing the prizes to come tumbling down.

Mrs Walker ran her hands through her thick wiry hair. 'Dy-lan!'

Eve and Viv were going to put out picnic rugs near their stall the following day, so people could sit and eat their cakes if they wanted. They had a few folding canvas chairs too. Eve had taken them out of their van, but she'd leave them under wraps for now. She didn't want them covered in dew.

The vicar had moved on to help set up a play area beyond the fortune-telling tent. The sound of the gamelan on one side and free-range youngsters on the other would test Moira's patience… Eve arrived to help just as he crawled inside one of the tepees he'd put up.

'Are you all right in there?'

'Perfectly, thank you, Eve. I'm just remembering what it was like to be seven. I find I miss it occasionally.' His good-humoured face, topped by its thick thatch of grey hair, appeared in the doorway.

She grinned.

'Imagine having the run of a place like this as a child,' he said.

'I know! The games you could have...' She looked up over the top of the tepee, taking in the grounds and the hall again. She was vaguely aware of movement at one of the third-floor windows.

It was at that precise moment, as Eve's focus adjusted and sharpened, that she saw the figure in the window tip forward, their body bulky. Swathed in something? The scream rang out across the grounds. She remembered it afterwards: the way such an innocent scene was interrupted by something so horrific. She was conscious of a sickening thud, almost in the same moment as the shriek. She couldn't see where the person had fallen. There were too many stalls and people in the way. Nausea rose in her stomach and the vicar's robust face went white and slack.

Eve felt as though she was in a daze as she stood up straight and looked towards the hall. People were running over the lawn, between the tents, marquees and stalls. Eve and the vicar followed them, tripping over guy ropes and bumping into others headed in the same direction.

'What happened?'

Viv had appeared next to her. 'Verity.' She swallowed and then turned away from the scene in front of them for a moment as Eve moved forward. 'It's horrible. Horrible. She must have gone inside to fetch that marquee or gazebo or whatever it is that's under her. And then she fell from one of the windows. But how?'

The canvas Viv had referred to had partially cushioned Verity's landing, but not where it counted. Her head and torso had hit the flagstones directly. Bile rose in Eve's throat.

People had slowed as they reached the spot where the adventurer had fallen, as though they couldn't bring themselves to get any nearer. In another moment, Verity's team medic, Pete Smith arrived.

'Get back everyone!' he shouted, dropping down next to where his colleague lay, deathly still.

He was crouched between Verity's body and Eve now, blocking her view. At last, he stood up again, but he was shaking his head. 'Stay back. Someone call the emergency services. But tell them there's nothing they can do for her now.' His hand went to the back of his neck and he closed his eyes for a second.

After a moment of complete silence, everyone spoke at once.

'… throw the tent out of the window, rather than carry it down the stairs…'

'… very heavy canvas. The old-fashioned sort…'

More people gathered and the noise increased.

'… never liked that type of window. They look so elegant and tall, but they're too low. Dangerous. I'd be frightened to live here if I had children…'

'… must have got a foot tangled as she hurled it out. She leaned too far…'

And then one small, high-pitched voice rose above the others.

'Someone gave her a big push.' It was little Dylan Walker.

CHAPTER THREE

Eve was one of several people in earshot when Dylan called out. Another was Lady Belinda Seagrave, owner of the hall, Rupert's mother. Her sharp gaze met Mrs Walker's.

'Dylan, do stop making things up.' Mrs Walker had gone puce. She bent to take his hands in hers. 'There's been a terrible accident. Inventing things is only okay when you're playing, or at story time at nursery. Otherwise, it's lying. I have told you.'

Lady Seagrave looked on, her chin held high, eyes flinty, arms tightly folded.

Next to Viv, the Seagraves' blonde estate manager was also watching. Eve had heard her catch her breath when Dylan spoke. Her eyes were scared.

'I'm not lying! There was a face!' Dylan looked close to tears. He scuffed the toe of his shoe on the gravel that bordered the house and stared down at the ground.

When the estate manager spoke, her voice was shaky. 'I was looking up too. Something must have caught my attention. A sound maybe.'

'And did you see anything, Tilly?' Lady Seagrave's voice was clipped and controlled in the quiet that had descended on the lawn.

Of course, that was her name. Tilly Cotton. Eve remembered now. She looked too young to run the estate.

'No. No, I don't think so. Verity filled the window.' Her hands were trembling. 'I offered to help her carry the tent down, but she said she could manage.'

Lady Seagrave gripped Tilly Cotton's shoulder with a firm hand. 'It's not your fault. Verity was nothing if not independent. We all know that.' Her tone was hard and disapproving. She'd been one of the family members who'd closed ranks against Verity, Eve guessed.

It was only at that moment that Eve noticed the son of the house, Rupert Seagrave, had appeared. Verity's fiancé. He was standing to one side of the dead woman, his red-gold hair clutched in his hands, knuckles white, a look of anguish on his face. Eve could hardly bear to watch him. He sounded as though he was fighting for breath. When he moved towards Verity, Pete Smith the medic stepped forward again, coming between them. Rupert shoved him away and knelt by her body, his hair flopping over his forehead.

A moment later, Eve heard a syrupy, playful voice call out 'What's all the fuss about?' and a pretty young woman with a heart-shaped face and a mischievous twinkle in her eye appeared from round the side of the house.

'That's Cora?' Eve whispered to Viv. 'The Seagrave's ward? Rupert's cousin?'

Viv nodded as they watched realisation creep across Cora's face. Her eyes opened wide, and she put her hand over her mouth. A moment later she rushed towards Rupert and crouched down in front of him, close to Verity's body.

'Rupe! Oh my goodness. I can't believe—'

'This is all your fault!' He spat the words out.

Someone close to Eve gasped. His tone had shocked her too. His fists were clenched, his lips white.

Cora leaped to her feet again, moving back as she did so. 'What on earth do you mean?' Her jaw hung open. It was weird. For a moment she coloured, as though he'd slapped her, but then a look of concentration washed over her face, as though she was processing some bit of information.

Rupert paused for a long moment, as though he was struggling to control himself. 'You told Verity it was easier to chuck stuff out of the window, rather than carry it down the stairs. Yesterday, when she went to fetch the rugs from the attic.'

It took Cora a second to reply too, as though her focus had shifted. 'Well, it is easier!' she said at last. For a moment, she sounded like a child who'd been unfairly told off: petulant, her lower lip sticking out. Then she took a deep breath and edged towards her cousin again. His look told her not to come any nearer. 'The staircases in the hall are a death trap; you know that! The sweeping stone monstrosity is hard if you fall and the back ones are narrow. I've always thrown things out of the window. It never occurred to me that it would cause any danger.'

'I don't believe you were genuinely trying to help. It was the only civil thing you said to her while she was here.'

'She hated me!'

'You treated her like dirt!'

Eve had conducted interviews where relatives blamed themselves or others for the death of a loved one. Sometimes they contacted her after they'd calmed down, to ask her to forget what they'd said. But instinct told her there was something more going on here. Rupert couldn't really blame Cora for the advice she'd given. What else had she done?

'Quieten down, the pair of you!' Lady Seagrave was moving towards them at speed, stepping automatically round the tent that still lay under Verity's legs. Her focus was entirely on her son and his cousin; it was clear where her priorities lay. Their angry words would be the talk of Saxford St Peter for weeks to come.

Rupert was crying. Cora tried to approach him again, a determined look in her eye, but Lady Seagrave put a hand on her arm and gave a quick shake of her head.

At that moment, Sir Percival Seagrave appeared, his eyes on Verity. 'I was round at the stables,' he said. 'It's true then?' He bent towards the dead woman. There were tears in his eyes, Eve noted.

She only had a moment to focus on him before a team of paramedics dashed round the side of the hall. Within seconds they were attempting resuscitation, though Eve knew Pete must have already tried. She watched as they shook their heads at last, and made the decision to stop. After that they proceeded more slowly, moving the crowds of villagers back, one of them speaking quietly with Rupert. Belinda Seagrave's focus was elsewhere. Following the direction of her gaze, Eve saw two uniformed police officers, a man and a woman, had also arrived, and were walking swiftly towards the scene of the accident.

'What's going on?' Her tone was imperious.

'Please accept our deepest condolences, Lady Seagrave,' the male officer said.

Rupert turned his tear-stained face towards his mother. 'The paramedics were just explaining that police officers always attend if there's an unexpected death.'

Belinda Seagrave's frown deepened.

'It's our job to establish the circumstances, ma'am,' the woman added. 'Once that's done, we're able to give the ambulance team permission to continue with their work.'

'I see.' She stepped towards them. 'Allow me to tell you exactly what happened.'

In a moment, she'd explained that Verity was fetching a heavy tent from the attic and had evidently decided to save time and effort by throwing it from the third-floor window. 'If you grow up in a place like this, you're well aware of the low windows and sheer height of the building. Verity came from a very different walk of life; she can't have taken the care that's needed when you lean out.'

The officers exchanged a glance.

'Did anyone see her fall?'

At that moment, Dylan Walker managed to wriggle free of his mother's grasp and bounded towards the officer and Lady Seagrave. 'I saw a face at the window. The person who pushed her!'

'Dylan!' Mrs Walker was after him. Eve saw a look pass between her and Belinda Seagrave. 'Don't be silly!' She gave the policeman an apologetic grimace. 'He's always making up stories. Tilly Cotton was looking up at the window too, weren't you, Tilly? And you didn't see anyone.' Eve could tell by her tone that she really wanted to believe that version of events.

The estate manager hesitated. 'Verity filled the window and in the sunlight everything behind her looked dark and shadowy.'

Eve didn't miss Tilly Cotton's twisting hands.

'Did anyone else see Ms Nye fall?' the female officer asked.

Eve put up her hand. 'Yes, but I'm afraid I was way down the garden. I couldn't even tell who it was until I got closer. I wasn't near enough to see if there was anyone else at the window.'

The man nodded. 'Which room did she fall from?'

Everyone looked up at the building.

'From mine.' The chief executive of Wide Blue Yonder spoke quietly, but it wasn't a sign of control. Her voice shook.

'Your name please?'

'Jade. Jade Piper.' She explained her role.

The officer nodded, a frown tracing its way across his brow. 'Any idea why Ms Nye would choose your room, or drop the tent out of that particular window?'

Jade Piper shook her head.

There was an awkward pause. 'You didn't invite her to use your room?' the man said at last. 'Or accompany her?'

'No.'

'Are all the bedrooms on this side of the house occupied?'

Lady Seagrave's no-nonsense gaze met his. 'Not at all. We have a large number of bedrooms here. Several are still empty. Verity could have used any of them.'

Jade Piper flushed.

Belinda had moved closer to the police officers now. She was saying something, but Eve couldn't catch her words.

'Of course,' the female officer said, 'we do see that. I've got little ones and they tell tall stories, too.'

Lady Seagrave gave a brief smile that didn't reach her eyes.

'All the same,' the officer continued, 'under circumstances like this we have a standard procedure we have to follow. I'm sure you understand.'

'Standard procedure?'

'A local detective inspector will need to come out.' The woman smiled sympathetically. 'We'll get them here as quickly as possible. In the meantime, I suggest we take everyone's contact details, just in case we need to speak to anyone again.'

Belinda Seagrave's face was like thunder as the policewoman and her male colleague marshalled the family and villagers round the side of the hall, well away from Verity Nye's body. Within moments they'd organised the visitors into two queues, ready to note down their names and addresses.

As Eve waited in line, she tried to come to terms with what had happened. Thoughts of Verity as she'd stood giving her talk to a roomful of unruly teens filled her mind – overlaid by the sight of her broken body on the flagstones under the dark windows of Seagrave Hall. It was unthinkable that such a force of nature was no more. Could someone have robbed her of her future?

She'd had secrets – that seemed certain. And she'd spoken of the way bits of the family had closed ranks against her. 'Talk about knives out,' she'd said. Of course, she probably hadn't meant it seriously. But the words, coupled with clear signs that both Belinda and Cora Seagrave had disliked her, hovered uneasily in her head. And what about Dylan Walker? He might be young, but he was insistent. Would anyone interview him? And if they did, would they listen?

She and Viv gave their details to the female officer and were told to wait just a little longer, until the detective arrived. After the villagers had been dismissed, back to their pitches, the uniformed officers erected a makeshift barrier to protect Verity's privacy – what little the poor woman had left of it.

Eve was glad the detective had been called in. She was keeping an open mind, but after what she'd observed that morning, their presence seemed warranted. She wondered who was on duty, hoping it wasn't—

'Oh look,' Viv said to Eve, glancing up the lawn from where they were waiting under the cedar tree, 'it's your friend DI Palmer.'

Eve took a deep breath. She'd had several run-ins with the man when she'd first come to Saxford. She'd been writing the obituary of a murder victim and inevitably she'd gathered information that was relevant to the case. She'd made the mistake of providing evidence that was more useful than what he'd dug up. Meanwhile, Palmer had jumped to conclusions, pursued the wrong suspects, and been irked whenever Eve passed on her findings.

She had a nasty feeling they'd clash on this occasion too – because Eve couldn't help thinking that Verity would be a fascinating person to write about. But there was more to it than that – covering her life story would allow Eve to find out more about her contacts, and who might have wanted her dead. Maybe her fall had been accidental, but doubts crowded Eve's mind. If the police opened an investigation and Eve wrote the obituary, she and Palmer would end up interviewing the same people; it was a recipe for friction.

The detective inspector greeted the Seagraves with plenty of sombre nods, then turned and conversed with the female uniformed officer for a few minutes.

At last, he motioned for the crowds of villagers to gather around him. Sir Percival and Lady Seagrave stood nearby, next to their son. Rupert's face was pale and crumpled. His mother's expression, which had been like granite when Palmer arrived, had relaxed just a little. Cora was behind her, talking earnestly to the male uniformed officer, a good-looking young guy with thick dark hair.

'Thank you for waiting and giving over your contact details,' Palmer said, when everyone was in earshot. 'I have access to the notes my colleagues took when they spoke to you earlier, and understand that the two adults who were watching as Ms Nye fell saw no one behind her at the window.'

Eve felt obliged to raise her hand and his withering look rested on her.

'Ah, Ms Mallow. I noted you were one of the two people. How fortunate that you happened to be looking in the right direction.'

He sounded as though he doubted her word. He probably thought she was after attention – he seemed to think that was what drove her. In fact, Eve preferred to shine a spotlight on other people. She glanced up and caught Lady Seagrave's look, cold and wary.

'To clarify,' Eve said, 'I was too far away to tell whether or not anyone was with Ms Nye, up at the—'

'Yes, yes,' he said. 'It's all in the notes.'

But it wasn't what he'd implied.

'The fact of the matter is that the only person claiming to have seen someone push Ms Nye is three years old and prone to telling untruths.' He glanced at Mrs Walker. 'As three-year-olds often are, of course.'

The woman blushed. 'That's right, Detective Inspector.'

'My colleagues' actions were conscientious,' his tone made it sound like a criticism, 'but there's no reason to detain you any further. Constable Bygrave will contact the coroner's office and make further necessary arrangements now. I believe the family would be grateful if you could leave your stalls standing today, to give them some privacy in the immediate aftermath of this terrible tragedy.' He glanced at Lady Seagrave, who stepped forward.

'The fete will be cancelled, of course. Tilly will be on hand tomorrow morning to help you dismantle your pitches.' She nodded at the estate manager.

A mature woman who looked faintly familiar had put a hand on Rupert's arm and was guiding him towards the house.

'Terrible bad luck,' Palmer said to Sir Percival. 'My sincere condolences.'

So Eve wouldn't clash with the detective inspector after all. He had no intention of taking the matter further. She knew he hated effort and complications, especially on a hot day, and most fervently when it involved the well-to-do of the neighbourhood. It made her all the more determined to pitch for the job of writing Verity's obituary. Could he really just walk away when a vibrant young woman had lost her life? Be so certain that it was a simple accident? Eve couldn't.

She and Viv went to fetch their bags and then walked slowly back up the grass, skirting round the stalls, next to other villagers deep in conversation.

As they approached the hall, making their way towards their van round the front, Eve passed Cora Seagrave. It was pure luck that she had to pause, due to someone just ahead of her stumbling over a discarded mallet. She cast her gaze to one side and caught Cora's look. The woman's eyes were turned towards where Verity Nye lay, behind the screen. Eve saw her face relax, like an actor whose performance is at an end, and then a smile spread across her lips.

CHAPTER FOUR

Viv drove them back to Saxford and dropped Eve off by the village green. A minute later, she'd returned to the cool sanctuary of her seventeenth-century thatched home, Elizabeth's Cottage. It was her haven, sitting on a lane that led down to tranquil marshes and the estuary – a place where she could hear the call of curlews from her bedroom window, and smell the sweet honeysuckle twined round the hedgerows outside.

Gus, her wire-haired dachshund, bounded through the house to join her the moment she reached the front door. She bent to give him a hug, which was met with a startled look. The embrace wasn't unusual, but the firmness might have been. She was so pleased to see him and anchor herself back in normality.

'Bit of a day, Gus.' She walked through to the kitchen, which was farmhouse in style but on a small scale, and refilled his water bowl. 'Looks like last night wasn't a coincidence after all.'

He watched her with his head on one side, eyes concerned. They'd both slept badly and woken to what seemed like the sound of thudding feet, out in the lane. Eve's cottage had a turbulent history. It was named after Elizabeth, who'd lived there in the 1720s and hidden a servant boy to save him from the gallows. He'd stolen a loaf of bread from his employers to feed his starving siblings. According to legend, he'd crouched, shivering and terrified, under her house, while a hue and cry ran up and down the tiny road searching for him. It was called Haunted Lane for the thudding feet you were meant to hear late at night: echoes of the men who'd been sent to hunt him down. The villagers said hearing the footfalls signified danger.

Eve didn't believe in ghosts, but she and Gus had dreamed up the thudding feet before, and each time they'd heralded trouble for the village. She'd tried to explain them away, citing everything from indigestion to her uneasiness working its way into her dreams. But it was hard to rationalise the experience this time. She didn't even know the Seagraves; what could have caused her to worry subconsciously about her visit to the hall?

That evening, Eve and Viv sat at the rear of the Cross Keys, at a wooden table that overlooked the pub's sweeping lawn, which ran down towards the River Sax. They'd both wanted a chance to talk through their shock but had fallen silent now. Eve's eyes were on the brackish estuarial water. The tide was coming in and the wading birds were being forced further and further up the mudflats to feed. Their eerie, melancholy cries echoed the events of the day. The conversation she'd had with Verity Nye, and the words she'd overheard in the tent, went round and round in Eve's head.

'I can't stop hearing her hit the ground,' Viv said.

Eve had pulled on a thin cardigan, despite the warmth of the evening. She hadn't stopped shivering since she'd arrived back in Saxford. It had taken a while for the reaction to kick in. Over at Seagrave Hall she'd felt oddly numb and separate. Everything going on around her seemed unusually vivid, in heightened colours. People's whispered comments echoed loudly in her ears. Now everything was muted, and a tugging sadness pulled at her insides. If only they could turn back the clock and alter the terrible course of events.

Gus seemed to have picked up on her mood. Both he and the pub's schnauzer, Hetty, had quietened down quickly after Eve had entered the Cross Keys' garden. Their brief rough-and-tumble felt as though it had been for the sake of form. Now, they were lying down together like an old married couple.

At that moment Jo Falconer – one of the three co-owners of the pub – approached their table with two plates laden with food.

'This is what you need.' Her voice was as robust as usual, though a little gruff.

Jo was the Cross Keys' head chef and, like Viv, she believed good food, honestly prepared, could cure most ills. She'd happened to be in the bar when they'd turned up and had told them what to have: chicken, bacon and leek pie with new potatoes. They both felt so shell-shocked they'd just thanked her and agreed. She'd told them what to drink too. They each had a glass of Beaujolais in front of them. ('No good going for a white after a day like this,' Jo had said, as though it was obvious.)

'Thanks, Jo.' Viv looked up at their hostess. 'You'll head back to Seagrave Hall tomorrow, I guess, to pick up your stuff?'

'Toby'll go with one of the bar staff while Matt and I carry on here.' Matt was her husband, Toby his brother.

'What about you?' Jo looked at Viv.

'I'm going to stay at Monty's and sell the cakes we would have taken to the fete. We'll donate the proceeds to Wide Blue Yonder in Verity's memory. Eve's going back to the hall.'

'I'd have to anyway,' Eve said. 'I need to ask Rupert Seagrave if he'll speak with me.'

Jo's eyes were sharp and interested. 'You'll be writing Ms Nye's obituary?'

'That's right. *Icon* magazine have commissioned me.' She'd called them when she'd arrived home, knowing someone else would offer to do the job if she didn't get her pitch in quickly.

'Should be an interesting one,' Jo said darkly.

It was true, and the uneasiness Eve already felt gave her pause. Dylan Walker's words whirled round in her mind. Had Verity really been pushed? She kept replaying what she'd seen herself, from way down the lawn by the play area, but it was no good. She'd been at the wrong angle and simply too distant to know what had happened. But Verity had had complications in her life; people who'd rather her marriage didn't go ahead. And Tilly Cotton's reaction made Eve wonder too. She remembered the way the estate manager's hands had trembled when Lady Seagrave asked if she'd seen anything. Her answer had sounded uncertain: *No. No, I don't think so. Verity filled the window.* The thought sent her insides quivering. Did Tilly know or at least suspect someone had been up in the room with Verity? Had she seen a shadow? Someone's hand on the woman's shoulder? And if so, why hadn't she admitted it?

But even if writing about Verity turned out to be a dangerous job, she was committed to pursuing it. What did she amount to, professionally, if she turned her back? Obituary writing was her career, but investigation seemed like part of her role now too. And the case felt personal, after her conversation with Verity.

'The Seagraves are an odd family,' Jo said, breaking into her thoughts. 'I wonder what they thought of Ms Nye. She and Rupert were due to marry at St Peter's.' She nodded in the vague direction of the church, which was beyond the pub. 'They'll have met with Jim. He might be able to tell you a thing or two.'

'Thank you. I'll ask him.' Eve would appreciate the vicar's input. He was clear-sighted and worldly-wise; kind and thoughtful, but not a pushover.

Jo shook her head and turned back towards the pub building. Just before she walked inside, she glanced at them again over her shoulder. 'Eat up now. I know it's a warm evening, but my food should be enjoyed piping hot.'

Viv raised an eyebrow and Eve was relieved to see the wry look back in her eyes, if only for a moment.

'Your parents-in-law know the Seagraves, don't they?' Viv's husband, Oliver, had died young, but his mom and dad still made their presence felt at Monty's, which had once been his business.

'They're frenemies. My in-laws' estate adjoins theirs. Their manor house is older – as they point out to everyone who visits – but it's smaller too, and of course their land doesn't run down to the beach. Though it is bordered by the main road to Walberswick.' She gave a broad smile. 'And the one-upmanship about the age of the houses doesn't really wash. There have been Seagraves around this area just as long as Montagues. There was an older house on the site of the current hall, but it burned down. The family clung on, rebuilt, and here they are today.' She raised her glass to her lips. 'Jo was right about the Beaujolais. And this food.'

Eve took a sip of her wine too. 'I think I might feel almost human by the time I've finished. Just as well. I need to start thinking about how I'll tackle Verity's obituary.'

'Are you sure you want to go ahead with it? What if she really was pushed?'

'That possibility makes me all the more determined to write about her. Palmer's clearly closed his mind to anything but accidental death. I feel I owe it to Verity to take the work on – to dig for information to check he's right, as well as to do her justice in my piece. I know we only exchanged a few words, but I felt some kind of affinity with her. And it was odd, what she said about the Seagraves.' Eve filled Viv in. 'When she talked about the family closing ranks, I'm assuming she meant Lady Seagrave and Cora. Sir Percival seemed affected by her death – he was in tears.' Had Verity known that something wasn't right – more than just the usual family tensions? Of course, she wasn't your standard bride-to-be if she was only just winding up an affair with Pete Smith.

'Well, take good care until you know what you're dealing with.' Viv sat back in her seat for a moment. 'How do you think Rupert will feel about talking to you? Isn't it hard to approach someone so soon after a sudden death?'

Eve prepared a forkful of pie. 'It's not too bad. People often find talking cathartic. It's an opportunity to pay tribute to someone they loved – or let out some pent-up frustrations if the relationship wasn't so healthy. But I'm sure it'll be harder for him than most. Their marriage was imminent, and she died so young and in such a tragic way. I won't put any pressure on him, of course. I'll just ask gently and see if he's willing.'

Viv swallowed a mouthful of her food and nodded. 'Who else will you want to talk to?'

Eve had already formed a mental list. 'Jade Piper for one.' As the chief executive of Wide Blue Yonder, she'd be invaluable.

'She looked harassed today, didn't she?' Viv said. 'I suppose she must have had to dance to Verity's tune if she wanted to keep her onside.'

It was an interesting dynamic. Jade could probably provide a dual perspective for Eve's obituary. She'd see Verity as an impressive figure who'd likely worked well as a patron, but also have views on a personal level. It was that kind of interview that could give her piece real depth. And there'd been tensions between the pair of them – that day at least. It was something Eve couldn't ignore.

'I felt a bit sorry for her,' Viv said. She was very much on Jade's side. Jade had pushed for local businesses to supply the fete, rather than getting larger caterers from nearby towns to step in. The household names could have afforded more in sponsorship, but supporting Viv's one-woman business fitted with Jade's ethos. Being involved had given them lots of free advertising.

'Yes. She looked stressed. But Verity seemed conciliatory when she realised Jade was losing patience.' Maybe she was the sort who wanted everything done urgently, but then took a step back when it was clear she'd overstepped the mark. Eve remembered the look in

Jade's eye as the adventurer turned away. However hard Verity had tried to make peace, it hadn't quite worked. It would be interesting to know why.

'So Jade was staying over at the hall, evidently,' Viv said. 'I wonder why Verity chose to throw the tent out of her bedroom window.'

Eve did too. 'Perhaps it was just nearest to wherever the tent was kept.' But if it had been her, she'd have chosen one of the unoccupied rooms. It hadn't looked as though Verity and Jade were close enough to wander through each other's quarters casually. Eve might prefer hard facts, but that didn't stop her speculating.

There was a lot more she needed to find out from Jade Piper.

CHAPTER FIVE

The light was fading gradually. To the west of the Cross Keys pub, the sun was low in the sky. The water of the River Sax had turned to gold. In the pub garden, strings of lights that ran along wooden frames had just come on, making the cream umbrella over Eve and Viv's table glow.

Eve loved the Cross Keys as much as she loved the whole village. If there was trouble, something to ruffle the peace and order she so appreciated, there was solace in the familiar surroundings of her adopted home.

'I bumped into Sylvia just after I called *Icon* magazine,' she said. Sylvia was her photographer neighbour, who lived diagonally opposite her on Haunted Lane. 'She's emailed me the pictures she took, to help me pick out the people I might want to speak with.'

'That sounds handy. I lost track, to be honest. Let's have a look.'

Eve pulled her phone from her pocket and glanced surreptitiously over her shoulder. Jo didn't approve of mixing work and technology with her carefully prepared meals, but for Eve, it was the perfect combination. The pleasure of a good meal, combined with food for thought, was second to none.

'Right. So first we have Verity Nye and her contingent.' Sylvia had started with Verity herself. The woman had glanced up as the photograph was taken. Eve's neighbour had captured her dynamism and the spark in her huge dark eyes. She was standing next to the diving gear she and Pete had been going to show people at the fete;

a smile lit her face, apparently an unstoppable reaction to the kit that reminded her of her passion.

'Sylvia's captured her zeal,' Viv said. 'She's a first-rate photographer.'

It was true – the portrait was excellent. It was as though Sylvia had seen into Verity's soul, even though she'd only met her an hour or so before she'd taken the shot. Eve could see why her work was in demand.

'Next, we have Pete Smith, the medic on Verity Nye's diving team. He's accompanied her on expeditions before, and he was down to go again, to their upcoming cave dive in China. He'll certainly be on my list of interviewees to approach.'

He seemed cool and confident in his open-necked white shirt, an easy smile on his lips. Blue eyes, blond hair and tanned.

'Good-looking bloke. Not surprised you want to talk to him!'

Eve gave her friend a look. 'He's got to be twenty years younger than I am and he's way too smooth. Moira's got a massive crush on him though.' She'd heard the storekeeper mention him as they'd waited to give their details to the police. She'd looked rather warm in her fortune-teller's costume.

'Be fair! You can see why!'

Eve put her fork down for a moment and folded her arms. 'I want to interview him because I hope he'll provide a key part of Verity's story. He'll be able to fill me in on how she operated, and what she was like as a leader under pressure.' She switched screens on her phone. 'I found this article about a previous cave dive where something went wrong.' She turned the screen towards Viv. 'One of the team, Ruby Fox, got stuck and they had to rescue her. It sounds as though timing was very tight. Dealing with extreme situations tends to show subjects at their best or worst. She sounds heroic in the coverage. But I think there's a lot more Pete Smith *could* tell me, beyond stories of their adventures.'

Viv's eyes lit up. 'Sounds intriguing.'

Eve recounted the conversation she'd overheard between him and his boss in the main marquee.

'Wow – that raises a few questions.' Viv sipped her Beaujolais, her eyes on the setting sun. 'So Pete Smith was keeping an eye on someone, and being too obvious about it. And he said he was acting for both their sakes.'

Eve nodded. 'And then he seemed to switch tack. He wanted to talk about making things work, but Verity said they'd already gone over that ground. She told him it was over.'

'Pretty suggestive, I'd say. You've got a good memory.'

'I replayed it all in my head while we were cleaning the tables.' And she'd written it all down too, sitting in the quiet of the dining room at Elizabeth's Cottage. She thought of Dylan Walker again. She still didn't know where this was going, but it paid to be thorough, and to keep a grip on information once you had it.

She swiped back to Sylvia's photos again. 'Here's Jade Piper, the charity manager, and that's the last of Verity's party.'

Jade looked polite but constrained: as though she'd been trying to get on with something when she'd been caught on camera. She was rather beautiful: sophisticated, with high cheekbones and rich brown hair, but her eyes looked troubled and she was biting her lip. She'd been wearing a businesslike shirt, open at the neck, and a gold pendant with a red gemstone. Her sunglasses were perched on top of her head.

'Right,' said Viv. 'So, two potential interviewees, Pete and Jade, medic and charity manager. Who have we got next?'

'The Seagrave family.' Eve called up the picture Sylvia had taken of Lady Belinda Seagrave. As well as a firm jaw, she had a dead-looking gaze. Eve had read that signified a lack of empathy; people's eyes normally made constant micromovements in response to what they were feeling – except in those who couldn't feel or process their emotions. She turned the screen so Viv could get a better look.

'Doesn't that photo just sum up her personality?' Viv said with a shiver. It was as though she'd read Eve's mind.

'Sir Percival seemed more human.' She scrolled to Sylvia's photograph of him, which showed a man with a relaxed smile. He looked well fed, well turned out and comfortable in his own skin. Eve guessed he enjoyed life.

'He might be a bit *too* fond of human interaction,' Viv said. 'I heard Jo call him a "giddy old goat" once.' She glanced towards the pub's interior. 'Maybe that's why Belinda always looks so grumpy. I've never been sure what that expression means, but I saw him giving Verity the eye earlier today, and he put an unnecessary arm around Tilly the estate manager's shoulders too. She was remarkably forbearing about it. I can't imagine having to work for someone like that.'

Eve felt mad on behalf of both women, and wondered how Rupert had reacted. The next photograph was of him. The picture showed off his classic good looks – a chiselled jaw and perfectly waved copper-blond hair. His conventionality shone out. He and Verity must have been an interesting mix. Maybe she'd looked to him for stability – a port in a storm when she came home from her death-defying exploits.

And then came Cora: adopted by her uncle and aunt after the tragic death of her parents. Eve remembered the look on Belinda Seagrave's face as the young woman tried to remonstrate with Rupert earlier that day. Her expression had been harsh. Was Cora treated like one of the family, or the cuckoo in the nest? Verity's words had suggested there was discord up at the hall. Sylvia had captured Cora's knowing smile, and the mischievous glint in her eye. She was remarkably pretty, but she looked dangerous too – the sort who could reel people in, and knew it.

Viv grimaced. 'Seeing her is making me relive the moment she arrived on the scene after Verity fell. Blimey, that was awkward.

She seemed so pleased to find herself centre stage when everyone looked at her. And then to watch her face as she realised what had happened.' Viv put her hands up to her cheeks. 'The way she kept trying to justify herself was hell to watch. I mean, I could understand her motives, but it wasn't the moment. There was something childlike about her, don't you think?'

But Eve remembered the way Cora had relaxed later, when she'd thought no one was watching. She didn't buy her as an innocent.

'So, that's the family: Percival, Belinda, Rupert and Cora. Anyone else?' Viv had taken another forkful of pie and was craning forwards.

Eve scrolled on. 'The staff at Seagrave Hall, or at least, the permanent employees. The trouble with Sylvia's portraits is that they make me want to speak with everyone, whether they were involved with Verity or not.' She peered at the first photo.

'So I gather from Sylvia's email that this woman is Ivy Cotton – mom of Tilly the estate manager. She's the housekeeper at Seagrave Hall. I saw her put an arm round Rupert's shoulders and usher him inside, once the police were wrapping everything up. She looks familiar.'

Viv nodded. 'Been with the family forever. I've seen her in the shop before.'

'Ah yes, of course, me too. And maybe at Monty's?'

Viv nodded. 'She's been in. Not often though – she always seems to be in a rush. I don't get the impression she has much time off.'

Eve could believe that, just looking at the photo. She had one of those faces that was kindly, but anxious, her eyebrows a little kinked, her mouth a little pursed, brow gently furrowed. In the photograph she was smiling, looking up from a window she'd been polishing. The smile managed to look sad.

'She was a lot more motherly than Lady Seagrave, when she was dealing with Rupert,' Eve said.

'Belinda doesn't set the bar very high.'

'True. I somehow thought they'd be more open and giving. After all, they're happy to welcome the hoi polloi into their grounds each year.'

Viv's expression was sour. 'I think that's more of a feudal thing, rather than a sign of easy-going generosity. They're very conscious of their place in society. Supporting local causes and patronising the villagers is all part of the package. It goes with having had a presence in the area for so many generations.'

Eve scrolled to the final picture, which was of Tilly Cotton, Ivy's daughter, the youthful estate manager. Sylvia had captured her dashing between stalls. She'd managed to get a sense of her brisk energy and the fact that she belonged. It was clear she'd been checking things over. Her wavy blonde hair, white T-shirt and pale denim dungarees made her look incredibly young, but Eve guessed that was deceptive. If Ivy was her mother, she'd probably be in her late twenties or early thirties.

'What did you think of her reaction, when Dylan Walker said he saw someone push Verity?' Viv said.

It was the element that was hardest to ignore. 'She seemed very uncomfortable. She might not have actually lied, but I think she could imagine Dylan being right. And who might have been up there if he was.'

She thought again of Verity standing opposite her, sympathising over Ian's text – and then of Palmer, obsequious towards the Seagraves, and dismissive of everyone else. She needed to find out more, whatever the dangers.

CHAPTER SIX

The following morning, Eve was at home, halfway down a mug of black coffee, just toast crumbs left on her plate. Thoughts of Verity Nye filled her mind. Her memory of the woman was so vivid; it seemed impossible that she was gone.

A text telling her it was time to book a dental check-up pulled her out of her reverie, and reminded her of Ian's message the day before.

She must have let out some kind of sound at the thought. Gus appeared at her feet, his soulful brown eyes on hers, his head up against her knee. She bent to make a fuss of him. His ecstatic response made her feel a little better.

Why couldn't Ian just butt out? She'd tackled him on it before. He dressed his regular messages up as 'staying in touch', 'keeping things amicable' and 'maintaining good lines of communication' for the sake of their twins. But Nick and Ellen were clear-sighted adults; he could contact them direct if he wanted. She knew what he was up to: he enjoyed feeling noble and superior. She imagined him sitting there smugly over a latte on the cruise liner, smiling at Eve's replacement, Sonia, and congratulating himself on being such a modern man. He might have split up from Eve, but hey, he still looked out for her welfare, and thought about her before he went off and enjoyed himself.

'He's such a jerk.'

She downed the rest of her coffee and got up from the table. Her dachshund, sensing action, leaped up too and did a giddy sideways scamper.

'At least he bought me you.' He'd given her Gus as a present, without asking, after he'd walked out. She was infuriated by his presumption, but with the dachshund it had been love at first sight.

A short while later she was running with him along the beach. She needed to clear her head before driving over to Seagrave Hall. Feeling irritated by Ian, or weighed down by sorrow at Verity's death, would throw her concentration off. The sea breeze in her short hair and the feeling of release as she ran set her up for the day. Gus seemed just as happy. He moved like a furry brown dart along the pebble-strewn sand, his shiny black nose pointing north towards acres of beach, deserted except for the gulls swooping overhead. At last, she turned her back on the North Sea, its waves glinting in the July morning sunlight, and headed back up the estuary path towards Haunted Lane and home.

Up in her bedroom, its wooden beams reaching over her head, she got ready for her visit to the Seagraves. She needed to be smart if she was going to talk to Rupert, to show her respect, but she'd also be lugging tables and packing up Monty's kit. She opted for a summer trouser suit – patterned in willow green – that she knew would wash well. It probably wouldn't show grass stains either. She dressed it up with some smoky quartz earrings, picked up the notes she'd made after the pub the previous evening and went to say goodbye to Gus.

In under ten minutes she was driving Monty's van over the River Sax, then doubling back round the other side of the estuary to reach the hall. It gave her an eerie feeling, parking on the gravel forecourt at the front of the house. The memory of what had happened less than twenty-four hours earlier was still fresh in her mind. The view of Pete Smith standing over Verity Nye's body, her legs flung out at an unnatural angle, would stay with her forever.

She was met by Tilly Cotton, the estate manager. The woman was biting her lip and staring at the array of vehicles in front of her. Several stallholders must be there already, dismantling the arrangements they'd made for the fete.

When she spotted Eve, she managed a smile. 'Please just come and go as you need. Let me know if you want any help.'

Eve thanked her and asked if it might be possible to have a quick word with Rupert Seagrave. 'I'm not sure if he's aware that my profession is obituary writing. I've agreed to complete a piece on Ms Nye for *Icon* magazine. I realise this must be the most appalling time for him, but I know some people find paying tribute to a loved one therapeutic. I'd be hugely grateful if he was willing to speak with me.'

Tilly Cotton nodded. 'I can certainly ask. I'll come and find you, to let you know.'

'Thanks.' The woman seemed more controlled today, but Eve couldn't forget her expression when Dylan Walker said Verity had been pushed. What did she think had happened? And what had she seen?

Eve walked down to the spot under the cedar tree where she and Viv had left their belongings. As she neared her destination, she saw that Moira Squires from the village store was hard at work too, removing her fortune-telling paraphernalia from the emerald-green tent she'd been lent. She was back in her normal gear: a figure-hugging floral dress and high-heeled shoes that made her wobble as she walked on the grass.

'Oh Eve!' she said. 'What a thing to have happened! I still can't believe it. And you saw her fall!'

'Only from a distance. I'd gone over to the play area to see if the vicar needed a hand.'

Moira shook her head. 'I was still inside my tent, but I'd no one with me at the time. I heard her scream. Horrible.' Underlying her shocked tone was a certain wide-eyed breathless excitement. 'I dashed out and found Daphne just beyond the tent door. Poor dear, she was white as a sheet. I'm sure it was just as well I was there to keep an eye on her. I expect everyone will want to know about it when I get back to the shop. I've left Paul there, looking after things.'

Anyone quizzing *him* for details would be out of luck. Grunting was his favourite form of communication. And when Moira was back, the customers wouldn't have to ask. The information would be forthcoming whether they wanted it or not. Of course, in Eve's case, Moira's penchant for gossip tended to come in handy…

'Viv said you were practising your fortune telling on a few of the key players yesterday.'

'Well, that's right, I was!' She put her hands on her hips. 'I spoke to Cora, Rupert Seagrave's cousin.' Her face took on a disapproving expression. 'I do have a way with people. I might not be a professional fortune teller, but I sense things, and I can tell you that I wouldn't like to take her into *my* family.'

'I'd heard the Seagraves adopted her after her parents were killed in a plane crash.'

'That's quite right. They had a private jet.' (Her tone said, *Well, if people will do these things…*) 'Of course, it was tragic, but I understand the Seagraves have raised her just as though she was Rupert's sister. She's had every benefit.'

That was interesting, but 'every benefit' often referred to money rather than emotional support. Eve wondered who Moira had been talking to.

'You have friends who know the family?'

'Well, of course, Molly – that's Mrs Walker' – Moira glanced over to the tombola stall, where the woman had arrived to tidy up – 'is one of the cleaning staff here, working under the Seagraves' housekeeper. She's in the know.'

Eve was curious about Cora's fortune-telling session. She imagined Moira would have ensured it was a two-way process, what with her love of information. 'So you didn't take to Cora?'

Moira huffed. 'She enjoyed having an audience, and she made it clear she didn't really want my help.'

Eve raised her eyebrows.

'She laughed and said: "I don't know what I'm doing here! I'm an unstoppable force. I can predict my own future! And I can also safely divine that it won't please everyone."'

It sounded as though Cora Seagrave had big plans. But it was as Viv had said the day before – people tended to visit fortune tellers when things weren't yet going as they hoped. Was that the situation with Cora? What was she after?

Moira's mouth formed a thin line. 'She didn't take anything I said seriously. And then she skipped off out of the tent as though she was a child. And yet I understand she's in her late twenties. I thought her behaviour very odd. And did you see the way she pushed herself forward, after poor dear Verity had fallen?'

Eve nodded, but it wasn't just Cora's behaviour that had struck her; she'd been thinking about the timing too. Rupert's cousin had appeared from round the side of the house, after most people, though Sir Percival's arrival had been later still. Where had they been? 'Did you speak with Verity?'

Moira's look of frustration told Eve she'd been thwarted. 'Well, no. But of course, I knew she wouldn't have time. She was very busy getting ready for the fete. But I had her medical gentleman Pete Smith in. Now, there's a charming young man!' She touched her gleaming dyed-auburn hair as she spoke. She'd mentioned having her roots done before the fete. 'I will admit, he did giggle when I predicted he'd soon be travelling abroad.'

Eve smiled. 'Makes sense to start off with what you know, I guess.'

Moira nodded solemnly. 'That's what I thought. Anyway, although he chuckled for a moment, he suddenly pulled himself together, which I appreciated. Then he said: "In fairness, I'm glad to hear you say that. I've been looking forward to the dive in China, but nothing's certain in this world." There was a funny look in his eye, and he was so still for a moment. I honestly didn't know what to make of it. But a second later he was laughing again, and asking me all about the store and village life. A most engaging young man.'

Eve thought of the conversation she'd heard him have with Verity Nye. If she was ending their affair, maybe he'd been worried his job might be in danger too.

'I did offer to tell Jade Piper's fortune. You know, the woman who runs the charity, Wide Blue Yonder?'

Eve nodded.

'But she said she was too busy. And she looked very distracted, I must say.' There was a pause. Eve could tell there was more to come. 'But as I mentioned, I am quite good at reading people. I've told fortunes before, as a matter of fact, at a village fete several years ago.' She sighed. 'Something tells me that girl has problems. She seemed upset yesterday, well before dear Verity was killed.'

She'd always be 'dear Verity' to Moira now – no matter that she'd hardly spoken to the woman. Moira tended to adopt celebrities, even if they were unaware of the fact.

'Little Dylan Walker really put the cat amongst the pigeons, didn't he?' Moira's look was expectant.

Eve started to remove the ribbon from round the legs of the folding table. 'I suppose the police didn't speak to him?'

Her eyes widened. 'Oh no, I'm sure not! There'd be no need. Molly Walker came in for milk earlier this morning. She's very upset by the whole thing. Dylan's renowned for his tall stories. I hear his nursery teacher called her in before the end of term because he told her he'd been bitten by a snake on a nature walk. It caused quite a panic for a minute or two, what with all the adders on the heath.' She glanced over at the tombola stall again. Dylan, who was with his mother, was bouncing up and down and making loud frog noises.

'Loves to be the centre of attention.' Moira nodded wisely. 'And apparently he told Molly that the person who "pushed" Verity' – she raised her eyes to heaven – 'had "big shiny black eyes that sparkled". He obviously made the whole thing up. Most embarrassing for the poor woman, especially with her position here at the hall. Still, I imagine all the fuss will be over in a day or two.'

Mrs Walker wouldn't want to make trouble for the family, Eve guessed. Presumably not to the extent that she'd cover up a murder, but all the same – might Dylan be the boy who cried wolf?

CHAPTER SEVEN

'Rupert will speak to you now, if it's convenient?' Tilly Cotton approached Eve as she was carrying the last of the folding tables back to the outhouse. It knocked against the shin that was beginning to bruise from the day before.

'Do let me help.' Tilly took one end, so they were carrying the thing flat.

'Thanks. And thanks so much for asking Rupert about the interview for me. This must be such a terrible time for you all.'

Tilly's eyes weren't on Eve. She was twisted so that she could see behind her as they manoeuvred the table. 'It's an appalling shock.' Her voice wasn't quite steady. 'I've spent the whole day polishing and mopping, which isn't normally my role, but keeping busy with something manual has been good. My mother's been feeling off-colour since yesterday – the strain of it all – and of course there's a lot to do. We could have called the regular cleaners in, but they don't normally work on a Saturday, and the family needs some private time.'

Eve lowered her end of the table to the ground inside the outhouse and Tilly walked it into position.

'How long have you been with them?'

'I've lived here since I was a child. My mother has an estate cottage and she's been their housekeeper since she was twenty-three.'

Eve wondered about Tilly's father. She hadn't heard him mentioned, but it felt too nosy to ask.

'Let me show you into the hall.' Tilly took Eve through a door at the end of a long corridor. It was at the side of the house nearest the woods – the opposite end to the one she and the gang from the Cross Keys had used the day before, when they'd ferried food and drink into the Seagraves' kitchen.

'A house this size must be a bit of a rabbit warren.'

Tilly smiled. 'It is. I know every inch of it, of course. I used to play hide and seek with Cora and Rupert. There are two back staircases the servants used to use, as well as the grand lot in the centre of the house, so if you think you're about to be found, it's quite easy to escape.'

That was interesting. Eve was determined to keep an open mind about Verity's death – she wanted to base her thoughts on evidence – but she couldn't stop scenarios running through her head. It sounded as though sneaking down to the ground floor after killing her wouldn't be that hard. And there were plenty of exits too, as well as the two side doors. She'd seen at least a couple of rooms with French windows, as well as the grand front entrance which faced away from the lawn where the stalls sat.

Eve could see Rupert ahead of them now, standing at the bottom of the main staircase, a magnificent affair which divided midway between the ground and first floor, branching off to take members of the household to the west or east side of the building.

Belinda Seagrave was standing close to Rupert. They both had their backs to Tilly and Eve. Tilly had lowered her voice as soon as she'd seen them. Now she hesitated, chewing her lip.

'Of course I must speak to her, Mother!' Rupert's hair fell forward as he spoke. He yanked a hand through it.

It could only be a moment before they were spotted, and Rupert wouldn't relax in their interview if Eve acted like a member of the gutter press. She stepped forward, making sure her pump hit the tiled floor hard enough to make a noise. Lady Seagrave swung round, her look unfriendly, which wasn't a surprise, given what Eve had just overheard.

Rupert's skin looked almost grey, his eyes shadowed.

Tilly stepped forward. 'This is Eve Mallow, who's writing Verity's obituary for *Icon*.'

Rupert approached them quickly enough, his hand outstretched. In the same moment his mother swept up the staircase, gripping the heavily polished mahogany banister tightly. Eve had a feeling the grip was her way of controlling her anger.

Tilly turned to Eve. 'It's been nice to meet you. If you need anything else, please let me know before you go.' She retreated to a corner of the hall, where a basket of dusters and polish sat. As Rupert led Eve through to a dark room that was clearly a library, she saw Tilly pick up one of the dusters and get to work on the banister, carefully working in the wax polish, her gaze turning upward, towards the top of the building.

'Thank you so much for seeing me,' Eve said, as Rupert motioned her to a velvet-backed mahogany chair at a Georgian writing table. The room was lined completely with books, lit dimly by the one north-facing window, but also by a series of lamps on low side tables. Above the shelves were miniature alcoves that were home to marble busts and ornate vases, and above them, a white moulded ceiling.

Rupert closed the door and sank into a chair opposite hers.

'Please forgive my mother. She's very protective. Tilly must have mentioned you'd asked to see me.'

'It's completely understandable. I can't imagine what you must be going through.' Eve waited, not wanting to take her notebook out too soon. 'Did you see…?' She let the sentence hang.

He shook his head, like a cat trying to get water out of its ears. 'No. No.' He traced the embossed pattern on the leather tabletop with his forefinger and his cheeks coloured. 'I'd gone to the woods. For a smoke, as a matter of fact.' He shot her a quick glance. 'It was one of the very few things that infuriated Verity. She was so fit, so conscious of what she ate and drank. As for cigarettes – well, you can

imagine. But the build-up towards the fete has been a stressful time.'
He was tapping at the leather tabletop now; jabbing it repeatedly.
'I can't believe that's what I was doing when she fell.' Suddenly he
stopped and took a deep breath. 'But then I can't believe anything
that's happened in the last twenty-four hours.' He put his head in
his hands and pressed his forefingers to his brow.

Eve took the opportunity to grab her notebook from her bag.
She wrote his name at the top of the page. She'd record what she
could now and add her private conclusions later.

'You were here yesterday, weren't you?' Rupert said, removing
his hands from his face at last.

'That's right.'

'You probably heard me shout at Cora. I flew off the handle.'
His voice shook and his jaw tensed.

'That's completely natural,' she said gently.

'Cora didn't like Verity and it was entirely down to self-interest.'
Rupert continued as though she hadn't spoken. She knew that
look of determination. There was something he wanted to share.
He'd made up his mind and until it was out, he wouldn't focus
on anything else. The interesting thing was that it was about his
cousin. With her interviewees, it was normally something about
the person who'd died. She waited.

'Cora wanted me to go into partnership with her, to turn this
place into a hotel.' He raised his eyes to meet Eve's. 'As the eldest
son I inherit when I'm thirty, which is just around the corner now.'

The inheritance arrangement sounded unusual. Eve would have
to look into it, but for now she tried to imagine Belinda Seagrave's
reaction to Cora's plan.

'She had the idea that we could rent out most of the land here,
to bring in some income to support the venture too. I... well, for
various reasons I was considering it, but of course, my engagement
to Verity was bound to change things. This place would have been

her home.' He chewed his lip. 'Our relationship threw Cora's plans out of kilter.'

The very fact that he was telling her this made Eve's palms go sweaty. Why mention it? It was nothing to do with the article she needed to write. Was Rupert anticipating Verity's death would be ruled as murder?

And why highlight Cora's motive so blatantly? Did he suspect her? Or was he guilty himself, and looking to divert attention?

Whatever the truth, he was shaking with anger as he spoke of his cousin. Either he really believed she'd done it, or there was another reason.

He was watching her face, and pulled himself up straighter in his chair. 'I'm sorry – I can't think clearly. It's all been going round in my head, but it's Verity you want to know about. How can I help?'

'Maybe you could tell me where you first met.'

He took a deep breath. 'Of course. It was at a corporate event put on by my employers; a management consultancy in Mayfair.'

It figured that he worked in one of the smartest locations in London.

He closed his eyes for a moment, blinking away tears. 'They brought her in to lecture on one of her dives out in Egypt. You might have read about it. One of her team got stuck in a narrow channel between two rocks. The girl almost drowned, but Verity managed to get her out in the nick of time. It was so inspiring. Her experiences were a world away from anyone else's in the room. It was like a fresh breeze swirling around, stirring us all up. She was passionate and I found I couldn't stop looking at her.'

Eve imagined he wouldn't have been alone. She'd had the sort of looks that could bring a room to a standstill. And she could relate to his enthusiasm for Verity as a speaker. She explained she'd heard her talk too and Rupert's face lit up, just for a moment.

'*You'll* understand then. When she talked about the danger of the cave she'd been tackling, her eyes shone. They looked liquid; like dark pools with torchlight reflected in them.'

Eve could still visualise them too. Rupert looked as though he was in a trance, blinded by the memory.

'After the talk she mingled – or tried to. She was soon hemmed in by people who wanted to speak to her. I got the opportunity to talk to her myself at last, but it was quite by chance. She was excusing herself from a group that had been monopolising her and, in her haste, she bumped right into me. I'll never forget her smile and the look she gave me. It was as though her evening had suddenly taken a turn for the better.' He flushed. 'And it transpired we had something in common: we both came from Suffolk. She hadn't really talked about her background during her lecture, but she opened up then.' His tears welled up again now; and they brimmed over after a moment. 'I found her charming. She *was* charming.'

Eve made notes. Everything he said held her attention. What had made him utter that last sentence? It was clear Cora had disliked Verity. Had she gone out of her way to challenge his view of her?

'Did you get the impression she'd had a happy childhood?'

Rupert hesitated a moment. 'She was reluctant to talk about her parents. If I brought them up, she'd say, "Don't let's spoil the day."'

But he must have met them, surely? Their marriage had been imminent. Rupert seemed uneasy. She judged it best not to push; she could find out more from other sources, and she'd want to interview them anyway.

'I wondered how Ms Nye operated when she was preparing for a dive. Did she focus entirely on her project? Or was she able to compartmentalise, and spend part of her time socialising with people other than her team?'

It was natural to ask, but Eve was especially curious after overhearing Verity and her medic talking in the marquee. She'd been trained to watch her interviewees as she posed her questions. It was only polite to maintain eye contact for a start. Sitting there scribbling could look callous – needy and greedy. But the rule also meant you didn't miss clues: subtle reactions that might guide your questions in a particular direction. She was glad she hadn't looked down in this case. Rupert Seagrave had flinched. It was slight, but it was there – she'd touched on a sore point.

'She'd get very intense, very focused.' He took a quick breath. 'It was entirely natural, of course. Her adventures were dangerous. They needed meticulous planning.'

It made Eve wonder how the accident with her team member had happened. But if you were tackling some of the world's most perilous cave systems she guessed you could never be certain everything would go according to plan.

Rupert leaned on the table. 'The upcoming dive in China, after our marriage, would have been the first she'd done since our engagement.' He was gripping his left hand with his right, digging his nails into the flesh. 'I was worried about it, couldn't help myself.' His shoulders were stiff, his jaw set. 'But naturally, I had to learn to take a step back.' He took a deep breath, and his eyes met hers. 'She told me I was the only man who'd managed to do that, and I took pride in it. I gave her the space she needed. It wasn't easy, but I knew our partnership wouldn't work if I crowded her.'

It sounded as though Verity might have driven that message home. Because her freedom was essential to her? Or because she had something to hide, and if he clung to her like a second skin, he'd discover it?

Eve had liked Verity, but she hadn't known her. She had no idea what might come out as she researched her article, but she owed it to the woman to uncover the truth about her life. And her death.

CHAPTER EIGHT

Back at Elizabeth's Cottage, Eve was greeted enthusiastically by Gus, who leaped up (as high as he was able) and then scampered wildly round the living room. It was so nice to be appreciated. She bent down to scratch behind his ears.

A short while later they went into the back garden. Eve sat at the little round ironwork table with her tea, and Gus burrowed into the bushes at the end of the lawn in search of whatever had made them rustle.

Eve had her notebook open and began to add extra thoughts following on from her interview with Rupert Seagrave. They were things she hadn't wanted him to glimpse as they sat opposite each other, including her reaction to his outburst about his cousin Cora. She'd want to hash it all over with Viv when she got the chance. She was so intent on her thoughts that she almost knocked her mug of tea over when Gus bounded up the garden like a furry bullet, barking for all he was worth.

Looking up, she saw Cora Seagrave standing on her lawn, a guileless smile on her lips.

Eve sat there, in the warmth of the late July day, with goose bumps all over her arms.

'I knocked but you didn't hear me.' Her tone was eager and slightly breathless. 'I could see you sitting here from the lane, so I came round.' She put out a soft, perfectly manicured hand. 'Cora Seagrave.'

At that moment a text came in on Eve's phone. Viv.

Cora Seagrave – incoming.

So she'd sought her at the teashop first; that explained how she'd found Elizabeth's Cottage. Eve was so busy snatching up her phone, it took her a second to remember her notebook was in full view, covered with her thoughts on Rupert. Cora's eyes were on it as she took a seat at the table, the smile still playing around her lips.

'I saw your van when you came over to Seagrave Hall today,' she said.

It belonged to Monty's and carried its branding, phone number and web address.

'Percival mentioned you'd interviewed Rupe for the obituary you're writing about Verity. I know I'm on the periphery, but I'd so like to talk to you too.'

Gus had stopped barking and hunkered down, his eyes on Rupert Seagrave's cousin. Eve sympathised. She felt compromised, having the woman on their territory without invitation. But it was an unexpected opportunity. Cora hadn't been a close connection of Verity's and Eve had worried asking for an interview would seem weird. The visit would allow her to explore some of the questions teeming in her head.

So she ignored the disquiet building inside her. 'Would you like a cup of tea?'

'That sounds lovely.' Cora sank back in her chair. The sun was in her eyes and she shaded them with a hand for a moment, before taking out some sunglasses from the bag she had with her.

Eve took her notebook into the kitchen and swapped it with the one she normally used for shopping lists. She was already worried Cora might have glimpsed some of her private notes.

A few minutes later she was back outside with a tray laden with tea, sugar, a pitcher of milk, teaspoons and a plate of shortbread biscuits she'd brought home from Monty's. Cora had risen from her seat and was saying hello to Gus; it looked like she'd won him over, which made Eve ridiculously uneasy.

Once Cora had seated herself again, and had her drink in front of her, Eve opened the shopping list book. 'Tell me what you'd like me to know.' It wasn't uncommon to have someone approach her in relation to an obituary, rather than the other way about. Friends and relatives of the deceased often felt they had unfinished business: records to set straight, the need to correct a misconception or simply the desire to feel included.

Cora tucked her glossy chestnut-brown hair behind one ear and leaned forward. 'Can I talk to you in confidence?'

Eve took a deep breath. She presumed Cora appreciated that the obituary she wrote would end up in print. 'If you don't want to be quoted, I can still take what you tell me into consideration to inform my article.' But she'd want firm evidence before she accepted what the woman said.

Cora nodded. 'That's good. The fact is, Rupe might be a bit of an unreliable witness.' She giggled and Eve was reminded of the school playground.

Was there any chance Cora had an idea what her cousin had said about her? Had she come in order to cover her back? Or to get her revenge?

Eve had her pen poised, but her eyes were on her visitor. 'Unreliable? Why is that?'

'Can't or won't see the truth.' She paused for a moment and smiled. 'Or at least, I assume that's still the case. I didn't want you to miss out on a more unbiased account for your obituary.'

'You must have seen quite a lot of Verity just recently, I suppose?' Eve said. In reality she supposed nothing of the sort, but uttering the words 'you hardly knew her' would be undiplomatic.

Cora was beaming at Gus again, but turned to look at Eve now. 'A little of Verity went a long way. She only came up to Suffolk on

Wednesday, but seeing her at every meal, slinking round the hall, stroking her future possessions, gave me a good idea of her character.'

Eve made an effort to relax her shoulders and keep her face neutral, despite Cora's loaded words. 'I gather she and Rupert would have moved into Seagrave Hall quite soon?' It made Eve wonder. Moira had said Cora had had every benefit, living with Belinda and Percival, but where did she stand when it came to inheritance?

The young woman raised an eyebrow. 'That's right – on Rupert's thirtieth birthday. He'll take possession on his own now. It sounds archaic, but Percival claims it's the height of modernity. Most homes like Seagrave belong to the senior members of the family until the husband dies, whereupon the widow gets shoved out into a dowager cottage, and the male heir takes possession of the family home. Percival has what he seems to regard as a groundbreaking arrangement where Rupert will get to appreciate the hall when he's still young, with a view to bringing up a family there. But it still gets handed down the male line, of course. Don't you just love the patriarchy?'

Eve agreed with Cora on that score, but siding with the woman made her uneasy. 'Sir Percival and Lady Seagrave will have to move out then?' Eve couldn't imagine Belinda would enjoy being ousted. And maybe especially not if Verity had been moving in. She was sure the woman had disapproved of her son's bride-to-be. When she'd commented on her independence, she'd made it sound like an insult.

'There's a rather grand "cottage" on the estate the aging parents are destined to occupy. It'll be a wrench for Belinda, but Percival doesn't mind. And he's such a spendthrift; it's just as well he won't be living in the grand old money pit any longer.' She giggled again.

'Do you live on the estate as well?'

Cora nodded and a frown clouded her face. 'I've got a cottage too.' She crossed her arms. 'Not at all like the one that Percival and Belinda will occupy. It's just into the woods. Dark as hell.' But now the smile was back. 'But at least I have my own space. I'd decamped there for a coffee yesterday, shortly before Verity fell, but I was on my way back at the fatal moment. I couldn't imagine what was going on when I saw people running towards the hall. And then, when I rounded the building, everyone was standing there like zombies.'

Underneath it all, Eve guessed Cora didn't think much of the villagers and their stunned reaction to what had happened. Maybe she was still embarrassed that she'd pitched up on the scene, laughing. But perhaps she had a dark side to her character – the same lack of empathy that her aunt Belinda displayed. She wasn't dead-eyed like Lady Seagrave, but Eve still felt she had some kind of disconnect with reality. Though she wasn't guileless. Eve thought again of the way she'd relaxed the day before, once she thought no one was watching. She'd understood the need to act, even if she lacked the emotional awareness to play her role convincingly.

'So, what was your experience of Verity?'

'She didn't treat Rupert well, that's for sure. It was all smiles and loving looks to his face, but she was always sneaking off to plot and plan with Pete Smith. You've met him?'

'Not yet.'

'He rushed away from the hall yesterday as soon as the police had taken his details. He'd travelled up with Verity, in her car, and Percival invited him to stay on. No one thought he'd want to travel after what happened, but I've never seen anyone cut and run so quickly. He called a taxi to take him to the station.'

'I asked Tilly Cotton if she might contact him for me, to see if he'd be prepared to give me an interview.' She'd caught the estate manager before she'd left, after she'd finished with Rupert.

'Good luck with that.' Cora ate one of the shortbreads Eve had put out in a single bite. If Viv could see, she wouldn't be impressed.

Her food was meant to be savoured. Besides, Eve would run out of treats if Cora carried on like that. 'Anyway, when Verity wasn't closeted with Pete Smith, playing doctors and divers, she was busy charming Percival.' She tossed her head. 'He didn't approve of her at first – her background's pretty low – but her surface appeal won the day. In the end it was hard for Rupert to get a look-in.' She shrugged. 'He was behaving like a deluded fool. So, for your obituary, I just wanted you to understand that she might have been exciting, sexy and adventurous but she was also two-faced and wily. So now you know. Will you write that?' She seemed to take it for granted that her opinion would trump anyone else's.

'I have to make my work evidence-based. But I'll be speaking to a whole bunch of people, and what you've told me will feed into what I know. I'm grateful to you for coming to see me.' *But now, I'd be happy for you to go.*

Cora leaned forward. 'I haven't finished yet. Rupe told you how he and Verity met, I suppose?'

'He did.' She wasn't going to confirm the details.

Cora nodded. 'I expect he said they bonded when they found they both came from Suffolk? You can bet your bottom dollar he showed her a photograph of Seagrave Hall on his phone. I imagine she fell in love on the spot.' She paused, elbows on the table, the smile making her heart-shaped face dimple. 'Unless, of course, she already knew exactly who he was, and she engineered their charming little meet-cute.'

That was quite a conspiracy theory. But Eve felt a moment of doubt. She remembered Rupert saying Verity had literally cannoned into him and then gazed up into his eyes. It could have been planned. Rupert implied she'd been instantly pleased to meet him, and Verity had made Eve feel the same way when they met. For a second, she questioned the way she'd taken that at face value.

'Rupe blames me for Verity's accident because I suggested she should throw some rugs out of the window a couple of days ago. To be honest, I'm amazed she followed my advice, but the tent she went to fetch yesterday was much bulkier, so maybe she saw sense and got over herself. Either way, it was hardly my fault she tossed herself out with it.'

Her callous words were chilling and Eve had to focus to look beyond them. It *was* interesting that Verity had followed Cora's advice. Eve had overheard Tilly Cotton volunteer to help her get the tent. She'd responded with an irritated laugh and pointed out diving was excellent for upper-body strength. It certainly sounded as though she'd been intending to lug the thing back down the stairs. If she and Cora had sparred, wasn't it likely she'd bring the thing down under her own steam, out of pride, even if it was a tougher job than she'd thought? After all, she could have dragged it if it had proved too heavy to carry.

'Anyway,' Cora drained her tea, 'Rupe was predisposed to be angry with me. I'd told him Verity and Pete Smith were having an affair, half an hour before Verity fell.' She smiled and blinked.

Eve put her cup down and it rattled on the saucer. The possible affair wasn't a shock, of course, but Cora's actions and the way she relayed them so casually took her breath away.

The young woman held up her hand. 'Oh, I didn't have proof.' She laughed her tinkling laugh. 'But I smelled that cloying scent Verity wore on Pete's clothes – and then there was their body language. Of course, Rupe refused to believe me without concrete evidence. Or at least, that's what he said. He looked pretty angry though. It's a shame. We'd been getting on better until I mentioned it. I thought he'd realise I've got his best interests at heart. He's a bit of a chump sometimes.'

CHAPTER NINE

Soon after Cora left, Eve took Gus along Elizabeth's Walk, towards the estuary and the marshes. She hardly saw the gorse to either side of her and the reeds up ahead. Her mind was focused on Cora Seagrave. She couldn't get her tinkling laugh out of her head. She'd told Rupert his fiancée was having an affair without proper proof. She'd been so cruel and reckless.

Assuming her version of events was true, her accusation must have hit home. Earlier that day, Rupert Seagrave had flinched when Eve asked about the time Verity spent closeted with members of her team. Maybe he'd been suspicious even before Cora had spoken out. But she said he'd wanted proof, so presumably he hadn't already had it.

What had he done next? Slunk off into the woods, if he was to be believed, to brood over the news. And an hour later, Verity Nye was dead.

Cora and Rupert had each made it clear the other had a motive for killing her. Were they simply letting rip, after their argument? Or were they afraid, and pointing the finger, now that one small boy said Verity had been pushed? Eve didn't have any influence – but she'd write her article. They might think it was safest to put forward their own stories.

She looked up and saw Gus was waiting at the end of Elizabeth's Walk, at the turn onto the dirt path that ran alongside the estuary. His look was accusing and she dashed to catch up as he trotted ahead again, down the track with the marshes on one side, and a ditch and fields on the other.

'Sorry, Gus. Sorry!' She knew he hated it when her sense of priorities put something ahead of rushing down to the sea. 'But it's just so weird, you know?' She bounded forwards now in an attempt to redeem herself. All around the air was filled with the smell of warm grasses, mud and brackish water, where river met sea. By her feet lay a carpet of marsh violets, dancing in the light breeze, their pale lilac flowers quivering. She followed Gus down into some reeds he was investigating. Beyond, out on the mudflats, a pair of redshank waders were dipping their bills into the shallows, their soft grey-brown plumage decorated with droplets of water that reflected the light. As they raised their heads, they began their insistent repeated tune. People called them the sentinels of the marshes.

It was so strange to look out onto such an idyllic scene when the natural order had been fractured by Verity's death. After a moment, Gus scampered back up to the main path (after one last, longing look at the birds) and dashed purposefully towards the coast. Eve ran after him, and the brief peaceful moment was broken. What would she discover next?

Whatever it was, it might come via Robin Yardley, gardener to almost all of Saxford St Peter. He was due to visit Eve that afternoon and her pulse quickened at the thought. His appearance tended to have that effect anyway, ever since Viv had pointed out how good-looking he was. Eve wished she hadn't highlighted the fact; it filled her mind each time they met now, and made her feel awkward. Luckily, he only tended her garden once a month. But it wasn't just Viv's teasing that made Eve's heart rate ramp up. Robin had a secret, too. When Eve first arrived in Saxford, she'd uncovered part of it, through a series of chance encounters and a lucky guess. She knew he'd once been a police detective. Why he'd gone underground eleven years earlier, changing his name and his job, was more of a mystery. But he had one contact on the local force: DS Gregory Boles, DI Palmer's deputy (and his brains, as far as Eve could see). Robin might have inside information on the investigation into Verity's death.

Back at the cottage, after their run on the beach, Gus had a long drink of water, then went to stretch out under the dining table in the shade and enjoy a well-earned rest. Eve tried to concentrate on her research into Verity's life.

She already knew she'd been born and brought up in a large local village called Stoningham. She'd uncovered the information before she'd met the diver, but now she went back to it with fresh eyes. She clicked on the first link and found a photograph of the house Verity had grown up in. It was an anonymous-looking terraced place, tidy, with cream walls. She googled the street next, to find houses that were for sale there, and their descriptions. 1960s. Two bedrooms, two receptions. The place looked respectable and conventional. Verity's life had taken her in all kinds of directions: from unremarkable beginnings to some of the most dangerous places on earth, and if she hadn't died, she'd have moved into a grand country home – and one day become Lady Seagrave, when Rupert inherited the baronetcy.

Eve considered Cora's accusations. 'I can believe Verity might have been having an affair with Pete Smith,' she said to Gus, as she leaned back in her chair. 'It fits with the conversation I overheard.' The words came back to her. 'We can still make this work!' Pete had said, but Verity had told him they'd said all there was to say. 'Of course we can't "make this work". How can you not see that?'

It still surprised Eve. She hadn't had Verity down as someone who'd go into marriage deceiving her partner like that. But you never really knew what someone was dealing with unless you were standing in their shoes. All she could do was dig as deeply as possible to try to make sure her impressions were just.

'But Cora implied she was marrying for money too.' Eve peered under the table. Gus had his eyes closed. She decided that meant he was concentrating; she wasn't just talking to herself. 'I'm not sure that fits.'

Character-wise, Eve supposed it was possible. Verity had been independent, by all accounts, but if she was amoral and unsentimental, she might have seen sourcing funds in return for marriage in the same light as getting them from a sponsor in return for advertising.

'But it still doesn't make sense,' she said aloud. 'Cora implied Sir Percival's a spendthrift, and the hall must cost an enormous amount to keep up. If he's frittered away his cash, there's probably not much left for Rupert to inherit.

'Cora talked about Verity "stroking her future possessions" too – to imply she relished the idea of being lady of the manor, I suppose.' But Eve thought again of Sylvia's photograph of the woman: the spark in her eyes when she was showing off her diving kit. 'Take it from me, Gus, that's definitely out. She liked being in the field, taking risks, hitting the headlines.' Eve guessed she'd have hated standing in an elegant drawing room, drinking sherry and discussing the cleaning rota with Ivy Cotton.

So if money and position weren't the driving forces behind her marriage, she must have loved Rupert. But then why the affair with her medic, if that's what it had been?

Eve shook her head. Understanding more about the hall and the way it functioned might help her investigation. After a moment's thought she wrote an email to Tilly Cotton, to ask if she could look round the place and its grounds. People would be interested to contrast the stately home with Verity's more usual habitat – forbidding cave systems in faraway exotic places. It was a legitimate part of her story.

When she glanced down, Gus had opened one eye.

'I know what you're thinking, but I have to push myself forward if I want to get to the bottom of what happened.' The chance to speak with Tilly Cotton again was important to her too. Had she really seen someone behind Verity at the window? Eve shook her head. She was sure she hadn't imagined the woman's reaction. Maybe she could get her to confide if she got to know her better.

She pushed the thought to one side for now, and set about finding a way of contacting Verity's parents. Their names came up in articles about the dead adventurer, and eventually she found an email address for her father on some kind of church website. He was part of a committee who organised evangelical work. She sent him a message, expressing her sympathy and asking if it might be possible to talk to him about his daughter.

After that, she turned her attention briefly to Cora. Her background wouldn't help with the obituary – but she was a key part of the Seagrave family jigsaw puzzle, and she'd hated Verity. Eve couldn't get the woman's smile out of her head; it made her skin crawl. The results of the search were interesting. Rupert said Cora had wanted him to team up with her, to turn Seagrave Hall into a hotel. It had seemed off the wall at the time, but her findings showed it wouldn't be her first foray into the hospitality business – she already had one failed venture to her name. She'd invested in a boutique hotel down in London. *That must have cost her a fortune.* The article described her as an heiress, who'd invested 'family money'. It looked as though her parents had left her well off when they died. So were Percival and Belinda also planning to leave her anything? Or would their money go to Rupert alone? If their funds were dwindling, and Cora had already inherited a substantial sum, they probably felt they could leave her out. Eve couldn't imagine Belinda Seagrave weakening, just because Cora had lost hundreds of thousands in her failed business venture.

So that left Cora starting from scratch, unless she could sweet-talk Rupert into helping her. It sounded as though she'd been making progress, until Verity had come along and her plans had been cast aside. It was interesting that she'd made any headway in the first place. Why had Rupert almost agreed? The financial situation at the hall might be dire, but surely developing the place into a hotel would have involved a lot of initial outlay. And Eve couldn't imagine Belinda and Percival would approve.

Cora clearly had a persuasive personality, but maybe there was more to it than that. She made a note to find out.

'She seems like a nasty piece of work,' she said aloud. 'When Rupert shelved the hotel idea, it looks as though she tried to drive a wedge between him and Verity.'

Would Cora try to talk Rupert round again, now that his fiancée was out of the way? No wonder she'd been so keen to come across as sympathetic, the day of Verity's fall. She'd be working hard to get Rupert back onside. Had she seriously imagined her accusations about Verity would be met with warm words of thanks?

Even if she wasn't the killer, her lack of empathy made her dangerous. Rupert might have committed murder on the back of her words.

CHAPTER TEN

Eve was jolted out of her thoughts by the sight of Robin Yardley in her back garden, his charcoal grey T-shirt bleached by the sun. As she watched through the casement window, he put down a box of tools.

She closed her eyes for a moment and focused on the matter in hand. Maybe he'd be interested in what she could pass on, as well as vice versa. It was clear he missed his old work; when a new case came up in the village, he couldn't resist keeping an eye on progress.

She shook her head as she watched him. Locally, apart from her and DS Boles, only the vicar knew something of his background. And Jim Thackeray liked and trusted him, that much was clear. Eve had dug into Robin's history, not because she doubted him, but because it was in her nature. That spring, she'd made it her goal to try to uncover his past, using Boles as a starting point. Surely they must have worked together once? It would explain the amount Boles passed on, and the clear rapport between them. But she'd found nothing. Whatever his story was, it was buried deep.

She went out to say hello and offer him a drink. Gus followed her and immediately rolled over to have his tummy tickled.

Robin laughed and crouched down to oblige, but after a moment he glanced up at Eve. 'Are you all right?' His blue-grey eyes were concerned, though a smile lit his weather-worn features. Viv would call them rugged. She pushed her friend out of her head.

'After yesterday, you mean?' The scene came back to her: the scream, the thud and the sudden silence. Then crowds of villagers running towards the hall. She nodded. 'I'm okay.'

His brow was furrowed. 'I heard you saw her fall.'

That was Saxford all over. Everyone knew everything within a matter of hours. News rippled out and Robin ran into a lot of locals, thanks to his work. He might be careful about what he said, but Eve guessed they weren't.

'My police contact mentioned it,' he said, answering her unspoken question. He stood up now, and Gus righted himself too before pottering off down the lawn.

Robin always referred to Gregory Boles as his 'contact'. Eve had the impression he didn't want to highlight the man's name, but going through Boles' history with a fine-toothed comb hadn't unlocked Robin's secrets.

'Right.' She took a deep breath, and wondered if Boles shared Palmer's view, that she always wanted to be in on the action. She wouldn't want Robin to think that. 'I couldn't see what happened; I was too far away. But the first officers on the scene asked who'd seen her fall, so I felt I had to speak up.'

He nodded. 'And I hear you'll be writing her obituary.' She must have frowned, and he answered with a half-smile. 'I was weeding at the pub early this morning.'

'Jo? Well, you heard correctly.'

He picked up some secateurs he'd brought with him, ready to start work. 'The police have decided to take Dylan Walker's story seriously after all. They believe Verity Nye was pushed.'

The hairs lifted on Eve's scalp. She'd felt in her gut that it was likely from the outset, but hearing him say it aloud still snatched the breath from her lungs. Cora and Rupert Seagrave's words crowded into her head.

'What changed their minds?'

'According to my mate, the coroner wasn't satisfied. A post-mortem took place this morning at his request, and the pathologist found bruising on Verity's upper right arm. She was gripped from behind. And the mark at the rear was the strongest, indicating the pressure the killer exerted to thrust her forward.'

Eve pictured the scene: Verity at the low Georgian window, heaving the bulky canvas over the sill. The noise from down below, as people called to one another, hammered in tent pegs and put the junk gamelan through its paces. And behind Verity, someone stepping stealthily into the room, ready to pitch her forward… It was no wonder she hadn't heard them coming.

She was conscious of Robin again, watching her face. 'You already thought Dylan might be telling the truth?' he asked.

She told him about Tilly Cotton's reaction when Lady Seagrave asked if she'd seen anything. 'Her hands were trembling. She said she didn't think so, and that Verity filled the window. I wasn't sure she was lying, but I thought she was in doubt, and that she could believe it might be true. She looked so stunned and upset, but of course, she would, in any case.' Eve visualised the woman's face. 'I think maybe she can imagine at least one person having done it. And Dylan looked so injured at not being believed, too. Not like a kid telling tall stories.' She remembered her twins' expressions when they'd made things up as young children. They'd always over-acted, and there'd been a hint of mischief behind their wide-eyed tales. 'But then Moira mentioned Dylan said the killer had "shiny black eyes that sparkled" and I guessed no one would take him seriously after that.'

Robin's smile brought out his laughter lines. 'That mystery's been solved, I hear.'

'Sounds interesting.'

'Earlier on today outside the village store, I gather Dylan told his mother – very firmly – that it was Mrs Barclay who'd pushed Verity Nye out of the window. The woman was present at the time, so Dylan obligingly pointed her out.'

'Mrs Barclay the octogenarian?'

He nodded.

'Who does all the work for Save the Children?'

He nodded again. 'The same.'

Poor Mrs Walker.

'All was embarrassment and confusion, according to Moira Squires, but then Dylan started to go on about her shiny black eyes. Mrs Barclay was wearing sunglasses.'

'Oh!'

'My mate says Mrs Walker rang the police station a couple of hours ago to explain, but after the post-mortem they'd have contacted her if she hadn't got there first. So now Palmer's looking for a killer who wears sunglasses, had a grudge against Verity Nye and who was unaccounted for when she fell.' He shook his head. 'But I think sorting out alibis might be difficult. Most people will have been focused on setting up their stalls, and then staring up at the window or down at the ground where she'd fallen, rather than noticing the faces around them. You get that moment of shock, when everyone's pretty much oblivious to everything but the main event.'

It was true. Eve had already noted down her memories of what had happened, but they were patchy. She knew she'd run up the lawn with the vicar, and that Viv had appeared at her side at some stage. Apart from that it was just noise and confusion, until gradually she'd taken stock again. She guessed the villagers' memories of peripheral details would already be fading – blanked out by the horror of Verity's death.

'Anyone with a firm alibi that you know of?' Eve knew Robin wouldn't mind her asking. He was well aware of the danger she put herself in, each time she wrote about a murder victim.

The gardener shrugged. 'The police will need to do more interviews before they can be sure, but I understand they've spoken to the family and permanent employees.'

They must have managed to catch Cora after her jaunt over to Saxford.

'Lady Seagrave claims she was talking to Matt and Toby Falconer when she heard the scream. Assuming they confirm that then they're all in the clear. Sir Percival says he was at the stables and Rupert in the woods.'

'He told me that too – said he'd gone for a smoke because he felt stressed.'

Their eyes met for a moment.

'And Cora told me she'd gone back to her cottage to escape the mêlée for a while. She said she was just crossing the grounds again, towards the back lawn, when Verity fell.'

Robin raised an eyebrow. 'You're well-informed! I gather she's given the police the same story.'

'She paid me an unexpected visit earlier. I'll tell you about it, but finish your round-up first.'

'It's a deal. So, Ivy Cotton was cleaning windows at the western end of the house, and Tilly was driving in a loose stake to stop a tent from toppling over.'

Eve would need to note it all down. 'Any news on the other main players?'

'They've spoken to Pete Smith by phone, pending a formal interview. He says he was arranging a display of diving kit in one of the tents when Verity fell, so no one can vouch for him either. And they're chasing up Jade Piper, the charity manager, to get her story too. I should know more soon. For the villagers, I understand it's already established that Mrs Walker and Dylan were together.'

Eve nodded. 'And I was with Jim down by the play area. Sylvia was photographing Jo Falconer setting up the beer tent. She mentioned it when she emailed me the photos she took. And Moira told me she and Daphne ran up the lawn side by side.' It was Daphne who'd set up the junk gamelan at the fete; she lived with Sylvia.

A faint smile crossed Robin's face. 'Sylvia sent you photos? It's good to know you've got mugshots of the suspects.'

Eve took a deep breath. 'And there are still plenty of them.' Of Verity's closest contacts, only Lady Seagrave appeared to have an alibi.

Robin nodded. 'The police will interview the villagers next. I'll let you know if I hear anything useful.'

In the meantime, she'd have to be on her guard with just about everyone she interviewed. She swallowed, her mouth dry. 'I've already found a couple of people who had possible motives for the murder. And this is where Cora's unexpected visit comes in.' She explained what Cora and Rupert had said about each other. 'So Verity was standing in the way of Cora's business interests, and Rupert might have been jealous to the point of violence, if he believed Cora's accusations about Verity and Pete Smith.'

She told him about the conversation she'd overheard between the pair. Robin's expertise and inside information had been invaluable in the past. Once again, she was going to be interviewing the same group of suspects as the police, in danger of uncovering the murderer unexpectedly, in a situation she couldn't control. She wanted all the help she could get.

His eyes widened as she spoke. 'That raises a lot of questions.'

'You said it. What's the police's focus?'

'It's early days, but they're anxious to speak to Jade Piper.'

'Because Verity fell from her bedroom window?'

He nodded.

Eve wanted to talk to her for exactly the same reason – she was a key interviewee.

Robin's blue-grey eyes were on hers. 'Watch your back, won't you?'

She smiled. 'You don't have to tell me twice.' Inside she felt nerves tickle her stomach, but they were only partly due to the dangers she might face. The feeling of urgency to get on with the job, and work out who had done this terrible thing, set her on edge too. 'Drink?'

'A pint of water would go down well.'

She went to fetch the swing-topped bottle she kept in the fridge, poured a glassful, and took it out to him.

'I have to go to the village store. Do you want anything?'

He shook his head. 'I'm good, thanks. Feel free to leave Gus here.'

She wanted some more of the still lemonade the store sold; it was perfect for quenching her thirst in this weather. Five minutes later, she pushed open the door of the store, setting the old-fashioned bell jangling, and realised it was Moira's husband Paul behind the cash desk. He'd just about accepted Eve as a fixture in the village but that hadn't made him polite. He objected to anyone who wasn't Saxford born and bred. He served her without meeting her eyes and she was out again in seconds. When Moira was there it tended to be a twenty-minute operation.

She let herself back into the relative cool of the cottage and waited for her eyes to adjust to the light levels of the shady thick-walled sitting room. Through the window she could see Gus pottering happily around the flowerbeds. Robin never minded having him as company. He'd paused in his work to answer his mobile, his back to her.

She was on her way through to let him know she'd returned, close to the open back door, when she picked up on his conversation.

'… turned out to be a dead end, but there's more to work through. I'll report back soon; I can't talk now.'

His tone was serious. What was that all about? Eve paused where she was instead of calling out but Gus must have heard her. He scampered towards the house, causing Robin to turn and spot her too.

'That was quick.' He'd put his phone in his pocket.

Eve put the lemonade into the fridge and walked into the back garden. 'Moira's AWOL.'

'Ah.' He was smiling, but there was a slightly uncertain look in his eye. Was he wondering if she'd overheard his conversation?

'I'd better let you get on.' She hated that expression. Why had she used it? She always felt it meant the person speaking was anxious to get away but too cowardly to admit it. Which in this case was true.

He raised an eyebrow. 'It's certainly almost impossible to talk and prune at the same time.'

She gave a rather forced laugh and scuttled back inside. Gus was watching her with much the same look on his face as Robin. They both thought she was being weird.

In the quiet of the dining room, its six-paned casement window open onto the back garden, she sat and tried to concentrate on her work. She was looking for useful contacts who hadn't been at Seagrave Hall on Friday: people who'd dived with Verity, or other adventurers who'd known her, and old friends who might have another take on her life. But although lack of focus was never normally her problem, her gaze kept drifting upwards towards Robin, who was doing something technical-looking to the magnolia tree. What had he been talking about on the phone? She could understand him excusing himself from the call – he might not want to stop if he was busy – but she was sure there was more to it than that. He'd prefer her not to have heard, she was certain.

For the umpteenth time she glanced into the garden, and he finally caught her at it. He raised an eyebrow before turning back to her tree, where he got to work with his secateurs.

CHAPTER ELEVEN

St Peter's church in Saxford was packed on Sunday morning. Together with the pub and Monty's, it tended to be especially full when the villagers were in need of solace. Jim Thackeray, the vicar, paid tribute to Verity in his address. He didn't refer to the revelation that her death had been murder, but Eve could feel the knowledge pressing down on the shoulders of everyone there. The police had made the official announcement early on Saturday evening. As Jim spoke, memories of Friday flooded through her mind: the awful scream, the vicar's jaw going slack in the doorway of the tepee, then rushing up the lawn with him.

She glanced around the beautiful white-walled building with its angel roof – a stark contrast to the horror of events at the hall.

She'd never been a regular churchgoer, but Jim was no ordinary vicar. He encouraged attendees of all faiths and none, and considered every villager a member of his flock. Even pets were welcome, and Gus seemed to like St Peter's. He was settled happily at her feet and tended to go unnoticed, though he occasionally joined in with the singing.

Jim was just as at home in the Cross Keys as the church. Moira Squires didn't approve, but Eve knew he was casting his net wide to find people who might need a listening ear or a word of comfort. The fact that he enjoyed a whisky with his work didn't bother her. She had a lot of time for him.

Viv was in the pew next to her, and as the final hymn faded, she uttered the words Eve had been expecting. 'I need an update.'

'This afternoon – when I'm at Monty's. I know, I know.' She was responding to the exasperated look in her friend's eye. 'But I want to catch Jim. Jo Falconer said he was booked to officiate at Verity and Rupert's wedding – remember? And you know what he's like; he might have useful insights. It's all the more urgent now Verity's death's definitely murder.'

Viv heaved a heavy sigh. 'You have a point. But I want *all* the information you have this afternoon. It's horrific that she was pushed. I know we considered it, but having it confirmed has knocked me for six.'

'I know.' The news had been all over the village in record time. People had stopped her to talk about it as she'd given Gus his evening walk on Saturday. It had taken three times longer than usual, but it had been interesting. No one she'd spoken to could alibi anyone significant. It was as Robin had feared. Most had been so focused on their work that they had no idea what other people had been up to.

'This afternoon then,' Viv said, picking up her bag and edging her way towards the nave.

Eve followed. St Peter's huge arched doorway, oak with iron studs, was pulled back and she walked out into the sunshine that bathed the churchyard. Jim Thackeray exchanged words with each of the congregation and Eve waited to one side, not wanting to disrupt his routine. When the last one left he looked round and spotted her and Gus.

'Eve! How nice to see you.'

Gus had been sniffing round the gravestones, but he dashed over now and presented himself for tummy tickling. Jim Thackery was a great bear of a man, and well into his sixties, but he bent down to oblige with no problem.

'I'm sorry.' He had further to go than most people, thanks to his height.

'Not in the least. I wouldn't be this agile if it weren't for Gus. If he ever gets bored of this ritual I shall have to take up yoga.' He was upright now, and his eyes turned serious. 'How are you, after Friday? Even I feel shaken, and I didn't see it happen.'

'I'm okay, but I can't get it out of my head: both the fall and the conversation I had with Verity shortly beforehand. I liked her.'

He nodded and looked down at her with sympathetic eyes. 'We met, when she and Rupert asked to be married here, and I liked her too.' He sighed. 'Can I shock you now by doing an impression of Moira Squires?'

'That sounds alarm— I mean unexpected.'

He grinned suddenly. 'I mean in her role as fortune teller. I divine that you are writing Verity's obituary, but you plan to investigate her death too. You were worried from the start that the police weren't taking the matter seriously enough. And you're here to see if I can shed any light on her character. How did I do?'

'Spot on, and no crystal ball required. I'm impressed. Would you mind passing on your thoughts?'

'Not in the least.' His brow furrowed. 'But as your vicar, my first comment has to be to take care.'

'Understood.'

'And because I trust you and your motives, I will tell you as much as I can – in strict confidence.'

'I really appreciate it. Now that DI Palmer and his team are on the case that ought to be enough, but I get the impression he's loath to cause problems for the family. And I probably don't have the same... constraints he has.' She wasn't after favoured treatment from the local gentry, so her mind was open, whereas she suspected Palmer would move heaven and earth to prove one of Verity's outside contacts was the killer. 'I'd like to be involved, for Verity's sake.'

The vicar's eyes twinkled, just for a moment. 'I understand perfectly. Would you like to come to the vicarage for a cool drink? Or we could walk around the grounds. That might please Gus better.'

'I think it would. Thank you.'

St Peter's had been built in the 1600s. As well as the graveyard that surrounded it, it was bordered by the ruins of an older church.

They were eerie at night, casting odd shadows in the moonlight. But by day it was fascinating to walk around the walls, half tumbled down, and look through the ancient windows to share the view parishioners in the 1400s had seen. When the old church fell into disrepair, bits of it had been used to help construct the new one, but the previous structure was still clear.

Gus made a beeline for a low-lying bit of wall and lifted his leg.

Eve stepped towards him but Jim Thackeray put out a hand to stop her and smiled. 'If the Lord is watching, his mind will be on world hunger, not on Gus.'

It made sense.

'So, to my meeting with Verity and Rupert. I don't know if you're aware of the way we vicars work, when a couple want to marry?'

She shook her head. 'Not really.' She and Ian had married in a registry office.

'We're nosy – it's our job. There are legalities to get out of the way too, but while we're sorting out the form filling, we also get to know the couple, if they're not regulars. Ideally, I want to build a rapport so they feel they can come back to me in the future, if they ever run into trouble.'

Eve imagined it would normally take years of friendship before someone would be willing to share relationship woes with their vicar, but the idea was sound. And Jim was informal; he could probably work faster than most.

'We spoke at the vicarage, and I left Verity and Rupert to chat when I went to make them some tea. Absenting myself gives couples a chance to discuss any last-minute worries privately. I didn't listen in, naturally,' he gave her a look from under his bushy grey eyebrows, 'but they sounded relaxed. Verity was quite forthright during our conversation. I could see maintaining her independence was important to her, and Rupert certainly seemed to support that.

He suggested readings from Kahlil Gibran's *The Prophet*, which are focused on loving but existing as individuals.'

They walked round the back of the ruins of the old church, towards an area of open grass that overlooked the River Sax. In front of them, reeds near the water stirred in the gentle breeze.

'They both mentioned Rupert's parents several times, which struck me as unusual. In-laws do crop up in conversation, but in this case it almost felt as though they were in the room. There was some discussion of whether Belinda Seagrave would approve of the Gibran readings.' He took a deep breath. 'Rupert became rather skittish in his comments.'

Eve tried to read what was behind the vicar's words. 'It almost sounds as though he was rebelling against his mother and enjoying it.'

A look of approval crossed Jim's face. She'd managed to divine what he was too tactful to say.

Eve wondered how deep Rupert's rebellion had been. Was it just his choice of readings, or his choice of wife? If it was the latter, his feelings might not have been built on solid foundations.

'Remember, they sounded relaxed together when I left them to talk,' Jim said, almost as though he'd read her mind.

'Their feelings seemed genuine.'

The vicar smiled again. 'Rupert said his father would be happy with the Kahlil Gibran.'

'Maybe Percival likes to live independently from his wife.'

Jim smiled and gave her a sidelong look. 'What an extraordinary conclusion to jump to, Eve. I certainly hadn't intended to hint at that.'

She smiled back. 'Of course not.'

'Rupert said Percival was a fan of Verity's and she said she was well aware of the fact. And then he apologised.'

'For his father?'

Jim had his back to her now and had wandered towards the water. Down on the mudflats, black-tailed godwits with their orange-brown summer plumage were probing for worms.

'Sorry?' he said, turning towards her with a vague smile.

She understood. He shouldn't be telling her any of this, and suggesting Sir Percival had flirted with Verity was a step too far, but she got it. Thank goodness Jim Thackeray trusted her and felt she had just cause to pry.

The take-home message was that Percival had been a creep, and Rupert was aware of it.

CHAPTER TWELVE

Eve walked through the heat to Monty's that afternoon, past gardens crowded with roses and lavender, their heady scent thick in the air. The sound of the bees and a blackbird's mellow song overlaid the voices of children playing on the village green.

Inside the teashop, the scene was just as colourful. The tables were covered with the same sea-green cloths they'd planned to use at the fete, and laden with Viv's trademark stylishly mismatched crockery and exquisite cupcakes. As usual, Eve cast an eye over the place as she entered, assessing the situation so that she was prepared for the work ahead. There were barely any spare seats. The outside tables overlooking the River Sax were all full. Out of the rear windows she could see the blue water, reflecting the sky above. There were gulls and waders aplenty on the sandbanks. The serenity of the scene was offset by the chat inside. Eve heard more than one person mention Verity Nye as she crossed the teashop to the counter, where Viv's son Sam was serving, alongside his girlfriend Kirsty. They both grinned.

'Mum'll be glad you're here,' Sam said. 'She's got some problem with the supplies for next week – but I think it's the need for information that's making her most desperate.'

Eve laughed. 'I'd better go out the back then.' She was down to do an admin session. Viv had taken her on to try to bring some order to Monty's. Eve was constantly fighting against the tide, but she enjoyed a challenge.

She walked into the teashop's kitchen to find Viv on her hands and knees, her rear half sticking out of one of the tall cupboards they used for spare flour and other ingredients.

'Everything all right?'

Viv jumped at her voice and knocked her head on a shelf. She emerged, rubbing her glossy blue-green hair.

'All the better for seeing you! Bear in mind, Eve, that I've had to wait' – she glanced at her watch – 'the best part of twenty-four hours for an update!'

Eve wasn't going to be deflected. She peered into the cupboard Viv had been searching. 'Sam said you had some kind of supplies problem. You might have to wait a bit longer for tea and chat if you want me to do my job.'

Viv gave a deliberate sigh. 'You're so strict. Honestly, I'm sure the admin can wait.'

'Have you got what you need to make up the cakes for tomorrow?'

Her friend avoided her eyes.

'I'll take that as a no. What's gone wrong?'

'You know when you asked me the quantities of ingredients I needed for the fete?'

'Yes?'

'And I told you. And you said was I sure?'

'Ah.' They'd made up the cakes before the fete was cancelled, and Viv had managed to sell them all the day before. Everyone who'd been planning to attend had visited Monty's instead, and donated to Wide Blue Yonder in Verity's memory. 'D'you want me to help Kirsty out while Sam goes to the cash and carry? I can catch up on the urgent admin after that and do the rest when I'm next in.' Eve made a mental note to insist on checking quantities herself next time. When Viv gave out information in an airy tone, while waving a dismissive hand, it was always a sign of trouble.

Viv gave her a winning smile. 'That would be fantastic. I wouldn't ask, only the cash and carry will close before we do, as it's Sunday.'

'That thought had crossed my mind.'

Three hours later, the crowds were thinning out, Sam had returned with the goods Viv needed, and much of the bake for the following day was prepared.

Viv appeared at Eve's shoulder as she put the finishing touches to Monty's weekly planner. 'No more excuses!' she said. 'I have an urgent need for updates, and everyone else in Monty's is talking about the murder. Did you hear about Dylan Walker accusing Mrs Barclay?'

Eve nodded. 'That, and rumours there's been a post-mortem on Verity, too.' She passed on the details without letting on it was Robin who'd told her. Even Viv didn't know about his past and his connection to Gregory Boles. It bothered Eve – she hated not being honest with her friend – but Robin wanted the secret kept, and she couldn't let him down.

'You knew all that – and you didn't tell me straight away?' Viv looked thunderstruck.

'Would we have got as far as bringing in emergency supplies on time if I had?'

'Erm… Well, fair point. It explains why they're so certain she was pushed. But now, Eve, we are going to sit at a corner table, where Kirsty and Sam will bring us strawberry shortcakes with elderflower cream and a large pot of Assam tea, and you will tell all!'

With the weekly plan sorted out, workers assigned to all shifts and plenty of flour and sugar in the cupboard, Eve felt relaxed enough to look forward to the debrief. Thrashing out the facts with Viv might help her see things more clearly.

Once they were settled, Eve took a bite of the dainty strawberry shortcakes – two layers of biscuit with elderflower cream and strawberry pieces in between. 'Perfection!'

'I thought it would be good to bring out a fresh summer recipe in time for August.'

'I love it.' The tea was refreshing too. The heat of the day was oppressive, but Sam had propped Monty's front and back doors open, making the most of the gentle summer breeze.

'So,' Viv said, 'obviously I want your news, but I'm feeling twitchy too. I know you were intent on investigating Verity's death when the police were convinced it was an accident, but couldn't you leave Palmer to it, now he's accepted it was murder? Playing sleuth just seems so risky.' Her eyes were serious, but suddenly she sat forward and looked more Viv-like. 'And I'd miss your help here if someone took you out. You know I'd never cope.'

'Gee, thanks!' Eve pulled a face, then stared into her tea, thinking. 'I hope Palmer does a decent job, but I don't trust him. He gets so blinkered – you know that. And I feel involved. I can't get my conversation with Verity out of my head. She confided in me, even if it was only in a minor way. It would be awful to let her down. And besides, there's every chance I'll discover something relevant while I'm interviewing. It would be crazy not to push a little further, to see if it amounts to anything.' She'd taken the same approach before. If something smelled off, she had to keep digging until she had the facts. The police wouldn't take her seriously unless her information stood up to scrutiny.

Viv took a sip of her tea and sighed. 'I knew you'd say that really. Just take care, okay?'

'I will. And if I find anything concrete, I'll take it to the police.'

Viv nodded. 'That's good – and I do see your point. Palmer needs a level-headed outsider to put him on the right track. I'm sure he'll suspect Jade Piper, given Verity fell from her window, and there's no way she's guilty. Look at the way she stuck up for Monty's and insisted on the Seagraves hiring us to cater for the fete.'

'I think it's possible to like good cake and hate someone enough to kill them at the same time.'

'Eve!' Viv looked at her as though she'd just claimed the world was flat. 'Honestly. But beyond her having good taste, who gets into the nitty-gritty of organising an event, right down to being bothered about the suppliers, if they're planning a murder?'

'I don't think this murder was planned.'

Viv paused, her piece of shortcake halfway to her mouth. 'You've already started to fathom it out! I love it! But what's your thinking? I suppose no one could know Verity would throw the tent out of the window, but Rupert Seagrave did say Cora had suggested it. Even if she didn't commit the murder, someone could have heard her give that advice and followed Verity upstairs, waiting to see if she'd take it.'

'It's actually Cora's suggestion that makes me think the murder was done in the heat of the moment.'

Viv's brow was furrowed as she took another bite of her strawberry shortcake. 'Explain.'

'It's clear Cora and Verity didn't get on. That's why Cora came to see me, in fact – to bad-mouth her.'

'Nice.'

Eve explained the dynamics involved, from Cora's thwarted plans to partner with Rupert to turn Seagrave Hall into a hotel, to her accusation about Verity and Pete Smith's affair.

Viv put her hand over her mouth. 'Blimey. So Cora and Rupert both have motives then.'

Eve nodded. 'So, anyway, it sounds as though tensions were running high at the hall and I'd guess all the main players on Friday knew the score between Cora and Verity. After all, they were all staying at the house, and Cora's a bad actress.'

Viv frowned. 'Okay. I'm with you so far. But why does that mean the murder wasn't planned?'

'I think Verity would have ignored Cora's advice about using the window on principle. And she scoffed at that type of labour-saving shortcut anyway. I heard her reaction when Tilly Cotton, the estate manager, offered to go and help her collect the tent. She laughed, but you could see it made her impatient; she didn't like people fussing. She knew she could manage. She was strong; used to swimming in extreme conditions. So no one would have imagined she was likely to be hanging out of a window at a precarious angle a few minutes later. I guess that means it was a last-minute decision on Verity's part, and whoever killed her was in the house for another reason, saw their chance and took it. They were probably in a complete state of shock afterwards. They might have fantasised about killing her before, but I'll bet they had no idea they were going to make it a reality that day.'

'Wow.' Viv sat back in her chair, frowning. 'But it makes sense.'

'And there's a second reason too. I've looked up falls.' She'd worked into the night on Saturday, checking every detail she had. 'Pushing someone from a height isn't a reliable way of killing them. People sometimes survive quite big drops, even if they're badly injured. And if Verity had landed more squarely on the tent, the cushioning could have changed the outcome too. Again, that points to someone overtaken by the moment. They didn't wait to plan and use a surer method. It was a big risk. Verity could easily have survived and identified them.'

'Onto the next question then. What on earth made her throw the tent out of the window?'

Eve let some more of the shortcake melt in her mouth. Viv's wares always helped her think. 'You're not going to like this, but maybe she wanted an excuse to go into Jade Piper's room.'

'What would she want in there?' Viv drained her tea and poured them each a refill.

'I have no idea. But Jade looked ill at ease on Friday.'

Viv sat forward in her chair and spoke slowly. 'You think she's got something to hide?'

'It's possible. I've called her office and left a message, asking for an interview.'

'I can't believe she's guilty,' Viv said stoutly. 'I really liked her.'

'I did too. But good people can do bad things. Especially if they're pushed to breaking point and act on the spur of the moment.' What could Verity have done that would make Jade do something so terrible? She couldn't imagine, but that didn't mean anything.

'I bet Palmer will go after her. She's just the sort he'll relish. A bit troubled. Kind. Defenceless.'

Viv had a point. But Jade Piper might still be guilty.

'So she's on your list of suspects?' Viv said, when Eve remained silent.

'She hasn't got an obvious motive. Whereas Rupert and Cora are right up there.' But she wanted to know more about Jade. There was something there, under the surface.

'And have you found anyone else who might have wanted Verity dead?'

'I wonder about Pete Smith.' Had he had time to run down the stairs and reach Verity's body as quickly as he had? It sounded as though the police thought so. He hadn't been on Robin's list of people who couldn't have been involved. 'If Cora's accusations about his affair with Verity are true, maybe he made one final attempt to persuade her not to end their relationship, and killed her when he failed. It would fit with the conversation I heard them having in the main marquee. He sounded angry then.

'Tilly's sent him a message for me, requesting an interview. He arrived on the scene before Rupert, Cora and Sir Percival, but I don't think he was especially quick. Rupert said he'd been for a smoke in the woods, Cora said she was on her way back from her cottage and Percival claims he was at the stables. And then Jade appeared from somewhere. I'm not even sure if she was last.' Eve cursed the shock that had blinded her to the details.

As she walked home, Eve weighed the suspects in her mind; the outsiders, Pete and Jade, versus the insiders, Rupert and Cora. Any of them could be guilty, but it was the Seagrave contingent that filled her with unease. It made sense that Tilly Cotton might protect a member of the family, if she'd caught a glimpse of the person who'd pushed Verity. And the Seagraves' hostility had been on the diver's mind. *Knives out.* Maybe even Rupert had lined up against her after Cora's accusations. Both he and his cousin seemed bound up with their own obsessions. Perhaps that removal from reality had allowed one of them to cross a terrible line.

Eve had only been home for five minutes when there was a knock at the door. The young woman on the cottage's front path introduced herself as Detective Constable Olivia Dawkins and showed her warrant card. Eve breathed a sigh of relief at not getting a personal visit from DI Palmer. Getting her statement about Friday would be below his paygrade, but that didn't usually stop him. He liked to intimidate her – or try to.

Eve invited DC Dawkins inside, where she accepted a glass of chilled lemonade. It was clear Gus approved of the woman. There was none of the suspicious trouser-leg sniffing or hostile stares he employed with Palmer.

'Do take a seat.'

The young woman seemed hesitant, and lowered herself awkwardly onto one of Eve's couches. 'Thank you. I understand you saw Ms Nye fall. Please could you tell me exactly where you were and what was happening beforehand? I'd like you to include everything you can remember until our officers arrived.'

Eve nodded. She'd been expecting the visit, so she'd gone over her notes again earlier in the day. She went through her movements, knowing they wouldn't help the investigation much. She guessed alibiing the vicar wasn't their top priority.

The constable noted everything she said, looking up periodically to nod her encouragement. And then she uttered the words Eve had been dreading. 'And is there anything you witnessed on Friday that might have a bearing on the case?'

The quarrel Eve had overheard from outside the main marquee filled her head, but she'd already decided her approach and it still felt like the right one. It wouldn't be fair to pass on the details without understanding the background, and she couldn't do that without more research. In reality, she was sure rumours of the affair would reach the police anyway, via Cora. Armed with that knowledge, she suspected Palmer would go doggedly after Pete Smith and Jade Piper. The revelation would give Rupert a motive for killing his fiancée too, but she doubted the DI would let that bother him. It would be up to her to look at the tensions between Rupert, Cora and Verity. Once she was armed with hard facts she could pass on proper information.

'Nothing I can think of. I guess you already heard about the exchange between Rupert and Cora just after Verity fell?' Every villager there had witnessed it.

The DC nodded. 'But please tell me about it yourself too, in your own words.'

Eve obliged. When she'd finished explaining how Rupert had lashed out at his cousin for advising Verity to throw equipment out of the window, DC Dawkins thanked her and drained her lemonade. Yet still she didn't get up. She'd put her notebook away, and was looking at her hands, which were twisting in her lap.

'Is there anything else I can help you with?' Eve asked.

'I… er… I have a message from DI Palmer.'

Gus tensed. And so did Eve. 'Yes?'

'He wanted to let you know that he's keen for you to steer clear of the murder investigation. I mean' – the woman's flush deepened – 'for your own safety of course. And for operational reasons.'

Eve bet that wasn't how he'd put it. 'I quite understand.'

'He said—'

Eve couldn't bear to see her squirm. 'Let me guess. He said to mind my own business and that if he finds I've gone beyond my brief he'll get an order to stop me questioning Verity Nye's contacts.'

DC Dawkins' face was a blotchy red now. 'That's pretty much it.'

Gus looked at the young woman with disappointment in his eyes.

Eve's adrenaline had kicked in. She imagined stamping on Palmer's toes in her sturdiest boots, but she tried to control her expression. DC Dawkins deserved a warm smile. It must be hell working for Palmer. 'Please tell the detective inspector that I understand his message.' *And fully intend to ignore it.*

The DC nodded, got up quickly and rushed to the front door.

Later that evening, Eve sat at the round ironwork table in her garden and watched the sun sink over Elizabeth's Cottage, streaking the darkening blue sky with gold. Gus put a paw up on her lap.

She turned to ruffle his fur. 'You're just as beautiful as the sunset! Yes you are!'

Her mind had been on Rupert Seagrave and his claim that he'd been in the woods when his fiancée was killed. Cora said she'd told him about Verity and Pete Smith's supposed affair half an hour before that. But she said he'd refused to believe her story, openly at least, without proof. She couldn't imagine he'd have left it at that. He might have wanted to challenge Verity – and maybe to search for evidence too. But what with all the organisation he wouldn't have had much time.

Would he really have gone off into the woods instead, to brood about the matter in private?

What if he'd lied? He might have seen his fiancée go inside the house to fetch the tent and followed her in for a quiet word. Or maybe he'd taken the chance to look round Pete Smith's room, to see if he could find evidence.

'I think Rupert loved Verity, Gus, and Jim Thackeray agrees.' She gazed into the dachshund's brown eyes. 'But that doesn't mean he's rational. What if he went into the house, full of pent-up rage and jealousy, found his proof and then saw Verity in such a vulnerable position? What then?'

CHAPTER THIRTEEN

Jade Piper had offered to see Eve on Monday morning. The Wide Blue Yonder offices were in London, but she was working with a group of young women in a town called Eastbury-on-Sea in Essex that day, so Eve's journey shouldn't be too bad. After giving Gus a run in the woods, she changed into the most lightweight interview clothes she had: a fitted knee-length sky-blue dress with a scarlet-trimmed neckline that gave it some punch. She had a jacket to match, but it might be a bit much. It was important to look serious and to make sure her interviewees knew she minded, and a suit could help with that. But Jade Piper would also be in the middle of her working day, putting in hours for the cause she championed. Eve wanted to look businesslike, but without overdoing it.

She'd already looked up Wide Blue Yonder when she and Viv had agreed to supply the cakes for the fete. She never went into things with her eyes closed. She'd dug deeper now and knew the organisation was more than just a career to Jade: she'd established it. Eve needed to mainline on questions about Verity, but understanding the charity manager might hint at the dynamics of her relationship with the diver too.

Jade's directions took Eve to the seafront on the south side of Eastbury-on-Sea, beyond the residential area. She parked on a wide tarmacked road outside the single-storey cream building that Jade had described, down to its clapboard exterior: the town's community rooms. The glass door at the front was unlocked, the main room inside empty, with a deserted stage area, scuffed parquet flooring, and slightly grubby yellow paint. But beyond the room, through double glass doors, Eve could see Jade. She was outside on a decking area with a group of girls in their mid- to late-teens, dressed in crop tops and shorts. Jade herself was wearing three-quarter length jeans and a Breton top. Eve was glad she'd ditched her jacket.

She strode through to join them. The glass doors creaked as she pushed them open, but Jade didn't notice her presence immediately. Eve could see the fire in her eyes as she spoke to one of the girls. The others were in conversation too – with each other. It was one of them that spotted Eve first, and got Jade's attention.

'Thanks so much for seeing me when you're busy.'

Jade's deep-brown hair flew in the sea breeze. 'That's okay.' Her eyes were still half on the group she'd got with her, but the look of anxiety Eve had noticed on Friday, well before Verity fell, was edging its way back into her expression too.

'You carry on making plans, okay?' Jade said to the group.

They nodded from where they sat, perched on a wooden bench and on the low walls that bordered the deck. They looked engaged. Eve felt they had metaphorical wind in their sails, as well as actual wind in their hair.

'It's a holiday session,' Jade said, as she and Eve went back indoors. 'But we meet regularly after school in term time too. I run this group because I live this side of London, but now we're expanding I'm recruiting trainers in twelve different hubs around the UK to provide the same service. Then hopefully they'll train more trainers, and the whole thing will mushroom.' She was slightly flushed, her eyes bright and intense. The worry that had crept into her face lost its grip for a moment as she spoke about her work. 'It's a good sustainable way of scaling things up.'

'It sounds brilliant. I'd love to include some of this information in the obituary I'm writing. It's feature-length, so I've got space to go into more detail than someone writing for a newspaper.'

'That would be great.'

Eve had noticed a news report saying Wide Blue Yonder had enjoyed an influx of donations following Verity's death.

'What sparked your interest in this area of work?'

Jade had taken her through to an office off the main hall of the community building now, and motioned her to a seat in front of a basic veneer-topped desk. She sat down herself and glanced out of the window for a moment at the girls in her group and the North Sea beyond.

'I had what most people would consider a fairly easy upbringing: middle-class parents, food on the table, books and so on. But my father was a difficult man. He wore down my confidence day in, day out. I lost any self-belief I might have had, but then' – she paused and swallowed, her hands held together tightly on the desk – 'then I saw someone who had it worse than I did. It was trying to help her that saved me.' She took a deep breath and turned to face Eve properly. 'A teacher had tried to help before that. She told me I was doing well, but it was all "Come along now, Jade, buck up! You can do this!" And I didn't believe her. It was seeing someone else just like me that gave me some perspective.'

'So that's your model now? You bring together young girls and women who've been through similar trials?'

Jade nodded. 'Their problems are quite varied, but the key thing is, they see each other, and they want to help. And they share. And before you know where you are, they're getting stronger and stronger because they've found something to fight for, even if it isn't themselves. Once that feeling of empowerment's unlocked, starting to battle for their own future usually comes next.' She was fired up again. 'We don't just get them to talk. They do things like self-defence, to improve their feeling of control in a difficult world. That lot out there' – she nodded towards the window – 'are a formidable support network now. They don't have to be friends; they back each other on principle.'

Eve was scribbling down notes, feeling enthused herself. 'I can ask the magazine I'm working for to include your website, so people can donate.'

Jade flushed and smiled. 'Thanks.'

The room was stifling but she didn't open the window. Eve guessed she wanted the girls outside to have their privacy. She must have seen Eve wipe her brow though; a moment later she offered iced water from a humming fridge behind the desk. Eve sipped from the glass Jade had poured her and tried to resist the temptation to raise the vessel to her cheek and press it there to cool herself.

'So what made you approach Verity Nye to be Wide Blue Yonder's ambassador?' Eve watched Jade's face. She could come up with her own answers of course: Verity's fame would provide brilliant publicity, and her daring might be inspirational to the young women Jade worked with, but Eve didn't want to make assumptions.

Jade gave the answers she'd expected, but she blinked quickly before she responded: a sign of stress.

'I suppose you must have to pick between a shortlist of people,' Eve said, 'and then sound them out to see who's best for the role?'

Jade sipped her water. 'I did my research beforehand, so I knew Verity wasn't doing anything similar already.'

'Did the job take up a lot of her time?'

'No, and the number of hours were specified in a contract before we started. She'd agreed to do a handful of special events each year, plus some limited mentoring.' For a moment Jade looked thoughtful. 'One-to-one sessions aren't part of Wide Blue Yonder's standard approach, but a sponsor came forward and liked the idea of organising an award with mentoring as the prize. I was in two minds, but it seemed like a good way to raise the charity's profile; it's easier to get publicity for a prize with a single stand-out winner than it is for good, solid day-to-day work.' She sighed and shook her head. 'You could speak to the mentee who won if you like. I'll give you the details.' She wrote them down on a sticky note.

'Thanks.' Eve tucked it into her bag. 'You must have known Verity quite well in the end. I can see you were very hands-on when it came to organising the fete at Seagrave Hall, for instance. I presume you saw her in the family setting if you ate together there?'

'Just at that one event. Normally I'd stay at a guesthouse so I could cover all the set-up, and Verity would arrive on the day unless she had a long way to travel.'

So if the adventurer had been looking for a chance to sneak into Jade's room, it sounded as though the fete had presented a rare opportunity.

'I was planning to stay at the pub in Saxford St Peter this time,' Jade went on, 'but Sir Percival insisted that I have a room at the hall when I arrived.' Her eyes were unreadable for a moment.

Eve considered Jade Piper's gleaming hair, deep brown eyes and fine figure, then remembered Jo Falconer having called Sir Percival a 'giddy old goat'. It was a light-hearted term for what might be a serious character failing.

'In the end it was handy to be on the spot. Verity approved and the pub let me cancel.'

'That's good. And what was Verity like to work with?'

The charity manager chewed her lip. 'She was used to being in charge. Collaborating wasn't her forte.'

Eve smiled. 'I saw her laying down the law about something when you spoke with her on Friday. She was gesticulating at the hall.'

'I covered the admin side of the events we did together. An ambassador is a figurehead, to draw in the crowds. No one expects them to act like a charity employee. But there are ways and ways of asking if you want someone to do something.'

Eve nodded. But she'd seen Verity trying to placate Jade too, and she'd looked sincere. Maybe she'd overstepped the mark one too many times. Given Wide Blue Yonder pushed young women to collaborate, it was ironic if they'd ended up with an ambassador who wasn't a team player.

'I was in the estate manager's office printing out a file for Verity when she fell from my window.' Jade's words came out in a rush.

Eve guessed the police must have interviewed her by now. She bet Palmer was going after the woman with his foot to the floor, thanks to that extra detail.

'I don't know why she chose my room,' Jade went on, 'but I guess it was most convenient.' Her shoulders were stiff and hunched as she sat forward in her chair. 'She wouldn't have worried about going in there. My bedroom was the equivalent of my office while I was working on the fete. We'd met there to discuss arrangements the day before.'

'That makes sense.' In reality, Eve was planning to analyse the matter once she was back in her car, but she saw Jade relax a little at her words.

'I didn't know she'd fallen,' she said now, her eyes wide, as though she was remembering. 'The estate office faces towards the woods, at the side of the house, so all the activity was out of sight, and the printer was noisy. I didn't hear anything.' Her knuckles were white as she gripped her glass. 'I went to fetch the paperwork I'd printed off, and walked out of the room. My mind was still on the speeches for the following day. But as I went into the corridor the side door to the garden was just swinging shut.'

Was that true? Had Jade narrowly missed seeing Verity's murderer leave the hall?

Jade's eyes were bleak now. 'I told the police, but I don't think they believed me. And I didn't see who it was.'

Eve felt a trickle of sweat snake its way down her back.

'I got outside just in time to see Pete Smith making sure no one got near Verity's body.'

'That no one got near?' Eve couldn't help herself. The words were odd. She'd have said 'injured Verity further by moving her' or something similar.

'That's what it looked like. I had a better view than some people.' She paused. 'He crouched down and checked Verity's vital signs, and made an attempt at resuscitation, but it wasn't how I was taught.' She glanced out of the window at her group of girls. 'I had to do a first aid course before I started running our youth sessions, so I noticed. Of course, at the time it never occurred to me that Verity was murdered, but since I found out, the thought of him keeps filling my head.'

CHAPTER FOURTEEN

Back in the dining room at Elizabeth's Cottage, Eve's head was full of the interview she'd conducted that morning. Jade said she'd told the police about Pete Smith – the way he'd kept people back, and his attempts at resuscitation that didn't match her memory of correct procedure. But Jade had the impression the police doubted her word. Maybe they thought she was trying to divert attention away from herself. Eve wondered what motive Palmer thought Jade had. She hadn't identified one, but it wasn't enough to reassure her. She'd had the opportunity.

Eve opened her laptop and looked again at the photograph that Sylvia had taken of her; she had sunglasses balanced on top of her head. And who was more likely to have dashed into her bedroom to fetch something, only to find Verity there, leaning precariously out of the window? If Jade had something to hide, she might have guessed why the adventurer had been in her room, and taken the opportunity to silence her. But what could Jade have to conceal?

She needed to find out more. It would be useful to speak with the young woman who'd won mentoring sessions with Verity. She found the contact details Jade had given her and dialled the number. After multiple rings, a guy answered and said she was away, volunteering on an environmental project in the Amazon. It certainly sounded as though the mentoring had spurred her on, but she wouldn't be easy to talk to.

Eve looked at Wide Blue Yonder's website to find more informa-tion on the prize. It had been a six-session mentoring programme with Verity, according to the charity's press release. The actress Kim Carmichael had sponsored the prize and hosted the award ceremony. Eve could see why the project had seemed promising in terms of publicity.

'This might be the lead I want,' Eve said to Gus, who'd just pottered into the dining room. She stroked his head. In fact, she was glad the mentee was abroad; it gave Eve an excuse to talk to the actress, and the woman was a much better bet when it came to investigating Verity Nye's murder. 'As the funder, Ms Carmichael would have been given updates on the project. She's probably aware of the dynamics between Jade and Verity.' Eve would have to explain her reasons for requesting an interview, but she had plenty of ideas for that. An account of the adventurer's charity work was important for the obituary, and including the actress would add colour and a fresh perspective. It would be good to speak with someone independent, who'd been involved, but not intimately. And her name would draw readers in. 'I even have myself convinced.'

She'd just called Kim Carmichael's agent to broker a meeting when there was a knock at the door of Elizabeth's Cottage. Gus bounded towards the sound and indulged in a barking frenzy, his tail wagging with excitement.

'You know,' she said to him, 'it's a little bit insulting that the arrival of a visitor makes you so ecstatic. I might be forced to assume my scintillating company isn't enough for you.'

Gus looked at her as she reached the front door and gave a little sideways bounce, his tail wagging still harder. It was clear she hadn't moved him with her comment.

She opened up and found Viv's brother Simon standing on the doorstep.

'Hello, you!' He gave her a warm smile and a kiss on the cheek. 'Long time no see.' He was always bouncy, but there was something artificially jolly about his tone today, which made Eve curious.

'You look well!' He was sporting a white open-necked shirt that showed off his healthy tan. He ran a riding stables, as well as dabbling in a number of other businesses.

'Thanks!'

Was he blushing slightly? He bent to scratch Gus, who'd rolled over onto his back. Eve watched him from the shadowy interior of the cottage as he stood upright again in the heat of the sun, the hedgerow of Haunted Lane behind him, alive with birdsong.

'Viv mentioned you're writing about Verity Nye. She wanted me to seek you out and tell you everything I know about the Seagraves as background.'

Simon had helped her with local intel in the past; he had fingers in a lot of pies and was a mine of information.

'I've worked with the family quite a bit over the years,' he went on. 'Helped them buy horses for their stables, that kind of thing. They're expecting a delivery of another one this week, only I don't suppose they've thought of it, what with everything that's happened. It was meant to be a present for Verity, as a matter of fact. A mare she could ride when she's at the hall.' He frowned. 'I'll have to call them about it, but it's not an appealing thought. I'll give them a day or two first. Anyway,' he met her eyes, 'I thought Gus might like a session at the Cross Keys, and you could come with us.' Simon bent again to fuss the dachshund, who'd jumped up at the mention of the pub. To him, it meant playtime with Toby Falconer's schnauzer, Hetty. 'Besides,' Simon added, 'I've been wanting a word with you.'

Eve's antennae quivered. What was on his mind?

Whatever it was, it was probably best tackled head on. Besides, a cool drink was appealing, and Simon usually came up with good information. She attached Gus's leash (and was met with a disdainful look), grabbed her bag and keys and followed Simon down the lane. Overhead, tiny brown and white sand martins flew, agile and swift, towards the estuary; their chirruping song filled the air.

'So, Viv tells me you're interested in the set-up at Seagrave Hall, as well as in Verity Nye's life story.' Simon gave her his twinkly smile.

'That's right. Verity gave a talk at the school where I used to work, and then I spoke with her shortly before she died, and we clicked.' The fleeting feeling of connection came back to her and she shook her head. She needed to be practical; it was all she could do now. 'I didn't really know her of course, but I liked her, based on what I saw. And Viv's keen for me to keep my ear to the ground too. There are rumours going round that the police suspect the Wide Blue Yonder charity manager, Jade Piper, and she took a liking to her.'

'Ah yes, she mentioned that.' Simon shot her a sidelong glance. 'And what do you think?'

'That Jade's holding something back. I interviewed her this morning and there were a couple of times when she avoided my eye. Once when I asked her why she'd set up her charity' – Eve remembered she'd looked out of the window as she replied – 'and once when I wanted to know how they recruit their ambassadors.'

'Interesting.'

'I admired her too. She's passionate and driven.' But then Eve thought of the zeal she'd seen in the woman's eye. Passionate and driven people might kill, if they thought their cause was worthy. A second later her mind went back to Verity and Pete Smith's conversation in the main marquee, an hour or so before she'd died. It sounded as though Pete had been following a woman around. Verity had told him to stop because he was making it too obvious, but he'd protested that it was necessary, to protect their interests. Could it have been Jade they were talking about? If they were after some kind of information, maybe Verity had decided to scout round Jade's room herself. But Eve couldn't imagine what she might have been looking for.

She sighed. 'Whatever the truth about Jade, she deserves to have someone on her side – at least to the extent that they're receptive to all genuine information, wherever it leads. And yes, I'm also curious about the family. I can't get Verity's death out of my head. She was so beautiful, and so vital. I suspect she could be impatient and brusque sometimes, because she was quick and driven herself, so she could have ruffled feathers that way, but there's obviously more to this.' Eve wished she could tell Simon about her conversations with Rupert and Cora Seagrave, but it wouldn't be ethical. It was bad enough that she'd confided in Viv and Robin.

She'd already created a spreadsheet detailing information relevant to Verity's murder. There were tabs for all the main players in her life. At the moment the family insiders, Cora and Rupert, were top of her list of suspects, but without a confession, or a witness, she couldn't imagine how she'd go about proving their guilt. Motive and opportunity weren't enough. She could only hope some general digging unearthed something unexpected. And in the meantime, she mustn't exclude the outsiders just because Palmer would give them top priority. Jade made her anxious, and she needed to speak with Pete Smith. Things between him and Verity had clearly been emotionally charged. And if Jade's story was true, and he'd failed to take proper action to resuscitate the diver, it pointed to his guilt.

Eve still suspected Tilly Cotton was trying to protect someone, which made a family insider seem more likely, but who knew how much she'd seen? If it was just a shadow, she might have jumped to the conclusion it was a Seagrave because of the tensions between them and Verity. And from far below, it was possible she might have mistaken Pete for Rupert. Each of them was fair, with a similar build. The fact that Cora and Jade were both brunettes put the icing on the cake. Eve couldn't narrow down her suspects based on what Tilly might have seen.

For a second, Eve thought how mad DI Palmer would be if he could see her notes and felt a small lifting of her spirits.

They crossed the pub's forecourt and went through to the shady interior, where Jo Falconer stood at the bar, fanning herself with a sheet of A4 card. That day's menu. Jo despised pubs that had set lists of food that rarely changed. Everything she produced was seasonal and cooked fresh. Her narrowed eyes had been focused on a guy with an untidy beard who Eve didn't recognise. He was talking on his phone about the murder as his plate of food cooled in front of him.

As Eve and Simon walked in, she diverted her gaze, gave them a wave and then handed them the menu.

Simon raised an eyebrow. 'Shall we?'

'It would be rude not to.' This came from Jo. She gave Toby, who was standing next to her, a deadpan look when he shook his head.

Jo put the fear of God into newcomers, but Eve and Simon knew her well enough not to be bullied. And Eve's mouth was already watering. It was late lunchtime. She chose salmon and samphire linguine. Simon went for mussels and fries.

'At least I know you two will appreciate your meals properly,' Jo said, nodding at the guy on the phone and not bothering to lower her voice. 'Some people round here are only focused on the copy they'll file for the rags they work for.'

Broadsheet or tabloid, local or national, Jo had no time for journalists unless they behaved themselves – and that included treating her food with the reverence it deserved.

Gus had spotted Hetty and they were performing their usual meeting ritual, which involved tumbling about the place in an undignified manner.

Jo pointed to the back door. 'Outside, you two. There's no excuse for roughhousing in here when the weather's like it is. Go on!'

'Oh all right then!' Simon laughed. 'Oh, I see. You meant the dogs.' They'd already shot into the garden, Gus with an anxious look over his shoulder at Eve. Jo made him nervous.

'Wine?' Simon said.

Eve shook her head. 'I'll never work this afternoon if I start this early in the day.' Simon's smile was undimmed, and Matt Falconer was on the approach. Toby outflanked his brother before he started badgering Eve with a rundown of his favourite whites.

'Sparkling water please,' she said to him, and he grinned and nodded.

Simon laughed. 'You're probably right. I'll have the Sauvignon Blanc.'

A moment later they joined the dogs in the garden, and sat in the shade of one of the cream parasols, looking down the lawn to the fields, marshes and estuary beyond.

'So,' Simon said, leaning on the wooden table between them, 'let's see what I can tell you.' He took a sip of his wine. 'I first got to know the Seagraves about twelve years ago, I suppose, when Rupert and Cora were around seventeen. There's only a month or so between them in age – Rupert's slightly older. As I said, I was involved in buying some horses for the family, so I saw quite a bit of them. Both the kids were mad keen on nags at that point. I think Rupert's more into cars these days, but Cora still came to make a fuss of the last new animal I delivered.'

'What do you think of her?'

'Very easy on the eye, obviously.' He grinned. Eve was glad he was honest. Viv had warned her from the start he was a flirt. Despite that, she'd gone on a few dates with him. He was charming and thoughtful, but their romance had fizzled out quickly. They were too different. A frown crossed his brow. 'I always got the impression Cora came to the stables for the attention, as much as to make friends with the latest family pet.' He paused. 'I say "pet" but at one time Percival bought shares in a racehorse. I advised against it, to be honest. He was charged over the odds, but the person doing the deal was an old family friend, and he went for it.' He chuckled. 'I can still remember Belinda Seagrave's expression when she found out he'd gone ahead. The hall must eat money, and I don't imagine there's enough to go round. If *he* ever gets tossed out of a window, I shall know exactly who's done it, even if I don't see Belinda standing just behind him.' He paused and coughed. 'Sorry. That was in poor taste.'

Eve hadn't minded his joke, but it wasn't like him. Why was he so excitable today?

'Anyway, back when they were kids, Cora and Rupert got on well.'

That must have been before Cora had blown her inheritance on her failed hotel venture and the need for more money had reared its ugly head.

Jo arrived with their food and set it down for them. They paused to thank her with all the ceremony she'd expect. Her attitude was fair; the salmon linguine smelled awesome.

'That was before I got to know Percival and Belinda better.' Simon picked up his fork, ready to attack a mussel. 'I mainly dealt with the estate manager back then.'

Eve thought of the woman she'd met. 'Tilly?' But she was close to Rupert and Cora in age.

Simon ate the mussel he'd extracted and speared a French fry, his expression darkening. 'No, not Tilly – her father, Walter Cotton. I didn't like him from the off, and when I turned up one day and saw a bruise under Ivy Cotton's eye, I was pretty sure I knew the sort of man he was. I was worried.'

'Were you able to do anything?' Eve twisted linguine round her fork. The salty samphire was perfect paired with the salmon.

Simon looked regretful. 'I tried to hint to her that I was standing by to help if she ever needed it, but it was difficult, because I hardly knew her. Anyway, I breathed a sigh of relief when I heard Percival had given him the sack. He disappeared from the area and

Tilly took over his job later. She's more than capable. She's grown up knowing the hall's business inside out.'

'When you say business…?'

'What it takes to run the place, grants they can apply for to help manage some of the land, a small sideline selling hall produce. She's been talking about developing that into something bigger. And last year she asked me if I knew anything about establishing a vineyard. I wasn't able to help, but she's resourceful; she'll have found out.' His dark eyes were far away. 'She and Rupert were sweet on each other at one point.'

Eve paused, her water halfway to her lips. 'I didn't know that.'

'A teenage romance. Not unnatural, I guess. She, Cora and Rupert had all grown up together. Then I remember turning up one day and the atmosphere was stilted. Tilly had given Rupert the push and a short while later I saw her out in Southwold with a new guy.' He finished another fry.

'I wonder if she's with anyone now.' Eve sipped her water.

Simon frowned. 'I think she is. I've seen her out with a bloke who owns a farm beyond Blythburgh.' He sat back in his seat. 'I'm not sure what else I can tell you, really. Except that Belinda and Cora have a personality clash. As soon as I started to deal with the Seagraves senior, after Walter was sacked, that became obvious. Percival was always indulging her. I guess that didn't help. I got the impression Cora made the most of his favour, but it could never replace what she'd lost, of course.' He sighed.

'The Seagraves seem to have very different ideas on just about everything,' he went on. 'I imagine Rupert didn't know where he stood when he was growing up. I wonder if that's why he fell so heavily in love with Verity. She was very different to what he was used to, from what I can see.'

'You might be right. She struck me as straightforward.' But then Eve thought of the conversation she'd overheard in the marquee.

She needed to be objective, to resist the urge to mould the woman into the character she wanted her to be.

As they continued their meals, with the water of the River Sax sparkling in the sunlight beyond the fields, Eve asked after Simon's stables, and they chatted about the teashop.

'And how's Polly?' she said. Simon had been dating the woman for a few months now; she was surprised he hadn't mentioned her.

'She's well.' He was blushing. It looked as though his whole face wanted to smile but was being overridden for some reason.

'What is it?' The answer came to her a microsecond before he answered.

'As a matter of fact, we've just got engaged.' His words came out in a rush and the blush increased. For a second his eyes were down on the table, but then he raised them to meet hers. His expression was uncertain. 'I wanted to let you know.'

'But that's fantastic! I'm so pleased for you! Congratulations. Oh, wow!' Too many words. She must stop now. Thank goodness she'd been firm and stuck to the mineral water. Gus had caught her tone and got up from under the table where he'd been shading himself from the sun. He looked expectantly from one of them to the other.

Simon did smile now – shyly. 'Thanks. I just… well, you know.'

Eve had a horrible feeling she did. He'd been concerned she might get upset. In fact, she was completely relaxed about the whole thing. So why had she overcompensated when gushing her response? She felt a blush come to her cheeks. She'd been reacting to *his* discomfort. And now he'd be convinced she was bothered. 'I'm really pleased for you both.' That was enough. 'I can't believe Viv never said anything! Though I haven't seen her since yesterday.' She was still surprised her friend hadn't bounded round to share the news.

Simon was full-on red now. 'Erm, actually, I haven't told her yet.'

'Why ever not?' She wasn't Polly's most ardent fan, but Simon was old enough to know what he was doing.

'Oh,' Simon drained his wine, 'you know. I just haven't managed to catch her. I didn't want to blurt it out in front of everyone at Monty's.'

Eve nodded. 'No. Right. Of course.' *Stop it.*

A short while later, back at Elizabeth's Cottage with Gus, she sank down onto one of the couches. 'You know what this means, don't you, Gus?'

Her faithful dachshund looked up at her, his melting brown eyes concerned.

'It means Simon was convinced I'd mind. He probably spent hours agonising about telling me.' She stood up and clutched at her hair. She'd not long had the pixie crop trimmed, so there was irritatingly little to get hold of. 'He even told me before Viv!' The colour came to her cheeks again. She'd had to cope with Ian, her ex, feeling guilty and sorry for her, even though she was really enjoying life without him, but it was much worse with Simon. He was a friend and neighbour. And his sister was her best friend and co-worker. They'd both be peering at her anxiously now. How could she make sure he knew how she felt, so he wasn't busy pitying her? 'Heck!'

Gus looked startled. She crouched down to give him a cuddle. 'Sorry. Normal service will be resumed shortly.' She went to the kitchen to fix herself a coffee. This was ridiculous. She needed to concentrate on Verity Nye.

She turned her mind determinedly to the facts as she spooned grounds into her cafetière. So, Tilly Cotton had once dated Rupert. She'd ended the teenage relationship and gone off with someone else, and these days she was dating a local farmer by the sound of it. Eve pictured the woman: fresh-faced, organised, dedicated. She could imagine her wanting to date someone just as active and dynamic. A guy who knew some of the issues of land management and running a business. But that didn't mean her old fondness for Rupert had vanished entirely. As the water boiled, Eve thought of her anxious face again, when Belinda Seagrave had asked what she'd seen up at the window. She wondered if Tilly thought Rupert had killed Verity. Maybe she even wondered what would have happened if she'd stayed with him, and he and Verity had never met. Was she protecting him? Did she know what he'd done? Or was it just a worry that was gnawing away at her?

At that moment, Eve's mobile rang. Viv. Simon must have passed on his news then. Cue an onslaught of sympathy Eve didn't need.

Putting her shoulders back and taking a deep breath, she accepted the call.

CHAPTER FIFTEEN

The aftermath of Viv's phone call made Eve all the more determined to focus on Verity's obituary. Anything to stop Viv's anxious tone echoing round her head; the call was kindly meant, but it had set her teeth on edge.

She snatched up her coffee, almost slopping it, then marched into the dining room at Elizabeth's Cottage and flipped her laptop lid open. A second later, she brought up the spreadsheet detailing people she wanted to interview for her obituary, then launched the one called 'Murder Suspects' too.

Eve wanted to know more about Rupert and Cora. Simon's information had helped, but she might discover extra details when she went for the tour of Seagrave Hall. Tilly had left a message, agreeing to show her round.

But for now, Pete Smith was her focus. What had gone through his head as he checked Verity's breathing and pulse? She imagined him staring down at her, alive but helpless, then performing resuscitation badly, knowing he was doing more harm than good. A chill rippled through her body, but Jade might have a reason to lie, and no one else had questioned the medic's actions as far as she knew.

Tilly Cotton's efforts to approach him on her behalf had failed. He wasn't answering calls or emails according to the message the estate manager had left. She couldn't expect Tilly to keep chasing him up. She got to work on Google, looking for other ways to track him down.

It was a moment later, when Eve was deep in her work, that Kim Carmichael called. In person. The thought of the multiple

Oscar-winner on the other end of the line did nothing to help Eve get her breath back. She'd thought she'd hear from her agent – if she heard at all.

'*Come and see me!*' It was weird to hear the familiar voice from her own phone. '*I'm bored as hell! I've got the builders in, and I've twisted my damned ankle so I can't go anywhere to escape them.*' She gave a gravelly laugh. '*Though one of them's just brought me a cup of tea, so I can't really complain! Can you come tomorrow for elevenses? Only I've got great-grandchildren descending this afternoon. Can you imagine? Love them to bits, obviously, but just think! Hammering from upstairs and toys everywhere.*'

She was down in north London, Eve knew. 'I'll be there. Please may I have the address?'

Kim Carmichael rattled it off, while Eve balanced the phone between her ear and shoulder and tapped the details into her laptop. They'd said their goodbyes when Kim suddenly spoke again.

'*Oh, I forgot. Bring cake, would you? Lemon drizzle!*'

Kim Carmichael's base wasn't far from the twins; they were both in north London. She messaged them in case they had time for lunch the following day. Her work on Verity Nye's obituary weighed on her mind; she ought to tell them what she was up to and besides, she missed them. It had been a couple of months since they'd met. After that, she made herself go back to chasing Pete Smith, but half an hour later she gave up. She'd found some online contact details but none of them elicited a response. She was forced to leave messages and hope he'd get back to her.

In the meantime, she did what she'd normally do: find alternative sources who could give a similar viewpoint. She began to identify other adventurers who'd socialised or worked with Verity according to reports in the press. After that she dug for ways of contacting them, from websites to PR agencies. She needed to know what it had been like to dive with the woman: to rely on her under pressure, to plan a trip and celebrate afterwards. Without that, the life story she wrote would be nothing. After leaving multiple messages, she moved on to look for childhood friends. She found a woman who'd been doorstepped by a journalist in the immediate aftermath of Verity's death. She'd been at school with her and now ran a gift store just down the coast, according to the article. Eve found the store's number, called and left yet another message. Could they really be so busy they couldn't get to the phone? Maybe the place was full of holidaymakers, given the season.

She sighed, got up from her chair and put her shoulders back. Nothing was going to fall into her lap that day, clearly. She needed a break.

'Walk, Gus?'

He bounded towards the door, his tail wagging vigorously.

She left the sandals she'd worn for her pub lunch and put on a pair of flip-flops instead. The path along the estuary would be cracked and dry; they'd had weeks of heat now, and little rain. Once she'd picked up her bag, Gus's leash (just in case) and his ball, she was ready.

'C'mon then!'

She let them out and Gus gambolled about in the lane as though he hadn't been walked for a month. He tore ahead and she followed him towards the path that led to the estuary, letting her mind drift to her visit with Kim Carmichael the following day. It might reveal a lot, and it would be fascinating to meet the woman. She could start by asking—

'Eve?' The voice behind her made her jump.

Rupert Seagrave was standing in the road. He looked pale but neat, wearing a white shirt and dark trousers. She paused, uncertain what to do with Gus well beyond her and Rupert back by the house.

He walked towards her. 'I was hoping for a word, but you're going out.'

'Taking my dachshund for an airing.' She glanced over her shoulder to where she could just see Gus, peering out from behind a gorse bush at the start of Elizabeth's Walk.

'Perhaps I could come with you?'

She hesitated. Her lack of progress had left her frustrated, and he must have more information, but going with him along the lonely pathway by the mudflats made her nervous. It was well out of earshot of the nearest house.

'I'll call Gus back. It'll be easier to talk inside.'

'No, no – I insist. I don't want to make you change plan.'

What the heck should she do? For a crazy moment she imagined being killed because she'd been too polite to put her foot down.

But in the awkward silence came voices. Two teenagers she didn't recognise appeared on Haunted Lane. As they approached she guessed they must be bound for the estuary path too and breathed a sigh of relief. She hoped it wasn't too obvious.

'Well, if you're sure.'

She turned back towards the direction she'd been headed, but he put out a hand. 'Perhaps if we just pause a moment…'

They waited as the teenage couple dashed past them. Laughing, they disappeared into the undergrowth.

Rupert wasn't quite meeting her eyes. 'It's just a little bit delicate. I'd rather not be overheard. Since the police confirmed Verity's death as murder, Seagrave business is everyone's business.'

At last he was happy for them to continue. At least Eve knew the kids couldn't be that far ahead.

'How are things at the hall?' she asked, as they strode along the dusty track, towards the high reeds that marked the edge of the estuary. It was too personal to ask how he was coping, but the more general opening would let him offload if he wanted to.

'Strained, what with the latest revelations. I still can't believe someone wanted to kill Verity.'

She glanced up at him. Was that really the truth? But she couldn't judge his expression; his eyes were focused on the way ahead.

'Cora…' He paused and shook his head. She could see the tension in his body, barely controlled. Eve tried to picture the conversation he and his cousin had had, just before Verity was killed. Cora telling him that his fiancée was sleeping with her team medic.

Rupert took a deep breath and started again. 'Cora and I had another row. She came to talk to me, and when I didn't respond in the way that she wanted, she did just what she usually does.'

They turned the corner to join the path adjacent to the estuary. Gus had paused to check they were on his tail. On seeing them he dashed off again, bounding as fast as his short legs would carry him. There was no sign of the teenagers who had reassured Eve. Rupert had fallen silent.

'What's that?'

'She's like a toddler!' His voice was uncontrolled. 'She said whatever she thought might cause me the most pain and anxiety at that moment. The first things that came to mind.'

He'd been staring ahead, but now he glanced down at Eve. 'She's been very pleasant to me in the last couple of months: calling me to see how I am, inviting me for coffee when she was in London. She was being too nice, but I fell for it. She kept it up for longer than she's done in years. But then she said something that—' He stopped abruptly. 'Well, anyway, you might already know all this. While she was hurling abuse at me, she mentioned she'd been to see you, and that she'd… she'd given you information she said would help with your obituary.'

He turned to face her fully now, and she stopped just as he had. She didn't want him behind her, where she couldn't see him. Her insides quivered. She was conscious of a distant shout. One of the teenagers. Close, but not close enough.

'We did talk,' Eve admitted. She couldn't tell him what Cora had said; it would go against all her rules. She needed to write her obituaries according to her own judgement, not let the content be fought over and influenced by others.

Rupert held her gaze for an uncomfortably long moment. He was so much taller than her. At last he nodded.

'Since she came to share some extra details with you, I decided I should too.' He paused. 'I've been told you've helped the police with their enquiries in the past and now we know it's murder we're dealing with, it's best if you understand the truth.'

So that was his reason for seeking her out. He wanted to manage her impressions. This was becoming an alarming game of one-upmanship. Neither he nor Cora were behaving like adults. Eve took a tentative step forward alongside Rupert and breathed again when he resumed walking too.

'I told you Cora was trying to persuade me to go into business with her, and turn Seagrave Hall into a hotel, as well as renting out our land.'

Eve nodded.

'And that naturally, I had to rethink that venture when I became engaged to Verity.'

'Yes.'

'You should know that Cora hadn't given up on her dream, even though I'd put the plans on hold. And she certainly thinks there's fresh life in the project now.'

He was silent for a moment. The repetitive call of a black-tailed godwit reached them from the mudflats beyond the reeds.

'I used to feel guilty about Cora,' Rupert said, running a hand through his red-blond hair. 'And it's been hard to throw that off. She inherited some money but lost it on a business venture. It wasn't entirely her fault, but my mother was determined not to give her any more funds to "fritter away", as she called it. And although Cora drives me crazy, we were like brother and sister once.' He looked up at the sky. 'I used to stick up for her when we were kids. My mother… well, it wasn't easy for her, taking Cora in.'

Belinda Seagrave hadn't treated Rupert and Cora as equals emotionally, just as Eve had thought.

'But Cora had a rough time too, and part of the reason she blew her money on the business venture down in London was because she wanted to escape. I didn't do enough to make her stop and think.' His sigh was just audible. 'But maybe my guilt was misplaced. My mother tells me I don't see people for what they are. And now I wonder if she's right.'

Was he thinking of Verity, as well as his cousin? Was he still uncertain about Cora's accusation – unsure which of the women to trust?

He pushed his hands into his trouser pockets. 'The hall's a problem. Turning it into a hotel sounds crazy until you understand the amount of money it costs to keep the place up.'

'But wouldn't you have to borrow a lot to convert the building?' It sounded like a risk.

He nodded. 'Yes, but the alternative would be to break up the estate, and sell part of it off. Times might change. Fortunes fluctuate. But the Seagraves have been on that land for centuries. When Cora made her suggestion, that seemed all-important. She's a Seagrave too, and we felt the same. We could have kept a portion of the hall to live in, and made enough money for the upkeep.'

Had he been willing to take risks, to protect the family's standing and its inheritance? He'd probably have had a battle on his hands when it came to convincing his mother, but he'd have more control, presumably, once he hit thirty. But then his fiancée had arrived on the scene, and everything had changed.

'You say preserving the estate seemed all-important back then,' Eve said. 'So you changed your mind?'

He nodded. 'Verity came in like a breath of fresh air and made me think again. Life had been so different for her. She had no ties. She didn't miss her family home in Stoningham.' Eve wondered again about her parents. 'And apart from that, she was always on the move. She'd be camped out near an underwater cave, or exploring a far-flung country en route to her next adventure. Even in London she never put down roots. She'd rent somewhere, then move on. She made me realise I was using the hall as a prop – something to make me feel more significant; better about myself. When I told her about Cora's idea, she asked why I was so against selling off bits of land. There's plenty I could let go. And two cottages, beyond the ones in use by the Cottons and Cora, and the larger house reserved for my parents. It wouldn't involve disrupting anyone.' He shook his head. 'Suddenly, I saw things in a new light. Selling off part of the estate seems freeing now, rather than disastrous. And it'll be a quick, risk-free way to solve the estate's financial problems.'

He was talking in the present tense. Presumably he intended to go ahead, even though Verity was dead. Could Cora have killed her and now be desperate because Rupert still wouldn't revert to her idea?

'On top of the land and the unused cottages there are the stables too,' Rupert went on. 'The horses have always been a ridiculous extravagance. And the hall will remain intact, for future generations.'

'Do your parents know about the competing ideas?'

'No, and they'd hate both of them. But the status quo isn't an option. Something's got to give.'

Eve thought of Cora's assertion that Verity had been marrying for money. 'Your cousin suspected Verity's motives?' The adventurer's approach would have released cash quickly, unlike Cora's solution.

'She did.' He paused. 'But she was wrong. Verity never suggested I underwrite her expeditions.' Eve still had the impression he was trying to convince himself. However furious he was with Cora, she'd put serious doubts in his mind. And of course, if the diver was hoping for handouts, she'd likely be subtle about it. 'Verity was worried the hotel idea would take up all my time, and with her travelling a lot too, we'd hardly see each other. And I agreed; when she came home, I wanted to be there for her – and to provide a calm environment, not a working one.'

What had Verity's real motives been? Eve wondered. It did look as though she'd been having an affair. And now Eve understood just how extensive the Seagrave estate must be, she realised Verity's plans could have released big sums. Enough to shore up the hall, with more to spare? It sounded like it.

How much would her expeditions cost? A lot, presumably: fees for the team, insurance, flights, subsistence, kit… Maybe she hadn't known the family finances were tight when she'd first met Rupert. And once she realised he wasn't quite the full-time sponsor she'd originally thought, she'd looked at the most practical way to release money quickly. Eve had the impression Verity would do almost anything to enable her boundary-pushing exploits. Yet she'd been independent. She'd talked about the importance of ploughing your own furrow. Which version of Verity was the real one?

'So you'd told Cora of your new plans?'

'I'd been working up to it. I'd already pulled back from the hotel idea, because of my marriage, but I hadn't gone into detail about selling the land yet. I think she found out though – from the way she's behaved and her accusations.'

'How could she know?'

'Verity and I had discussed it after she arrived at the hall. Cora could easily have overheard. She's always in and out; she treats it as an extension to her home.' He rubbed his chin. 'And she kept sidling up to me to try to talk more about her hotel idea. She knew I felt bad and she played me for all I was worth. I kept telling her to let it go.' He looked at Eve and the anger was back in his eyes, all trace of guilt and regret gone from his tone. 'She tried every trick in the book.'

Eve could see the beach up ahead now. Gus was leaping at the sight of a herring gull, as though with just that bit more effort, he'd be able to catch it.

Rupert probably hoped the accusation about Pete Smith was simply part of Cora's campaign – that she imagined he'd break off the engagement. But she wasn't sure he believed it. His hand was shaking slightly.

Out on the beach in the sunshine, with the sea breeze brushing her cheeks, Eve thought of Cora standing behind Verity Nye in the window of Jade Piper's bedroom. Seeing her chance. Fearing Rupert would never see things her way again. Acting on impulse without thoughts for the consequences – like a toddler – and gripping Verity's shoulder tight before thrusting her forward until her centre of gravity shifted, and she went plunging down towards the paving below.

And then she thought of Rupert in the same position, mad with jealousy, pushing the fiancée he claimed he'd loved to her death. Maybe afterwards he'd doubted his cousin and regretted his actions. Perhaps he was determined to do what Verity had advised in some kind of sick tribute, to show he realised he'd been wrong about her.

As for Tilly Cotton, Eve could imagine her protecting either of them, if she'd seen them behind Verity. They'd all grown up together – been thick as thieves as children. And she worked for the family; her fortunes were bound up with theirs. She might be striving to convince herself she'd imagined what she saw.

The journey back along the estuary path loomed large; she didn't want to take it with Rupert Seagrave by her side.

'Thank you for talking to me.' She turned towards her dachshund. 'I'll be some time; I need to make sure Gus gets his exercise. Please don't let me keep you.'

She breathed a sigh of relief when he turned to retrace his steps.

As she threw Gus's ball and watched him scamper up the beach, she reassessed her impressions of Rupert. His hands had shaken when he'd referred to Cora, no doubt remembering her accusations. It spoke of how seriously he'd taken her words, and of violent feelings – kept in check, but perhaps only just. He could have turned that barely controlled fury on his fiancée the day she died. One tiny extra nudge might have led him to act. Some action of Pete Smith's, a sign that seemed to back Cora's version of events. She could see him as a killer. But proving his guilt was another matter.

It was a good ten minutes after he'd left before her stomach muscles relaxed.

CHAPTER SIXTEEN

Eve caught Viv before opening time at Monty's on Tuesday morning and bought several slices of her lemon drizzle cake. It felt too disloyal to go elsewhere and besides, if anything was calculated to curry favour with an interviewee, it was her friend's cooking. All the same, it wasn't ideal. She and Viv might have spoken about Simon's engagement by phone, but that didn't stop her wanting more of a debrief. And she demanded the latest on what she called 'the case' too.

Eve had to promise a full update during her shift at Monty's that afternoon. It was hard to dash away, especially when her friend found out who she was visiting.

'Get me an autograph!' she called as Eve reversed out of the door.

Eve was looking forward to her visit; interviewing Carmichael was a fascinating prospect, and on top of that, the twins were free for lunch.

Kim Carmichael's place was a palatial four-storey townhouse in Belsize Park. A man in paint-spattered overalls answered the door, grinned and nodded Eve through to a large living room that ran from the front to the back of the house, with a floor-to-ceiling bay window at one end and French windows at the other. The garden beyond was full of roses, but also builders' equipment: a stand for sawing wood and a cement mixer.

'You see how I let them take advantage?' Kim said, laughing. Her iron-grey hair had been up in a bun at some stage, but a lot of it was coming down. She was sitting on a pewter-coloured velvet chesterfield couch; one of her feet was bandaged and raised on a padded stool.

A moment later the sound of a drill disturbed the peace and elsewhere in the house Eve could hear hammering.

Kim put her hands over her ears for a moment and opened her eyes wide in mock anguish. 'I was so glad when my agent called and mentioned you wanted a word. I've been cutting down on the number of contracts I sign of late.' She shrugged. 'Age finally getting to me. A few aches and pains. And this!' She pointed to her ankle. 'But it's driving me up the wall. I hate not being active. I thought rescuing the house from its hideous state of disrepair would distract me. Well, it has! But not in a good way.' She leaned forward slightly and Eve realised how thin she was. 'Did you bring the cake?'

'I did. I have a friend who runs a teashop, so I bought it there. It'll be good.' She didn't like to admit that she worked at Monty's too. What would Kim Carmichael think if she knew she was talking to an obituary writer who waited tables to make ends meet? But then looking at the woman, Eve had a feeling she might not mind in the least.

'Excellent!' She clapped her hands together. 'Sorry to ask, but could you make tea? It's a bore, but I'm really not—'

Eve was already on her feet. 'Of course.' She made for the door.

'Turn left and it's on the right,' Kim said. 'No idea what state it's in. The builders make it their own during the day. Use any mugs! Just a dash of milk!'

The kitchen was large and square and overlooked the back garden, like the living room. It was currently builder-free, so Eve put enough water on for just herself and Kim, then searched multiple cupboards for teabags and something to drink out of. The mugs she found were large and old-looking, the glaze marked by multiple fine cracks.

'You managed to find some without chips!' Kim said, as she picked hers up, five minutes later in the living room. 'And you unearthed the decent plates too. Well done!'

Eve had brought a cake slice through to serve Viv's lemon drizzle and forks in case Kim wanted one, but she picked the slice up in her fingers.

'Oh my!' Her smile was broad as she finished her first mouthful. 'Does your friend do mail order?'

'Maybe she should.' It got Eve's mind working. Part of her role was to look out for new business opportunities.

'She definitely should! Please ask her to add me to the mailing list. So, you want to ask me about Verity Nye. I was surprised. I had a fair amount to do with her over the charity event I hosted, but I assumed you'd target close friends and family.'

Having predicted the question, Eve was prepared. Savings and her part-time job at Monty's were funding her efforts to unearth Verity Nye's killer, but she was glad to be there for other reasons too. Quality and originality in her obituary writing mattered to her.

'It's always useful to speak with people who were less personally involved with a subject. It's hard to tell an authentic story when you write about someone famous. Their persona's often fixed in the public's mind, but digging deeper can tell a different tale. Friends and family are sometimes too emotionally involved to be objective, or just unwilling to be honest. I want to write something original, that gets to the heart of what Verity was like. I need to cut through the gloss and find out what's underneath.'

Kim took a swig of her tea and nodded thoughtfully. 'Diligent. And I see what you mean. What would be the point, otherwise?'

Eve felt immediate warmth towards the woman. She'd worked out what drove her in under a minute, whereas Ian, her ex, had never understood.

'And if I say I thought Verity was awful, will you quote me directly?'

Eve was in the process of sipping her tea, which hopefully covered her surprise. Not that anything about her hostess should come as a shock. She wasn't Eve's average interviewee.

'I'm not saying she *was* awful.' Kim's brow furrowed. 'I just like to know where I stand.'

Eve put her mug down on the tray she'd brought through from the kitchen. 'I'll be guided by you. I won't quote you unless you're happy to be quoted. And I can refer to what you say in a general way: "Professional contacts sometimes found Verity Nye hard to work with. One said…" and so on, or I can be direct. And I never invent or exaggerate.'

'Good!' Kim ate some more of her cake. 'Let's talk then, and if you send me your notes before you decide what to add to your article, I'll let you know what I'm happy to put my name to. Agreed? Fire away!'

'For background, maybe we could start with how you got involved with Wide Blue Yonder.'

'Ah, well, guilt trip.' Kim shifted her injured foot on the stool. 'I was approached by a charity working with young actresses and asked to donate my time by mentoring one of them. But honestly' – she gave Eve a look that invited her to sympathise – 'it didn't fit with my attempts to cut my working hours. It was one of a flurry of requests that arrived within days of each other. And the charity concerned was working with very well-to-do young things. I'm not saying mentoring wouldn't have helped them, but they already had every other benefit. I sat there after I'd turned them down, feeling guilty, but after a while I realised I could still give something back. I got the idea of sponsoring someone else to mentor young women instead. And I wanted to work with a charity that raised aspirations in people who really needed help. Of course, sponsoring Verity Nye as a mentor took me outside the realm of acting, but I liked the idea of being general rather than specific. Acting's a tough business and there are plenty of other opportunities out there.' She leaned forward and laughed. 'Verity's job wasn't to mentor a budding adventurer, of course – that would be even more niche – she was just meant to show the person she was partnered with what's possible if you're determined and don't take no for an answer.'

Eve noted the use of 'meant to'.

'She was happy to give her time for free, so I covered travel expenses, a venue and so on – and bigged the award up in the press.'

'And did it work out?'

Kim sighed. 'Not in the way Wide Blue Yonder wanted. They thought telling the story of Verity Nye and her work with one girl would draw the newspapers in, and be more compelling for potential donors too. They wanted to use the publicity to boost their income to fund work with larger groups.' She shook her head and ate a little more cake. 'You're probably aware, but their ethos is all about building strong support networks – women empowering women – and they wanted the mentoring to reflect that.'

'But it didn't?'

The actress gave a crackly laugh. 'No it did not! I'm not sure why Verity's approach was so mismatched with Wide Blue Yonder's. You'd think they'd have checked her views before they took her on.' She reached for her mug. 'She'd made her own luck without support, apparently, and discouraged the mentee from leaning on anyone else. The charity administrator said the girl had written a report about the first session, as they'd agreed, but it was all about how relying on others leaves you weaker, and makes *them* weaker too.'

Definitely off-message. 'So Verity had effectively poured cold water on the idea of joining one of Wide Blue Yonder's mutual-support groups?'

Kim grimaced. 'Quite! By the end of the first session, the mentee didn't even want to partake in the rest. Don't get me wrong; she was really fired up, from what I hear. But Verity's actions went down like a bucket of cold sick with the charity. And I somehow found myself feeling responsible!'

Once again, Eve wondered about the charity's recruitment process. When she'd raised the subject with Jade, she'd glossed over it.

'What happened in the end?'

Kim laughed now. 'Well, that's the joke! Jade Piper was keen not to leave it at that and I ended up mentoring the girl myself. It took a while to coax her into accepting extra sessions, but at last I convinced her. We met five more times in total. And after all that I enjoyed it.' She sighed. 'Lesson learned. The mentee's doing really well now, but whether Verity or I spurred her on is anyone's guess.'

Eve wondered. Perhaps the best approach would depend on an individual's personality. Creating support groups seemed less risky, but Verity had clearly believed in her own methods. She really hoped she could talk to the adventurer's parents or a school friend to get a better idea of what had shaped her views.

'I wonder what made Wide Blue Yonder choose Verity.'

'Ha!' said Kim. 'I wondered too. I watched some videos about her dives. Hair-raising and certainly inspiring for a certain group of people. And she hit the headlines frequently of course. But I can't help feeling there must have been other candidates whose views aligned better with the charity's. That's what the administrator thought too.'

Eve had finished her cake. 'Excuse me?'

'Wide Blue Yonder's administrator talked to me about it when she called to update me on the problems they were having. She said she'd been worried about Verity from the start. She tended to lose patience quite quickly, and felt people should snap out of it if they were going through a difficult time. I gather there was no proper interview but when she came in for a visit, it seemed Jade Piper had already agreed the details of her partnership with the charity in principle. Odd, I thought.'

*

Fifty minutes after leaving Kim Carmichael, Eve was sitting in the arts centre where her son worked. Nick had just finished what he referred to as an 'intriguing' meeting with a group planning to perform the history of weaving through interpretive dance. Ellen was there too, after escaping from the patent-law firm she'd joined, following a two-hour session with a man who'd invented a new type of nose-hair trimmer.

'You couldn't make it up,' she'd said. 'Not that you'd want to.'

They'd come to the art centre's café, with its long beech-wood tables and mobiles overhead mounted on wires. Eve had told them about the case. Now, Nick and Ellen had their heads on one side, silent for a moment as they ate the pasta salads they'd chosen.

Nick shook his head. 'I don't know, Mama. You do get yourself involved in some weird stuff.' He was half laughing. Eve loved that he and Ellen still called her by the same fond, traditional name she'd adopted for her own mother. It sounded funny and touching said in an English accent by adults in their twenties.

Ellen laughed, but Eve could see the worry behind her eyes. 'I'd no idea villages were such dangerous places. It's like you've walked into one of those television crime dramas. There's always a murder at the fete. If I'd known what you were up to, I'd have warned you not to go.'

Eve joined in the laughter, but she reached out to squeeze her and Nick's hands too. 'Poor Verity was only up from London for a few days. It's still not clear whether trouble followed her or lay in wait at the hall. But I see your point, and I'll be careful. I wouldn't mind your take on the dynamic between Cora and Rupert Seagrave.' Eve had been obsessing about it. As an only child, like Rupert, she kept imagining what it must have been like to be presented with Cora and encouraged to treat her as a ready-made teenage sibling.

'Growing up together as cousins from part way through child-hood could be fun,' Ellen said. 'But it would be a big adjustment – and maybe a weird dynamic.'

Nick nodded. 'Going through life in each other's pockets, yet with totally different experiences. One destined to rule the roost and one only a temporary fixture.'

Ellen shuddered. 'What must it be like for Cora, staying in her cottage by the grace of the elder Seabrooks? It doesn't sound like a healthy set-up, whichever way you look at it.'

It all fitted with what she felt. The tensions that had come to a head were enough to make her focus closely on the pair. She looked into the twins' concerned eyes and hesitated. Would they feel more relaxed if she told them about Robin? It made a difference, having someone with police experience watching her back. She let go of their hands and picked up the coffee Nick had bought her. 'Want to know a secret?'

They both grinned. 'Not bothered,' Nick said, and Ellen tossed her head nonchalantly.

'Ha ha.' She filled them in and made it clear they mustn't tell a soul.

The twins exchanged a glance.

'What?'

'This is meant to reassure us, right?' Nick said. 'Because however odd it might seem that a former detective goes around in secret, masquerading as a gardener, he's definitely a good 'un because the vicar likes him?'

He and Ellen both laughed, and Eve raised her eyes to heaven. 'Okay, put like that I see your point, but you've met Jim.' They'd been to stay with her over Christmas. 'Surely you'd trust his judge-ment?' She was glad she hadn't told them about the mysterious phone call of Robin's that she'd overheard.

'Actually, that's fair.' Ellen took a forkful of her pasta salad. 'And it's not just you. Gus likes the vicar too.'

'I rest my case. His opinion is sound.' Eve took a spoonful of the soup she'd opted for.

'So I guess gardener-cop guy gets a free pass,' Nick said, the laughter still in his eyes. 'And if you've taken a shine to him, who are we to argue?'

'Taken a—' She shook her head. 'I haven't taken a shine to him. Seriously. But he's a good neighbour.'

They exchanged a glance again, and their secret smile: the one they used when they'd caught her out in some way.

Nick's innocent gaze met hers. 'I was just teasing, Mama.'

CHAPTER SEVENTEEN

Eve was with Viv in the kitchen at Monty's late on Tuesday afternoon.

'I still say Polly's too old for him.' Her friend's brows were drawn down.

'Viv, Simon's forty-four. Polly can't be more than early thirties.'

'I mean in real terms. He only acts around twenty-five.'

'He's always seemed remarkably mature to me. Look at his success in business. And he's a thoughtful friend.'

'Thoughtful friend! That's such a disappointment. I was convinced there'd be passion between you.'

Eve tied the strings of the apron she was wearing rather fiercely. 'Do give it a rest. How are things with your guy, anyway?' Viv had a man she'd been seeing on and off for over a year now, in a nearby town, and Eve wanted to change the subject.

'He's asked to see me again tomorrow night.' She spoke as though he were hair she'd only just washed, but which needed doing again already.

'You're fed up with him?'

She shrugged. 'He's all right, but there's no need for him to overdo it.'

Eve sensed marriage wasn't on the cards for her yet. 'Better get on with the baking, I suppose.' The description of what Viv had in mind was daunting; Eve felt she'd be lucky to get home in time for supper.

It was a special order, a celebration cake for a twenty-first birthday, and Eve was there to learn. It was to be an eight-layer chocolate and gooseberry cream confection, with candied almonds and homemade white chocolate truffles on top. Two of their student regulars, Angie and Tammy, were covering the teashop while she and Viv got creative.

'All right then,' her friend said. 'We can talk about my brother and bake at the same time. Don't think I didn't notice your attempt to divert me.'

'If you stop going on about Simon, I'll tell you what Kim Carmichael said about your cake.'

Viv turned towards her, as she tucked her sea-green hair into her baker's net. 'Did you get her autograph?'

Eve took a deep breath, pulling a net over her own pixie crop. 'It would have been unprofessional to ask. But she wants to go on the list if you decide to start a mail-order service. And if you do, she'll be putty in your hands. You can ask for her signature then – on the bottom of an order form.'

Viv's blue eyes opened wide. 'Wow. Well, it's a thought.' Her brow was furrowed as she reached for a mixing bowl.

Eve had managed to sign up the famous rapper, Billy Tozer, for a regular order a few months earlier. He lived locally, but if supplying celebrities took off they might have to hire more staff. 'It would need a lot of planning.'

Viv shot her a sidelong look. 'I know! But I'd like to explore the idea. What else is new? Did you get anything useful on the case?' She pushed the recipe she'd written in front of Eve.

'Yes.' She went to fetch the sugar for the candied almonds. Viv was letting her do them on her own. Small steps. 'I don't know what it means, but I think there was something weird about Verity Nye's appointment as Wide Blue Yonder's ambassador.' She explained the interview with Jade Piper, which had made her curious, and then Kim Carmichael's report. 'It looks to me as though Jade insisted on having Verity, in the face of some opposition. Whether Verity wanted the role for some reason, and was in a position to force Jade's hand, or it was Jade who singled *her* out, I don't know. But there's something going on. And there's a second oddity too.' It had come to Eve as she'd driven home from seeing Nick and Ellen. 'Jade gave me the contact details for Verity's mentee. So she *wanted* me to get the story Kim just told: to understand Verity's views, and how they didn't match the charity's.'

Why had she done that? It had made Eve question Wide Blue Yonder's recruitment processes, which wasn't in Jade's interests. But it had also highlighted Verity's viewpoint, which some might call harsh. Was that what she'd wanted Eve to see?

'You were supposed to find information that made Jade look less suspicious, not more.' Viv frowned at her, over the flour she was sifting. 'Do you seriously think she might be guilty?'

'I don't know anywhere near enough to tell, but I can't ignore the evidence. I'll just have to keep digging until I get to the truth. It'll be better than not knowing.'

'I suppose… How will you find out more?' For Viv, the whole case centred around the woman who'd championed Monty's. She tended to be pretty partisan when it came to her own venture.

Eve thought again of Jade's sad, serious face and the way she'd avoided Eve's eyes when she'd asked what drove her to set up her charity. Assuming she was innocent, Eve wanted to find the truth for her sake too. Not because of her support for Monty's but because she'd looked troubled. But then if she'd killed a woman, how else would she look? 'Everyone's got an internet presence. I'll research her personally now, rather than her charity, and I'll go deep.' She always did.

'What about Simon? Did he say anything helpful before coming out with his ridiculous news?'

'He told me about a teenage romance between Tilly Cotton and Rupert Seagrave – which she ended, apparently. It made me wonder whether sentimental feelings might mean she'd cover for him, if she thought he was guilty. She might have just seen a shadowy figure that fitted his physique; that could make her worried, but hesitant about coming forward.'

Viv looked thoughtful as she reached for the butter. 'I could see that. And if that's the case Jade can't be the murderer. She's not at all like Rupert physically.'

Eve put water and sugar into a pan on the stove. 'But we've got no way of knowing what Tilly saw. For what it's worth, I could see her covering for Cora too. They all ran around together as kids. And Cora and Jade are both brunettes of a similar height.'

Viv was silent.

Eve turned up the heat. 'I had an unexpected extra interview with Rupert, as a matter of fact.'

Her friend's eyes widened as they met hers. 'How come?'

Eve explained his reasons for tracking her down.

'Wow. So, conclusions?'

'His feelings are all over the place. Cora drives him mad – her behaviour sounds very mercurial – but he feels she's been treated unfairly over the years. Reading between the lines, I'd say his mother's warned him she's manipulative, and after her claims about Verity and Pete sleeping together, he's come to the tentative conclusion that Belinda's right.'

'So Cora tipped the balance by slinging mud at Verity?'

'I'd guess so. And Rupert's either inconsolable because he spent the last half hour of Verity's life suspecting her, and maybe treating her cruelly because of it...'

'Or?'

'Or because he killed Verity as a result of what Cora said.' Eve still couldn't decide which was most likely. 'Either way, I feel like his feelings are hanging in the balance. He's confused and overwrought – and still not sure what to believe.'

'What he said makes Cora's motive for murder look stronger too. If the marriage had gone ahead, not only would her hotel idea have been out the window, but the land around her would have been sold.'

Eve nodded. 'Including the stables, which she enjoys, according to Simon. And without the hotel, she has no income or plans for the future, as far as I know.'

Viv shook her head. 'Maybe before long, Verity would have been knocking on her door, asking for rent. And of course, Cora was late arriving on the scene after she fell. She had time to do the pushing and then rush downstairs. Didn't you say she claimed she'd been over at her cottage? Very convenient.'

Eve nodded. 'I saw her come around the side of the hall when she arrived at the scene of the fall, which fits with that. But she could have slipped out of the front or side doors of the building, and still given the impression she'd walked from her house.'

'Sounds plausible.' Viv pushed her sinking hairnet up from the bridge of her nose. 'Honestly, what's wrong with the elastic in these things?'

'One more issue's occurred to me. Do you remember I told you I overheard Verity talking to Pete about keeping tabs on an unknown female?'

Viv nodded, causing the hairnet to fall forward again.

'Well, I'm starting to wonder if it was Cora that Pete was following, not Jade Piper.'

Viv brightened. 'Could be, now you mention it. Do you think Verity knew Cora was bending Rupert's ear about her hotel plan, and she was a potential threat?'

'It's possible. Having Rupert staying at the hall for a few days was a prime opportunity for Cora to turn up the pressure. Using Pete to make sure she and Rupert were seldom alone together could have been Verity's way of stopping her. And if she wanted

Rupert's cash to fund her expeditions, her and Pete's interests coincided.'

Would Verity have acted that way? Marrying for money still didn't seem to fit with her ideals, but then neither did deceit or an affair with her medic.

She made herself plough on. 'And there's one more interesting thing. Cora said Pete smelled of Verity's perfume. It was partly based on that that she told Rupert she thought they were having an affair.'

'Right.'

'But how would she have noticed, unless she'd been pretty close to Pete herself?' She ought to have thought of that before. 'Maybe he'd taken the task of keeping an eye on her more seriously than Verity realised.' She took a deep breath. So much of this was speculation. It made her uneasy.

'Oh yes – it's possible!'

Viv was adding eggs to her mix. Eve could never put them straight in like that. She had eggshell issues.

'Either way,' Viv went on, 'I feel like Rupert and Cora are much more likely suspects for murder than Jade. She doesn't even have a motive.'

Privately, Eve agreed; the facts so far made the Seagrave insiders seem more likely. But there was still lot more to find out. She hoped her research wouldn't shatter Viv's illusions.

CHAPTER EIGHTEEN

'I thought today would be a good day to choose.' Tilly Cotton, the Seagraves' estate manager, opened the door of her cottage, where she'd agreed to meet Eve on Wednesday morning. 'The family are all out. It just makes it a little easier – when everyone's feeling so fragile. Though I checked it would be okay to show you round, of course, and no one minded.'

Eve wondered about that. She guessed Belinda Seagrave might not have been too keen. She hadn't wanted Eve to interview Rupert. Had she been worried about his feelings, or concerned about what he might give away? Perhaps she'd sanctioned Eve's visit today to make the family look innocent. Knowing Eve wouldn't interact with Rupert and Cora might have calmed Belinda's nerves.

Tilly opened her cottage door wider and stood back. 'Come on in. I'll make us a coffee before we start the tour. Black or white?'

'Black, thanks.'

Tilly and Ivy Cotton's cottage was a tiny, tidy but cosy-looking place constructed from worn red brick. Eve guessed it might have been built in early Victorian times, later than the hall, but somehow it had the air of having been around longer. It looked more relaxed and fitted snugly into a clearing in the woods. Eve had left her car on the driveway that led to the stables, then followed a path to the Cottons' house.

The room Eve had entered was a living space with a brick floor and a large open fireplace.

'Do make yourself comfortable,' Tilly called from the kitchen.

Eve pulled out a lath-back farmhouse chair and sat at an oak dining table. Its surface was mostly clear, bar the odd bit of post and a couple of glossy magazines; Tilly must have been browsing them when Eve knocked. They were open on listings pages and Eve glanced at the box advertisements, which were for estate manager jobs.

The woman appeared at that moment with a dark-red coffee pot and small cups and saucers. 'Sugar?'

'No thanks.'

Tilly set the tray down and hastily grabbed the magazines, flipping them shut. 'Sorry. I should have tidied up better.'

'No problem.'

She bit her lip. Was she wondering if Eve had noticed what she'd been up to? At last she sighed. 'I've been having a look round for other positions.' Maybe she'd rather be upfront about it if there was a chance Eve had seen. 'To be honest, I thought making my next move when Rupert married Verity would be perfect timing. She'd probably have wanted to make changes anyway, so I wouldn't have felt guilty about leaving.'

'You feel responsible for the family?'

She hesitated. 'That sounds mad, I know, but I've been around a long time. They're used to having me here, but I've never seen myself staying for ever.' She glanced around the room. 'I love this place and Percival's been so kind to me, and my mum too. But I need to make a change. It can be a bit… oppressive.'

'But you're finding the thought harder, after Verity's death?' Eve felt sorry for her. She remembered what Simon had said. Did Rupert still lean on her for emotional support, even though so many years had elapsed since they'd dated? Was that what was oppressive?

Tilly's eyes were anxious, her jaw taut. 'You were looking up at the window when Verity fell too, weren't you?'

Eve nodded.

'Are you sure you saw nothing?'

Eve could hear the quaver in her voice. If someone else confirmed what she'd seen, half seen, or whatever it was, would she go to the police? But there was nothing Eve could do. 'I'm really sorry, but no. I'd only just glanced up because of something the vicar said. I was conscious of movement and then of… of a body pitching forward. But I didn't even know who it was that had fallen.'

The estate manager had her head in her hands.

Eve leaned forward. 'Tilly, if you think you saw something, even if you don't trust yourself or quite know what it was, please go and talk to the police. I mean—' She broke off. She didn't want to frighten the woman, but there was nothing for it. 'It might be safest to tell them. If you did see something, you could be in danger.'

Tilly shook her head. 'I don't think whoever targeted Verity would attack me.'

There was a long pause. Tilly closed her eyes for a moment, but then took a deep breath and began to drink her coffee.

Eve thought it best not to ask questions until they left the Cottons' cottage. She wanted to give Tilly a chance to think, in case her advice sank in. After a couple of minutes, the estate manager was on her feet.

'Shall we visit the hall first? And then we can tour the grounds and stables before I show you back to your car.'

'That sounds perfect. Thank you.'

Walking up to the hall from a distance gave Eve the full impression of its size and grandeur. The brick and white stucco building was majestic. Tilly took her round to the front where the main entrance sat under the portico, its grand columns gleaming in the strong sunlight. They mounted the steps and she opened up, using keys from a sizeable bunch.

'You've seen the entrance hall before, of course. We came in through the side door down that way.' She pointed, then guided

Eve in and out of a series of downstairs rooms. They were impressive but each created a similar impression when Eve looked closely. The elegant drawing room was a good example. There were busts similar to those Eve had seen in the library, a crystal chandelier and a carpet that looked high-quality. But when she focused on it, she saw it had threadbare patches, and the faded swagged curtains were frayed at the hems. And although there were several fine paintings on the wall, she noticed one area, over an ornate side table, where the lavish deep red wallpaper was darker in a rectangular shape, less faded than the paper next to it. Had the family had to sell the artwork that had hung there?

Tilly walked Eve towards one of the two back staircases which lay at either end of the house. Through an open door Eve spotted a desk and a printer.

'That's my office,' Tilly said.

It must be where Jade Piper had been when Verity fell. If she'd been telling the truth.

At the top of the steep narrow stairs was a spacious corridor.

'The family's rooms are all on this floor,' Tilly said, opening doors to reveal a series of four-poster beds and draughty bathrooms.

They climbed another flight of stairs, and Eve's skin prickled as she thought of Verity's final moments. Jade Piper's room had been on this level. 'I'm afraid Mum and I made all the guests put up with staying on this floor,' Tilly said. 'The rooms were clear and ready for use.'

So Pete Smith must have been up here too then. If Rupert had been inside the hall when Verity fell, looking for evidence of an affair between his fiancée and the medic, he'd likely made for this floor. He'd have been on the spot when Verity entered Jade's room…

'There's just the attic above,' Tilly said. 'But it's worth a quick peek. The servants used to live up there, and there's storage space too.'

The rooms were small and dark, with sloping ceilings, their windows hidden from the grounds by a stone parapet. 'They're so much less grand than the ones downstairs,' Tilly said, echoing her thoughts, 'but I still love them.' She put a hand on the wall and smiled for a moment.

Back outside, they walked across the lawns and on through the woods. After a minute or two, they came to a large clearing.

'Oh, I'd forgotten to mention the pool. It's rather far from the house, which made it more expensive to install.' She sighed. 'But it's wonderfully secluded.'

It was beautifully made, with a light stone and tile border forming steps down into the water. The cover was off, and it looked inviting. The woods surrounded it, so that anyone coming for a bathe would feel at one with nature.

Another five minutes' walk took them through the woods and out to the sea. It really was a large estate. She guessed looking after it would stand Tilly in good stead with any future employer – and that she'd be better off leaving before it became obvious that the family weren't managing, in case anyone laid the blame at her door. From what Eve had heard it sounded as though she'd been fighting a losing battle.

They were almost back at the stables and the Cottons' cottage again when they passed a large outbuilding.

'Rupert's fond of classic cars. That's where he keeps them. He doesn't have enough space down in London.' She glanced quickly at Eve. 'He hasn't bought one in a while.'

Maybe he'd been saving his money to patch up the hall. Perhaps he should have started that effort sooner. The thought was accentuated when Tilly showed her the stables. They were large, with four horses visible in the stalls. There was so much to maintain.

As they passed Tilly's cottage, on their way to Eve's Mini, they saw Tilly's mother, Ivy, the Seagraves' housekeeper. Tilly introduced

Eve and the woman responded politely, but her face was pinched, her mouth tight.

Eve wondered what would happen to Ivy Cotton if Tilly secured another job and moved out. Would Rupert let her keep hold of the cottage they currently shared? Or would he pension the woman off?

If he and Verity had discussed plans for the estate while they were staying in the hall, one person who could easily have overheard was Ivy Cotton.

As Eve walked slowly back to her car, she reviewed her visit. She turned to give Tilly a final wave. The woman was still anxious, that was for sure, and clearly she hadn't decided how to proceed. If she'd made up her mind to shelve the matter, she wouldn't have asked Eve what she'd seen. The thought of the killer watching Tilly, wondering if she'd make a move, left Eve feeling horribly helpless.

She sighed and walked on. Another take-home point was the state of the hall. It backed up the hints she'd had so far that money was tight. If her hunch was right, and the family were already selling paintings to pay the bills, there was no way Rupert would have been able to fund Verity's adventures without letting chunks of the estate go.

Was there anything else to note? As she fished her car keys from her bag, her mind strayed back to Tilly's mother Ivy – imagined her overhearing Verity and Rupert discussing their plans for selling off the estate. She'd be worried for her future, surely? Would she be strong enough to have tipped Verity out of the window? From what Robin said, Ivy was one of those who had no alibi at the time of the woman's death.

And of course, Tilly would be just as protective of her as of Rupert, and worried, yet certain the woman wouldn't cause her harm.

Eve shook her head. The impression she had of Ivy Cotton so far, that gentle anxious look she had, didn't make it seem likely. Nevertheless, it paid to be thorough; the woman might be an outside possibility, but she had a motive.

CHAPTER NINETEEN

Back at Elizabeth's Cottage, Eve ate a lunch of crusty white bread and cheese, with Gus to keep her company. Her mind was full of Tilly's words.

'She doesn't think the person who killed Verity is a threat to her,' Eve said to him. 'She must suspect someone at the hall, but am I right to home in on Rupert and Cora? And is *she* right to feel safe?' Sir Percival and Ivy Cotton hovered round her head too, like ghosts. Even Gus looked worried. Maybe he'd picked up on her tone. 'I can only hope that she'll think about what I've said and confide in me, or in Palmer, or someone.' She couldn't currently see a way to get hard evidence unless Tilly talked.

'The problem is, I've got no way of knowing she's certain of the killer's identity, and if she doesn't know for sure, then it's possible an outsider like Jade Piper or Pete Smith's guilty. I need hard facts.' She got up, and Gus, sensing her intention, dashed towards the front door. 'Viv's right,' she said, following him and slipping on her flip-flops. 'Jade's got no obvious motive, but I'm sure there's something weird about her connection with Verity.' Until Eve knew what that was, it was hard to form any kind of opinion.

Once they were back from a stroll through the woods, Gus dashed to quench his thirst in the kitchen and Eve got down to work in the calm quiet of the dining room. As she'd planned, she focused on Jade Piper as an individual now. The heart of a person's character was what drove them. In Jade's case, the charity she'd established was her life, but it seemed to be a symptom of her passion, not the root cause.

Eve scrolled through pages of links online, looking for anything that referred to Jade's life outside work. Other than Facebook and Instagram, the first four pages were full of hits related to her professional life, and social media was no help. She had all the right settings to protect her privacy. But on the fifth page Eve found the odd personal mention. She showed up on various JustGiving donation pages and some online petitions arguing for better housing and more support for people with poor mental health. One of the charity donations was to a Tim Piper, and her message (*So proud of you, my love. Hot food will be waiting when you get back! xxx*), coupled with the photograph of the man she was sponsoring – who looked around her age – made Eve think they were probably married. Or – she checked the date – had been four years ago. Something about Jade made Eve feel she was currently alone. She gave the impression of a person who held their head up high and kept going against the odds. Eve told herself off for being fanciful. She couldn't know that. But there had been pride in the woman's eyes, as well as sadness and some kind of bravery. She needed to find out what was behind that. The photo of the man in the JustGiving picture made her feel emotional; he had laughing friendly eyes. She hoped Jade was still with him.

It was only after trawling through two more pages of search results that she found another link that made her pause. It led to a website belonging to the 'Friends of Blackwood Burial Ground', and the mention was an acknowledgement of Jade's latest donation towards the upkeep of the site, coupled with a formal thank you for her regular visits and hard work. Eve looked at the address and her heart beat a little faster. It was in Norfolk, close to Thetford.

Gus had pottered in and was sitting at Eve's feet.

'You know,' she said to him, 'that's a very long way for Jade to travel on a regular basis to help tend the graves. It's out in the countryside, so she couldn't even get there by train. That kind of commitment has to mean something.'

Her dachshund cocked his head to the side.

For a second she thought of the man in the JustGiving photograph. She so hoped it was nothing to do with him. But Wide Blue Yonder had been going for years now, and Jade was based in London, just like the charity. If she had been married to him, and he'd died, it seemed likely he'd be buried in the capital. Perhaps she had a parent who'd been interred there. Eve remembered Jade saying how cruel her father had been, destroying her sense of self-worth. But perhaps it was her mother, or it was her dad but she still felt a sense of duty towards him. She'd seen examples of that before.

'There's only one way to find out more.' She glanced at her watch. Thetford was an hour and twenty minutes by car, but it was only mid-afternoon. Gus looked up at her hopefully as she rose from her seat.

'I'd love to take you with me, but it'll be a long and boring journey.' And possibly a fruitless search for information at the other end too. Why was she even doing this? But here was something that really mattered to Jade, a duty that governed how she spent her free time. And if it was that important to her, it was sure to mesh with her other concerns in some way.

Eve texted Angie, one of the students who did shifts at Monty's, to ask if she was free to give Gus a walk and some company that afternoon. Angie had done it before for extra cash, and she and Gus were friends. After that, she changed out of the dress she'd worn to Seagrave Hall into some cropped cotton trousers and a fitted T-shirt.

Angie texted back, promising to come at four. She already had a key, so there was no need to leave a spare hidden in the garden. It was against Eve's rules to do that anyway; it had led to trouble in the past.

'Angie's coming to see you! Yes, she is!' Gus looked ecstatic. 'I'll try to be as quick as I can.' He walked off, clearly unconcerned about when she might finally return, now that he'd been promised an exciting stand-in. She followed him and gave him a hug anyway.

Blackwood Burial Ground was an atmospheric place, at the end of a narrow byway called All Souls Lane, which was bordered by yew trees. Close to the entrance stood an old stone chapel, its windows dark in the strong sunlight. The graves were arrayed in front of her amongst more yews. The memorials were varied. She could see ancient stone angels, ornate crosses with what looked like Celtic markings on them, edging stones, flat memorials and upright headstones with detailed lettering. The burial ground was silent, apart from the sound of the birds. The site was bordered by woodland and up in the Scots pines Eve could hear rooks cawing. Somewhere closer at hand, a wren sang its sweet song.

Eve walked into the interior. She guessed there must be an area where more recent graves had been dug. It would make sense to begin her search there. If something was calling Jade to this place, week after week, she guessed it would be a grave of someone she'd known: one that was less than thirty years old.

She passed just one other person on her walk to the far side of the ground: a grey-haired man in worn brown trousers and a faded red and white checked shirt, open at the neck. He was neatening the grass next to an edging stone with a pair of long-handled trimmers. Pausing for a moment in his work, he wiped the back of his hand across his brow. As she stepped on a dried-out twig that had fallen on the ground he caught the sound, glanced up and wished her good afternoon. She returned the greeting and hoped her search wouldn't take long. She didn't want to have to explain what she was up to – or invent a lie to cover her tracks.

Over in a corner of the grounds, she saw a collection of graves with stones that looked brighter than the rest, next to a few plots that weren't yet used. The first she came to, on a part-complete row, was covered in wreaths and bouquets and the date on the stone was just the previous month. The man who lay there had only been forty-three. It made Eve's heart ache to think of all the loved ones he'd left behind. He had a story she'd never know, which would probably never make its way into any magazine or paper, but the number of floral tributes spoke of the ripples he'd left. She imagined them fanning out into tiny disturbances for people who'd hardly known him.

A second later she put her shoulders back and gave herself a shake. It was a pity she didn't have Gus with her; he'd have made her snap out of it. Mind you, he'd probably have tried to pee on the gravestones too.

As she walked down the row, the dates on the graves grew older, the flowers on them more faded and less plentiful. She switched into analytical mode to stop herself getting maudlin, and pictured Jade as a visitor. If she came regularly because she'd lost a loved one, she probably brought flowers on every visit. She glanced along the next row.

Sure enough, a couple of graves still had bouquets that looked fresh. She navigated round to where they were. The first vase contained pink roses. The plot belonged to a woman who'd died at the age of eighty-two. The name didn't set any connections going in Eve's head, but she'd google for more background if she drew a blank elsewhere.

She glanced over at the man tending the grounds again. She'd swear he'd moved closer. Maybe he was wondering if she needed help. She probably looked lost. Eve took a determined step towards the second grave in that row with a fresh tribute: this time a bunch of larkspur, with flowers of such intense blue they seemed to glow. She raised her eyes to the grave itself.

Ruby Fox.

Eve felt anguish tug at her chest again. She'd only been twenty-four when she'd died, four years earlier. As she stood there, looking at the grave and wondering what Ruby's story had been, the name settled in her head. Did it sound familiar?

Weirdly, Eve felt that it did, though she couldn't remember where from. The man tending the graves was facing away from her. She took out her phone and entered the name into Google. The result made her catch her breath.

It was the young woman Verity Nye had rescued during the cave dive in Egypt. Yet here she was, dead.

The burial ground around Eve faded and all the hairs lifted on her arms and scalp. What did this mean?

And then, a second thought came to her. Ruby and Jade. Two jewel names. Jade was Piper of course, not Fox, but the JustGiving page Eve had spotted made her think she might have married.

She went back to her phone and entered "Ruby Fox" and "Jade Piper" into Google at the same time in quotes. Her hunch went from being a longshot to a certainty, with a bank of evidence behind it. Both their names on a death notice for a woman called Amanda Fox – their mother according to the text. Ruby 'liking' Wide Blue Yonder on Facebook, years earlier. Jade's name on a sponsorship page of Ruby's. And so it went on.

She was so absorbed, she didn't notice the gardener had approached her until a shadow fell across her phone. She locked the screen and thrust it back into her bag.

'You're a friend of the family?' he said.

She nodded. 'I've met Jade. She seemed so sad.' It was true. Eve had sensed that without knowing the background.

He sighed. 'It's tragic. She and Ruby were very close. She'll be pleased someone else has come to see the grave.'

He looked at her curiously. She must seem like an odd sort of visitor; she hadn't brought flowers.

'I'd better be going, I suppose,' Eve said awkwardly, and made her way towards the driveway.

Back at Elizabeth's Cottage that evening, she and Gus settled down in the living room. Eve put her feet up on the couch, a glass of wine at her side, and opened her laptop. Jade's sister, Ruby Fox, had been rescued in difficult circumstances by Verity Nye, but what had happened after that?

She found several articles about her death, including an obituary in a local paper. She'd stepped out in front of a car and been killed instantly. The driver said she'd been looking the other way; the conclusion was that she'd been preoccupied and made a fatal mistake. The dive she'd done with Verity had been her first professional commission. She'd been so young.

'Awful,' Eve said aloud, and Gus got up and pottered over to her. She stroked his head. 'Poor Ruby – to follow such a dangerous profession and overcome an ordeal that threatened her life, only to be killed like that.' The thought that one moment of lapsed concentration could be so devastating was sobering.

For a second her mind returned to what Jade had said, about her motivation for setting up Wide Blue Yonder. She'd realised someone else was suffering worse than she was. Could this have been Ruby, the younger sister, who'd maybe found the undermining behaviour of their father even harder to cope with? She remembered again the emotion she'd heard in Jade's voice, and how she'd looked out of the window, avoiding Eve's eyes.

'I have to find out what happened between the dive and Ruby's death.' She looked down into Gus's melting brown eyes. She needed to know all of Jade's sister's story.

After a lot of digging, she found an article about Ruby in the *Eastern Daily Press*, talking about her struggle after returning home from Egypt. She'd developed pneumonia in the days immediately after her ordeal. But as far as Eve could work out, she'd made a full recovery.

She swung her legs down off the couch and bent to give Gus a cuddle. 'I don't get it, Gus. What do you think? Verity rescued Jade's sister during their cave dive in Egypt. So far, so good. It would explain why Jade was determined to champion her and have her as Wide Blue Yonder's ambassador.' She gave him one last pat, then rested her elbows on her knees, head in her upturned hands as she looked at him. 'But if she was eternally grateful for what Verity did, why not mention it when I interviewed her for the obituary?' She reached her wine and took a sip. 'Yet it's way too much of a coincidence for it to be unrelated. Ergo, Jade was not grateful for some reason.'

Surely it must have been that which had motivated her to recruit Verity. Had the adventurer known Jade and Ruby were related? Eve had never seen or heard it mentioned and guessed not. After all, they had different surnames, and Ruby had died four years earlier, well before Verity had been recruited.

Eve went back to her laptop and wrote up her notes on what she'd discovered. Jade's tab on her Murder Suspects spreadsheet now included a lot more detail, and three questions:

- *Jade clearly adored her sister, so why wasn't she grateful to Verity after she saved her?*
- *What were Jade's plans when she recruited Verity to Wide Blue Yonder?*
- *And why did Verity go to Jade's room? Had she discovered her and Ruby's relationship?*

Jade had gone from being an outside possibility as murderer to someone with a lot of explaining to do. For a second, Eve's mind ran to Tilly Cotton. But she'd been through this before. True enough, Tilly had no reason to protect the charity manager, but Jade wasn't dissimilar to Cora physically. If Tilly was trying to shield the family, and mistook one for the other, that would explain it. And on a sunny day, looking up at a dark window, it was entirely possible Tilly had seen nothing more than a shadowy figure behind the diver. She might not even know their gender. It was time to pay serious attention to Verity's outside contacts.

Eve's mind flitted to the gardener who'd seen her examining the graves at Blackwood Burial Ground. If Jade was there once a week to tend Ruby's plot, he'd be sure to mention Eve's visit to her. They hadn't exchanged names, but he'd be able to describe her well enough.

It might be best to tackle the charity manager head-on, rather than waiting for her to come to Eve. She picked up the phone and dialled her mobile number, her mouth feeling dry as she waited for an answer.

CHAPTER TWENTY

Eve woke on Thursday morning feeling anxious. Jade Piper said she'd be passing through Suffolk that day. Maybe she was travelling to a vacation session for one of the youth groups she organised, but if she was coming that far north, she might visit her sister's grave too. Eve was nervous about the timing. Jade had suggested calling at Elizabeth's Cottage late in the afternoon. If she was going to the burial ground, she'd probably have done it by then. Would the gardener who'd seen Eve be present?

But it was clear Jade was already on her guard. Eve had told her she had some extra questions, having spoken to Kim Carmichael. Instead of offering to answer them over the phone, Jade had suggested meeting in person. She must be wondering what Eve knew, and how best to tackle her. Monty's or the Cross Keys might have provided a safer venue for the meet-up, but Eve knew the conversation would be delicate; a public place wouldn't do. She'd just have to be prepared, in case things got out of hand.

She was still preoccupied when she walked over to the village store for some milk. It took her a moment to pick up on Moira's urgent, agitated tone.

'Molly Walker?' Her eyes were wide as she leaned forward on the counter, one hand over her mouth, her plum-polished nails gleaming in the store's strip lights.

The woman she was talking to nodded, her curly hair bobbing. She was clutching a block of cheese, but Eve had a feeling gossip was her real reason for being there.

'Is she still over at Seagrave Hall?'

Moira's customer shook her head. 'They've sent her home. She was in no fit state to carry on cleaning, and I don't imagine the family want external employees on site.'

Moira took a deep breath and puffed out her cheeks. 'Well, no! I suppose not.'

'She's being treated for shock, I hear.'

What on earth had happened? Eve felt a quivery sensation in her stomach.

At that moment Moira glanced up and saw her. 'Oh my dear Eve!' She turned to the woman she'd been talking to. 'Now, here's Eve Mallow, who saw poor dear Verity fall. She's writing her obituary.'

The other woman turned, and Eve looked from one glaze-eyed stare to the other.

'Paula here has some terrible news.'

Eve's breath caught.

'Poor Molly Walker found young Cora dead this morning. She was floating in the swimming pool at the hall, down in the woods.'

'It wasn't an accident,' the second woman said. 'She was beaten. They think she drowned while she was unconscious.'

Eve felt a chill spread through her. Cora's eerie smile came back to her, and the way she'd giggled as she'd told Eve how she'd given Rupert a motive for murder.

'Oh dear me!' Moira rushed out from behind the counter. 'We shouldn't have faced you with the news like that! You look quite pale. Would you like me to make you a nice cup of tea?'

Tea with Moira – and quite possibly her friend – was the last thing Eve felt like. She thanked the storekeeper and made polite excuses. She had Gus outside in any case. In the end she left without her milk, and Moira seemed to forget she might have had a reason for visiting, so she let her go.

She walked back across the village green on autopilot, hardly seeing the children playing, and other dogs being exercised. She almost bumped right into her neighbour, Sylvia, as she entered Haunted Lane.

'Trouble?' There was a knowing look in the photographer's dark eyes.

Eve swallowed and passed on the news. Sylvia put a reassuring hand on her shoulder.

'Moira offered to make me a cup of tea.'

'But you couldn't face it? Not surprised.' For just a second the woman's standard ironic look returned. 'Come and have coffee with us instead. Daphne's just made a pot.'

It wasn't the first time the pair of them had dragged her in when she'd been feeling awful. 'That sounds a lot more appealing.'

Sylvia laughed. 'I'd be insulted if you said otherwise. I wanted a word anyway, but after what you've just told me, I think it will do us all good to take stock.'

Eve followed her through the low front door of Hope Cottage. Like hers, it was a seventeenth-century thatched home, and had slumped down gently on one side. Eve loved it, and in a state of shock it provided almost as much comfort as her own house. The front half was much as it must have been hundreds of years ago, but Sylvia and Daphne had opened it out at the back to provide a large studio space which served both their careers. Daphne's latest ceramics were displayed on wooden shelves to one side. The cottage was full of cherished old furniture, polished, but showing the marks of time, as well as books, CDs and art.

Daphne entered the living room from the kitchen, coffee pot in hand, and looked up.

'Oh, how lovely!' But then her kind grey eyes met Eve's. She set the pot on the table, rushed forward and put a hand on her arm, just as the photographer had done, her look questioning.

Sylvia explained, without any of the to-do that Moira had employed.

'That's terrible!' Daphne ran a hand through her grey hair, disturbing the stylish cut. Her expressive face gave away her thoughts. 'Poor Molly Walker. And what must the family be going through?'

'*Some* of the family,' Sylvia said.

Daphne gave her a reproachful look.

'Well, it's true! And you already know what I was planning to share with Eve.' Sylvia made for the dining table, which was at the back of the living room, before the opening to the studio. 'And all the more reason to, with this morning's news. Come and sit down, Eve.'

She followed Sylvia over, wondering what was coming.

Daphne sighed. 'You're right. Let me bring another cup through.' The table was already laid for two. She turned to Eve. 'You must have something to eat as well.' She was quick on her feet. In a moment she was back from the kitchen with an extra cup and a plate: the beautiful set was her own work, Eve knew, aquamarine and iridescent.

Gus approached the table too, keeping to Eve's left, between her and Sylvia. He and the couple's marmalade cat, who was to Eve's right, didn't get on.

'No anchovy paste on toast today, Orlando,' Sylvia said to him, 'so you can stop licking your whiskers.'

Daphne had set a plateful of Monty's fresh blueberry breakfast cakes on the table. 'We decided to treat ourselves.'

'And now, I must say, the thought of a sugar boost is appealing.' Sylvia was a robust person; tall, cynical and with an almost permanent twinkle in her eye. It was unusual to see her looking so serious. She passed the plate of cakes to Eve; the sweet smell of fruit and dough was comforting.

As it became plain there was nothing of interest on offer, Orlando got down from the chair he'd perched on and walked disdainfully away from the table, his tail in the air. Gus lay down and relaxed.

'I've got photographs I thought you might like to see,' Sylvia said, pouring their coffees. 'Not from the day Verity died, but ones I've taken of the family over the years.'

'Thanks.' Eve picked up her cup. 'They commissioned you regularly then?'

Sylvia nodded and flipped her thick plait, streaked smoke and iron grey, over her shoulder, out of the way of the cake and coffee. 'I was looking at them yesterday, what with everything that's happened, and it occurred to me they tell a story, in a way. They're not relevant to Verity's obituary, but if you're looking for clues and want more background on the family?' She raised an eyebrow.

'Both those things. And all the more so, now that Cora's dead. She and Rupert involved me in their affairs, whether I wanted it or not.' She took a sip of the coffee, and hoped it would sink in and work some kind of magic. If it didn't, the blueberry breakfast cakes ought to. She savoured her first mouthful. They were made with buttermilk: soft and deliciously moist on the inside, but with a bite to their outer layer, which was encrusted with granulated sugar. Viv referred to them as 'strengthening'.

Eve swallowed the mouthful and sighed. 'I can't turn my back on what's happened.' What if she did, and Tilly was attacked? Or Palmer arrested someone who was innocent, and let a guilty person go free? And Verity deserved justice too. Eve still felt an odd connection with her, and a compulsion to understand what had made her a target.

They talked about Eve's work on Verity's obituary as they ate, and she was conscious of her neighbours' tact. Neither of them pressed her to confide more than she should.

After they'd finished, Daphne started to clear away, and Eve and Sylvia rose to help. They all went to and fro from the tiny kitchen, with its red-stained dresser and ancient oven.

'Right, let's get the albums laid out,' Sylvia said, fetching them from a tall white gloss-painted bookcase at one side of the living room. She put them down on the table and flipped the first one open between them as they all sat again.

'These are from the first session I did for the Seagraves after Cora joined the family,' Sylvia said. 'They're only small prints, kept for my own records, and to show prospective customers.' She laughed. 'I have stuff online now too, but I hadn't when I took these. Cora was fourteen at the time.' She stretched to reach a pair of half-moon reading glasses from a coffee table, then peered at the date in the album. She nodded. 'Fifteen years ago. Funny how much has changed.'

She turned the album so Eve could take a closer look.

'Family portrait?' Eve recognised Percival's genial smile. He'd been slimmer back then, his complexion less florid. Belinda hadn't changed much; her eyes weren't any more friendly than they were now, and her strong features had stood the test of time. Rupert had already been handsome. He was standing close to Cora, who looked uncertain. It was her expression that surprised Eve the most. She didn't look like the woman who'd glanced down at Verity's body with a heartless smile, or who'd laughed as she'd talked about hurting her cousin with her targeted words.

Sylvia's eyes were on hers and she nodded. 'Cora changed a lot. I think she was like an animal, learning how best to fit into a new habitat. Working out survival tactics.'

'That's a bit dramatic.' Daphne was frowning.

'It may be,' Sylvia said, 'but that's how it seemed.'

Eve thought of Rupert's suggestion: that Cora had jumped at the chance to move to London, to get away from Seagrave Hall. He'd said it made her risk money on a venture that was unsound.

'At that stage, she was new to the family and very unsure of herself. Grieving too, of course.' Sylvia pointed at the photograph. 'The older couple standing to Percival's left are his parents, Henry and Matilda. They were Cora's grandparents as well as Rupert's, and they lived on the estate. I think they helped Cora settle. Unfortunately they died within two years of this photograph being taken. One got cancer, the other had a heart attack. Cora had one loss after another.'

She turned over several pages at once, then went back and forth. 'Ah, here we are: the start of the next session I did for them.'

Eve looked at two pages full of group photographs.

'It's nice that they included the staff in the sessions,' Daphne said, leaning in to see more clearly.

Sylvia looked at her over the top of her glasses. 'I rather think the Seagraves enjoy that sort of thing: patronising their employees, having pictures of the old retainers.'

Daphne shook her head. 'Well, you would think that!'

'Is that Walter Cotton?' Eve asked, peering at a man standing next to a much younger Ivy. He was good-looking, but there was something about his eyes that told her he was dangerous. Or was she just being influenced by Simon's report?

'That's him,' Sylvia said. 'Younger than me by a good bit and not my preferred flavour in any case, but that didn't stop him making eyes.' She shuddered. 'Ivy wore a lot of make-up that day, but I wasn't fooled. I had a quiet word with Percival after the session. He hadn't noticed her bruises, but in fairness to him, he was outraged once I pointed out what was going on. Ivy was stuck too. If she left Walter, she'd be walking out on her job and home, with a daughter to care for.'

'What happened to him?'

'Sacked. He was out by the end of the week. I was relieved; I've always thought of Percival as a weak character but he went ahead and acted on that occasion.' She turned over a page. 'Here's Cora with Rupert. This is a year on, so she'd have been fifteen, and he just a little older.' Sylvia had managed to get a shot of them laughing. Cora looked carefree, and Rupert relaxed and at ease with her.

'The grandparents were still around then, and they balanced things. But then compare that with this portrait I took.' Cora was much more recognisable in the next one Sylvia indicated. The knowing smile was there, and it felt as though she'd erected a barrier: that she wanted to control what onlookers thought of her, and the way they reacted.

'The grandparents acted as a buffer between Cora and Belinda. But by this stage they were dead. I took Cora's picture first, because she rushed forward and oh my, the lady of the manor didn't like that. She made some cutting remark about pushing in.' Sylvia's eyes met Eve's. 'Rupert was conscious of the different way in which they were treated, I think. And where Belinda was harsh, Percival went the other way and always indulged her. Cora played him off against Belinda. And I think she encouraged Rupert's guilt too.'

'Sylvia!' Daphne was frowning.

The taller woman threw up her hands. 'That's just my opinion; she became manipulative, but she had every reason. It was a defence mechanism. Belinda's a poisonous piece of work and she never wanted her. Cora had to learn young and learn quickly. She became ruthless, but her aunt made her that way. And Percival made it easier for her to create divisions by spoiling her.' She shook her head and turned to Eve. 'It's best you know it all, if you might come face to face with her killer. Rupert seemed caught in the middle. He gets pulled in all directions like a flag in the wind, but at that point he trusted Cora.'

And Eve knew how much that had changed.

She wondered why Cora had been killed. Rupert could have done it in revenge for what she'd said about his fiancée. Or maybe his cousin had secret knowledge that made her dangerous to the killer, if she'd seen them do something incriminating. It might have been a detail she'd only realised was important later. That could explain the gap of a week before she was killed, if she'd finally confronted them. It meant Jade Piper and Pete Smith were still on the suspect list. Either of them could have targeted her if she knew they were guilty.

Now Eve had seen Sylvia's photos she felt differently about Cora. She should have made more of Rupert's guilt about the way she'd been treated, and her flight from home. It looked as though she'd gone from being a frightened fourteen-year-old to someone who'd remodelled themselves by necessity, as a form of self-defence. It was an unsettling background to her eerily childlike laugh, and willingness to use whatever she could to take control.

At that moment a text came in on her phone. She glanced at it quickly. Robin Yardley.

Meet me by the burned oak in Blind Eye Wood at 11? I've got news.

CHAPTER TWENTY-ONE

Blind Eye Wood covered the ground between the seaward houses of Saxford St Peter and the heath which overlooked the beach. Its name came from the days when smugglers had used it to bring contraband covertly from the mouth of the River Sax towards a quiet back lane leading south from the village. Everyone knew to steer clear of the woods if they saw a pinprick of light out to sea, or the answering signal of a lantern glowing onshore, giving the all-clear. The burned oak was a grand old tree near the centre of the woods, which still bore the scars of the lightning that had struck it many years earlier – a cleft running vertically down its trunk.

As Eve and Gus walked down Love Lane to meet Robin there, Eve's mind was full of what he might say. She still felt shaky at the thought of Cora, floating in the tranquil swimming pool she'd seen the day before. Gus dashed ahead on his extendable leash. She was pretty sure he only had rabbits on his mind.

Eve reached the old oak before Robin, and let Gus run free. He followed his nose, and found something tantalising under a fallen log, sniffing at the leaf matter on the forest floor. Eve scanned the trees for movement. Nature provided a soothing backdrop around her; sun-dappled quiet. The woods were rich with wildflowers, from the delicate enchanter's nightshade growing at her feet, to the headily scented honeysuckle which wove its way through branches, attracting bumblebees and white admiral butterflies. She couldn't help but think of the woods on the other side of the estuary, in the grounds of Seagrave Hall, where a murderer had watched and waited as Cora spent her final hours. She and the family had been down in London for the day, according to Tilly. Maybe Cora had come back tired and hot, and decided to go for an evening swim in the quiet of her family's woods.

The crack of a snapping twig underfoot made Eve start. There was Robin, in a fading black T-shirt and jeans, turning sideways to avoid a branch. He raised his hand and she returned the gesture.

As his eyes met hers, she suddenly remembered the call she'd accidentally overheard when he was last at her house, ended with a sense of urgency. What had he been discussing? It hadn't been your average conversation – all that talk about a dead end, more work to do and the need to report back. His look was appraising, and she was convinced he was thinking of it too, just for a second, and wondering if it had made an impression on her.

She looked away. 'I can't believe the news about Cora.'

'I know.'

'Do the police think she'd discovered the identity of the murderer, but kept it to herself for some reason?' Rupert filled Eve's head. If Cora had wanted leverage to get him to agree to her hotel idea, she'd sure as heck had it if she knew he was the killer. And the approach seemed to fit her way of operating.

She voiced the thought and Robin's blue-grey eyes met hers. 'That's a possibility. Or if she wanted money to start over, she could have tried to blackmail Jade Piper or the mysterious Pete Smith, if she knew either of them was guilty. Neither of them has an alibi, from what I hear.'

'The police still think it's Jade?'

'Palmer's like a dog with a bone; he won't let go of the idea. And anyone can get access to the estate. There are fences, and plenty of notices saying the place is private, but my contact says the perimeter isn't secure. There are various stretches that need replacing, and there's no security system.' He shrugged. 'Just not enough money to cover it all, I'd guess.'

Eve thought of Sir Percival and the cash he'd invested in a racehorse. Belinda Seagrave's disapproving face filled her mind.

Gus had finished snuffling under his log.

'Do you want to walk as we talk?' Robin said, looking down at him, a brief smile lighting his face.

'Sounds good.'

They kept pace, weaving their way through the trees.

Robin gave her a sidelong glance. 'So you probably heard Cora was hit on the back of the head as she was about to take a swim. The killer used a blunt instrument of some kind to knock her unconscious and left her to drown.'

Eve swallowed. 'I got the gist from Moira.'

'It's a step up in brutality from Verity's murder,' Robin said.

Eve had already pictured the sustained callousness of the killer, bringing their weapon down on Cora's head, hearing the crack, maybe, as it met its target. She couldn't imagine how someone could do that. 'I know.'

'I'm worried things are escalating. And whereas I can well believe Verity's murder was committed on the spur of the moment, it's entirely possible Cora's was planned. Apparently it was her habit to use the pool most evenings in summer. The family would know, and people who'd recently been guests at the hall would too. I understand they were invited to swim there when they were visiting, and Cora took a dip as usual.'

Eve closed her eyes for a moment. 'So it doesn't rule Jade and Pete out.'

'No.'

'Did any more alibis come to light for Verity's murder?'

Robin shook his head. 'Now, of course, the police are starting over, with reference to last night. I gather they've already interviewed the family and permanent staff. Sir Percival and Lady Seagrave have both told the police Tilly was burning the midnight oil in her office. They say they saw her when she arrived and heard her talking on the phone at around the relevant time too. The downstairs cloakroom's right next door to her workroom, so that all figures, but apparently they're behaving as though that gives *them* an alibi. My colleague had to point out that it doesn't. Tilly was engrossed in her phone conversations so she can't confirm hearing anyone use the bathroom, and they both knew she was planning to make some calls, so they could have made that up. Of course, they alibi each other, but no one gives that much weight.'

'And Rupert?'

Robin raised an eyebrow. 'Went to bed early, apparently. So no alibi, and it suggests he was out of sorts last night.'

'He'd find it easy to sneak down from his room and out into the grounds without being spotted.' Eve thought back to her tour of the house, with its multiple staircases and side doors. 'What about Ivy Cotton?'

'She felt unwell and left work early – went back to the cottage she shares with her daughter and, if she's to be believed, went to bed and slept until morning. Tilly says she looked in on her when she got home, around an hour after Cora died, and she was out for the count.'

'How are the police so sure about the time of death?'

'Cora hadn't had time to remove her watch before the killer struck her. She fell into the pool with it on, and it stopped. Apparently the time fits with when she'd normally take her evening swim too.'

Eve took a deep breath. 'Do you know what line the police are taking?'

'They're interested in the family's trip down to London yesterday. It sounds as though there was a domino decision to go. Rupert's not going back to work yet, but he needed to see someone in his office. Then Percival decided to travel with him, because he likes London. Reading between the lines, Belinda went because she didn't trust Percival to spend a day down there without getting into trouble, and then Cora hitched a lift too, saying she had some errands to run.'

'I wouldn't be surprised if she wanted to spend every second she could with Rupert.' Eve thought back to how she'd immediately tried to make up with him after Verity's fall. 'She was so desperate to get her hotel idea back on the agenda, and I guess Rupert would have been harder to persuade once he'd returned to the capital permanently.'

Robin nodded. 'That makes sense. My contact says Belinda gave the impression it was a restorative day out. After Cora had finished her errands, and Rupert his meeting, they went for a walk together along the Thames, apparently.'

'Cosy.' Eve thought of the way they'd each behaved when she'd seen them last. Could they really have buried the hatchet? But on consideration, she thought it was possible. Rupert had been furious, but also close to the edge, volatile and unsure of the trust he'd put in Verity.

'Both Simon Maxwell and Sylvia implied Rupert felt guilty about the way Cora was treated when she joined the family,' she said. 'I suppose that deep-seated feeling of responsibility might have come to the fore again.'

But Belinda wasn't a reliable witness in Eve's view; her story of a reconciliation might be just that: a work of fiction.

A half-smile played around Robin's lips as he glanced at her. 'What are you thinking?'

Eve took a deep breath. 'If Rupert's guilty, or Belinda thinks he is, it would be natural for her to gloss over his and Cora's recent arguments.'

'True. And if Rupert killed Verity on the back of the accusations Cora made, then decided she'd lied, a day of her intense lobbying over the hotel might have pushed him over the edge. He's very smooth, but that doesn't mean he wouldn't snap.'

'I believe you.' She thought of Rupert's shaking hands as he'd talked to her about Cora.

Up ahead something scuffled in the undergrowth, and Gus dashed off in pursuit.

'I'm fascinated that a creature with such short legs can move so fast.' Robin laughed and changed course so they were headed in the same direction as Gus.

'Dachshunds were bred as hunting dogs, so he's in his element.'

Robin sighed. 'And yet those melting brown eyes look so innocent.'

'Yes. He winds me round his little paws with that gaze of his.'

His smile was there again, but after a moment his look turned serious. 'The police are interested in the errands Cora did, down in London.'

'Do they know what they were?'

'She didn't tell the others, apparently, but Palmer's making much of the fact that Jade Piper's based there.' His eyes met hers for a moment. 'And so is Pete Smith.'

'He's another person I want to see, but he's ignoring my messages, just like Verity's parents. So the police think Cora sneaked off to try to blackmail Pete or Jade and then one or other of them drove up to Suffolk and killed her that evening?'

Robin nodded. 'Otherwise they can't explain the timing. And they're focused on Jade in particular. Verity falling from her room is still a factor.'

Eve's new-found knowledge about the charity manager sat heavy in her chest. It was a relief to confide in Robin, and she gave him all the details.

He whistled. 'Nice work. I think you and Gus have something in common on the hunting front.' He turned to face her.

'And on the short legs.'

He laughed and his gaze met hers. 'Your eyes are brown too. Have you found you wind people round your little finger?'

She felt a blush rise in her cheeks. 'Sadly not. I have to use Gus as a proxy.'

He grinned and they walked on without speaking for a moment.

'Are you going to tell Palmer what you found out about Jade?' Robin said at last.

She was glad he'd stopped teasing her, but the question left her uncomfortable. It had been playing round her head as she drove home from Thetford the day before. Since the news of Cora's death, she'd allowed herself to put it on the back-burner, but she knew she couldn't ignore it.

'I'd rather talk to her first. Get her side of the story.' She hesitated. 'She's visiting me at Elizabeth's Cottage later today.' He'd think she was crazy. And the plan, made that morning before she knew Cora was dead, seemed far riskier than she'd thought. The perpetrator had gone from being someone who'd probably killed on the spur of the moment, to someone who'd carried out a vicious attack, using a weapon they'd likely brought with them.

Robin's eyes told her the same thoughts were going through his mind. 'That could be a dangerous decision. You've concluded she didn't like Verity for some reason and had pulled her in close, with an unknown motive. That, together with Verity's subsequent death, makes Jade a worry from my perspective.' He folded his arms.

Eve sighed. 'I know. But she's so sad, Robin. I don't understand exactly what happened in the past, but she had a tough upbringing and lost her sister at a very young age. And she's passionate about the women and girls she helps. I feel I owe it to her to admit what I've found and give her the chance to explain. Besides,' she pulled a face, 'if I run straight to Palmer, he'll only say I "went beyond my brief".' But what if she was guilty? Doubt gnawed at her insides.

Robin's eyes were serious. 'What time's she due to visit?'

'Five. But she might clam up unless we're alone.' She guessed he might be thinking of 'happening to be in the vicinity'.

'I'll be subtle. You won't see me.'

'Aren't you worried someone might spot you stopping by my cottage when you're not due to garden?' She knew how cautious he was.

'No sweat. I'll bring a decoy shovel.'

She tried to hide what a comforting thought that was. 'Well if you see us having a dust-up, don't go using it to break a window. I'll leave the back door unlocked instead...'

'It's a deal.'

She turned to him. 'Thanks, Robin.'

'Think nothing of it.' It was a moment before he spoke again. 'The Seagraves are doing a press conference with the police today, over at the hall. It's at two. I thought you might want to go, if you can fit it in.'

She'd no business to be there if they were going to talk about Cora's death, but Robin was right. She'd certainly like to be present, and there were sure to be crowds of journalists in which to lose herself. Monty's wasn't a problem; her next shift was the following day – she was owed hours after all the work for the fete.

'I can make it. Thanks.'

CHAPTER TWENTY-TWO

Eve glanced at her watch as she waited with the other journalists on the sweeping gravel driveway of Seagrave Hall. She'd already seen DI Palmer and DS Boles being admitted by Ivy Cotton. Now, the waiting crowds were staring at an unattended lectern standing close to the grand front door. Presumably Percival, Rupert and Belinda were getting ready inside. She couldn't see through the dark sash windows. The glare of the sun made shadows of everything within.

'Which one of them d'you reckon did it?' a guy to her left said to a woman he was with. 'My money's on the dad. Rumour has it he was leching after Verity Nye. If she rejected him, he might have lashed out to shut her up. Maybe the niece saw him do it, which would have sealed her fate. I hear she's short of cash. Perhaps she tried to blackmail him.'

Eve didn't like the sound of Percival Seagrave's antics herself, but the way the journalist spoke, based entirely on gossip, bothered her.

The woman next to him chewed her lip. 'If Belinda Seagrave didn't have an alibi for the fiancée, I'd say it was her. Word is she didn't like either of the victims. Verity Nye was too common for her boy, if you can believe it, and Cora Seagrave was an interloper who got in the way.'

'But as she does have an alibi…'

'Yes. With that in mind, my bet's on Rupert. Not sure about a motive, but he's very dull to have hooked someone like Verity Nye. Maybe her reasons for—'

At that moment, a more general murmuring spread through the gaggle of reporters around Eve. She turned and saw they were twisting to look behind them. Someone had appeared in a red Mercedes, and pulled up to one side of the driveway, beyond where the press pack had parked. The windows were tinted, preventing anyone from seeing inside, and no one got out.

There was a certain amount of clamour as people went to try to speak to the driver and got nowhere, but a second later, Palmer appeared at the front door, leading the family out to the lectern, holding a microphone with a trailing wire. DS Boles brought up the rear, pulling the wire clear of the party's feet.

'Thank you for coming,' Palmer said. Eve hoped he couldn't see her. He definitely wouldn't approve of her presence. 'After the appalling second attack here at Seagrave Hall, the family have courageously decided to put out an appeal for information themselves.' He glanced at Belinda Seagrave for a moment. 'It should be noted that the hall grounds are easily accessible, and so anyone could have come in and attacked Cora Seagrave.'

Eve bet Belinda had told him to make that plain, with the rumour mill working overtime. Her face was fixed, jaw set. It was impossible to know exactly what was going on under the surface.

'In addition,' Palmer went on, 'it's perfectly possible to drive to the hall using back routes to bypass traffic cameras. As such we are appealing for witnesses: anyone who saw any unusual activity in the area should come forward, even if it seems irrelevant.' He paused and Eve analysed the expressions of Percival and Rupert Seagrave. Percival was crying. Rupert looked pale, shocked and frightened. But none of that was unnatural, whether he was guilty or innocent. 'I'd like to hand over to Sir Percival—'

But Belinda Seagrave glanced at her husband, her lips tight, gave a quick shake of her head and stepped forward.

'To Lady Seagrave, I should say.' Palmer coughed and moved back to stand next to DS Boles.

'I'd like to thank all our friends and neighbours for their good wishes.' Her eyes were dark and narrow. 'You can help us in our time of need by doing as the inspector says. We need to identify the person who's tearing our family apart.'

Her anger was barely controlled, but whether at the gossip circulating or the murderer, Eve wasn't sure. She was coming to understand that reputation meant everything to Belinda.

The woman paused now, with a look at DI Palmer, and turned to her son. 'Rupert also has something to say.'

Palmer blinked and DS Boles frowned.

'Yes.' Rupert's speech was unsteady. 'I-I can't quite comprehend what I've lost in the last week.' His voice cracked and he stopped.

The two journalists next to Eve exchanged a glance. What was going through Rupert's mind? The fact that he'd killed through jealousy, then killed again through fury, wiping out two women he'd once loved? Or that something beyond his understanding had taken control of his life?

'I – that is to say, before Cora was killed, I'd been thinking of how I could pay tribute to my fiancée, Verity. Now, I shall have to decide what I can do to honour my cousin also. But for today, I would like to announce that I intend to fund the cave dive Verity would have undertaken in China in her name. The team will remain unchanged, except for...' He broke down again. 'A young female diver who needs their first break will be chosen to take Verity's place. It would fit with her work for Wide Blue Yonder. And we have...'

His voice trailed away, but there was movement behind the bank of journalists now. The door of the red Mercedes opened, and Pete Smith stepped out.

Rupert moved back from the lectern, holding out a shaking hand in Pete's direction. Belinda took the microphone from

Rupert as the medic squeezed his way through the crowds to a burst of camera flashes. He wore dark glasses, but under them his face looked taut. What emotion was he hiding? Sorrow? Anxiety? Guilt? Eve wasn't sure.

Belinda handed him the microphone. Palmer and Boles had both stepped forward, having had their press conference hijacked, but Pete Smith was already talking.

'I want to thank the Seagraves for inviting me back here today, and Rupert for his support for the upcoming dive. When Verity first fell, the idea of going ahead with it seemed impossible, but he's right. It's what she would have wanted.'

The cameras were flashing again. Palmer was saying something to Belinda Seagrave, but not as though he was up for a fight. Meanwhile the press were enthralled, shouting out questions to both Rupert and Pete Smith. After a moment, the conference was shut down, but it was Belinda Seagrave who called it to a halt.

'It seems we need to finish now,' she said, with a sidelong glance at Palmer, but Eve had a feeling she'd have no qualms about continuing if it suited her purposes. She'd wanted to get their news out, but not to field a barrage of questions.

The press weren't content to give up. They swarmed up towards the house as Palmer and Boles ushered the family back inside, then pestered Pete Smith as he made his way back to his car.

Eve wasn't quite sure how she was going to get a look-in. The medic was at the centre of a scrum. The questions were intrusive ('Where have you been hiding?' 'How close were you and Ms Nye?') Over the top of the hubbub she heard his repeated response. 'No comment.' He still had his sunglasses on, and his voice was husky. It was going to take him a moment to send them all packing.

Eve decided to abandon her car for the time being and walk down the driveway instead. She was standing by the estate gates, in the middle of Pete Smith's escape route, when she heard a horn honk four minutes later. She turned and there was the red Mercedes. She peered at its tinted windscreen without getting out of the way, forcing him to wind down his window.

'Hello.' She walked nearer but without clearing his path. 'Mr Smith, I'm Eve Mallow. From Monty's teashop? My friend Viv and I were providing cakes for the fete.' She wanted him to see her in another context, not as part of the standard press pack.

Smith looked puzzled. 'Yes?'

'I understand you want to avoid the hacks up at the hall, but I work part-time as a freelance obituary writer. I tried to contact you about Ms Nye. My article's purely about her life and work – a way to let the public know about her character and her achievements. I just wondered if we could have a quick word about that?'

Smith glanced over his shoulder. 'They'll be on my tail any minute. I don't want to talk to anyone right now.'

'My article will appear in *Icon* magazine.' It was a quality publication. 'I'd really like to have your viewpoint, but I'm not digging for dirt. That's not my role – I just want to make Ms Nye's obituary rounded. If I don't speak with you, I know their readers will wonder why.'

She didn't normally try to manipulate her interviewees, but she hoped it was justified in this case. If Cora had been trying to blackmail him, he'd fit for both murders and if he refused to talk to her, it would make him look guilty. Answering 'no comment' to the hacks up at the hall was understandable, refusing to pay tribute to his dead diving partner, less so.

'Maybe if we talk you can tell everyone else you'd promised me an exclusive. It might get them off your back.'

Smith gave a sigh and nodded. 'Okay. I suppose I can give you five minutes. Not here though. What if I come to that café where you work?'

Thank goodness he'd suggested somewhere public. She'd just have time to quiz him before Jade Piper showed up.

CHAPTER TWENTY-THREE

'What can I get you, madam?'

Eve gave Viv a repressive look. Having an arch joker in attendance wasn't going to help. She turned to Pete Smith and handed him the menu. 'This is my boss, Viv Montague.'

The medic peered at Monty's list of wares. 'Just a pot of Assam, thanks.'

Viv gave him a thunderstruck look, which Eve ignored.

'Yes, that sounds perfect.' She guessed professional divers didn't mainline on cakes between expeditions. 'I'm sorry I waylaid you,' she said to the medic. 'I was hoping to interview you when I went back to Seagrave Hall to pick up our stuff, the day after Ms Nye died, but I missed you then.'

Smith nodded. 'I left on the Friday, as soon as the detective inspector dismissed us.' He put his head in his hands. 'It was just too hard, facing up to my feelings with all the family there. They must have wanted me gone, too.'

Eve remembered the violent shove Rupert had given Pete as he'd tried to reach the body of his fiancée. And then she thought of Verity inside the marquee earlier, apparently trying to end their affair, as he attempted to cling on.

'I can completely understand you wanting to deal with the grief away from Seagrave Hall,' Eve said, but in her head she was still thinking about his relationship with Verity, not the family.

How long had she been telling him the current situation wouldn't work? When he'd said he wanted to talk again she'd sounded weary and upset, but also frustrated and angry. Maybe that day he'd finally realised she meant it. If he had a violent temper, it could have been enough to make him kill her in that terrible moment inside the hall.

Smith chewed his lip. 'I don't think they quite understood about my relationship with Verity; how close you have to be when you're diving partners.'

It all figured. Eve felt sad. Their continued affair only fitted if Verity had never loved Rupert, but had decided to marry him for money.

'I guess being part of a tiny, close-knit team is outside the Seagraves' normal experience.'

'That's right.'

Viv had appeared with a tray. 'One lovely pot of Assam, your milk, sugar and cups.'

A moment later her son Sam also came to their table, carrying a plate of mixed shortbreads. He was blushing. 'Mum said you should have these. You know, just in case…'

Eve tried not to laugh. 'Thanks, Sam.'

'I won't if you don't mind,' Smith said.

'Of course not.' He'd be dead to Viv.

Eve reached for the notebook and her favourite black writing pen, both of which were always in her bag. 'So, how did your partnership with Ms Nye start?'

Smith gave a quick sideways look, as though she'd somehow put him on the spot, yet it had been an innocent question. 'A friend of a friend let me know she was looking for a medic. Obviously, there were other people interested too, but we clicked, and that's essential. If you're going to rely on someone one hundred per cent in dangerous conditions you have to know and trust them completely. If you get an equipment failure or something unexpected happens, giving way to panic makes the situation far more likely to be fatal. Those requirements mean suitable candidates are hard to come by.'

Eve took a sip of her tea. 'And I understand you and Verity had to cope with just that situation at the dive in Egypt, when Verity rescued Ruby Fox.' What had happened that day? She watched as Smith leaned back in his seat.

'We were exploring a couple of accessible caves before going down deeper when Ruby ran into trouble. We were navigating an area filled with water between two dry caverns and Ruby got wedged in a narrow section. She started to flail around. We carry strong lights, but it was impossible to see in seconds, because of the silt she kicked up. We managed to free her, but she knocked her mouthpiece out and got water in her airways before we could help her replace it. It was a close call.'

Eve imagined them working down in the murky depths, with almost no visibility. It sounded terrifying. 'How experienced was Ruby?'

His eyes narrowed. 'It was her first major dive with an expert team, but she'd trained hard. She was desperate for her big break. The problem is, it's difficult to predict how someone will perform in a crisis. You can workshop tricky situations as much as you like, but until the dangers are real, you don't know how you'll react.'

She'd touched a nerve. 'I can imagine what a brilliant opportunity it must have seemed.' Jade Piper's sad eyes filled her head.

'You may have read she got ill afterwards,' Smith continued, his handsome features taut. 'The pneumonia was rotten luck; it caught us off guard. I gave her a full course of antibiotics, but it's usual for patients to take up to six months to fully recover.'

'I understand.' Maybe other people had queried his actions in the past. Perhaps Verity had been lauded for performing a glamorous rescue, while the medic got questioned about why Ruby wasn't up to media interviews.

'And what was Ms Nye like to work with? You were with her for several years?'

'That's right, seven years and eight major expeditions.' He sighed. 'We each knew we could rely on the other absolutely. She was very passionate and driven. Businesslike, when it came to logistics and organisation. She was the right person to act as Wide Blue Yonder's ambassador; she minded about her work, and making a success of herself.' He paused. 'Though she certainly thought people should pull free of constraints to reach their limits.' There was a slight edge to his voice.

Free of constraints; there it was again – that hint that she'd favoured striking out alone to teaming up with others. And maybe that she'd started to see *him* as a constraint, when she wanted to end their affair. Perhaps he'd been worried he'd be dropped from the team, though he had a hold over her. He could have threatened to tell Rupert about their relationship if she'd decided to sack him. Eve didn't imagine Verity would have risked it.

For a moment, Eve considered confronting him about what she'd heard in the marquee. It would put her in the gutter-press bracket, but she had good cause. Faced with her knowledge, he might well give himself away. But if he was responsible not only for Verity's death, but also for Cora's, smashing her head in and leaving her to drown, it was too big a risk. If she asked him about the snippet of conversation, she was sure her suspicions would show in her face. Unless she could prove his guilt immediately, it would leave her horribly vulnerable.

'Could you tell me what planning sessions were like, before a dive?'

Smith was leaning forward again now, his eyes bright. 'Intense. We both loved our work. We'd look at every detail, check every aspect we could control. It was exciting, and of course if the other person feels the same way, you spark off each other.'

Eve made more notes in her book and nodded. 'And what about actually down in the water?'

'She was captivated by the experience; we both were. Safety came first of course,' he said quickly, 'but the sense of wonder and excitement we shared was irreplaceable.' He met Eve's eyes. 'It's not a sport, the sort of cave diving we do, it's exploration. Sure, it's dangerous, but everyone going into it knows that. Going to the moon was dangerous, trekking to the South Pole, climbing Everest, you name it. But if you look at it in terms of furthering our knowledge, reaching places where few other humans – sometimes none – have ever been… Well, then I guess it might be easier to understand Verity's motivation.'

Eve nodded. 'And what's your fondest memory of her?' Once again she watched him carefully. If they'd really been lovers, she wondered if she'd see some kind of confirmation there: a flush, a change in his eyes. Although there was nothing obvious, he opened his mouth to answer, but then closed it again. Was he worried he'd give himself away? At last he took a deep breath and spoke.

'Perhaps our first dive together, and the exhilaration we shared on reaching our goal.' It was a rather predictable answer, considering all the years they'd spent together. Eve was sure it wasn't the first thought that had come into his head.

'Did Ms Nye ever mention what her parents thought of her career?' For a second she allowed herself to imagine the pure, bottomless fear she'd feel if either of her twins took on something so dangerous.

Again, the medic looked wary. What was going on?

'She didn't mention them much,' he said, after a noticeable hesitation.

She nodded. 'I'm finding it hard to get hold of them, but I'll try again. So, you must still be in shock, I guess, but I hope preparation for the China dive goes well, once you're up to planning for it.'

He looked down into his tea. 'It won't be the same without Verity, but we'll start to look for a replacement in the next week or so. Time's pressing. I was surprised to get Belinda Seagrave's call about the funding. But grateful, of course.'

Did he suspect Rupert had discovered his and Verity's affair, if that's what it had been? And if he wasn't guilty himself, did he think Rupert had killed his diving partner? Realise that he was being bought off? He'd clearly decided to accept the cash and carry on. Whatever the truth, it made Eve wonder what kind of a man he was.

'What's next for you after that?' she asked, draining her tea.

'I've got a book deal, so I'll take a few months out to work on it.'

Eve could imagine him at a publisher's launch party, charming the attendees. 'Well, best of luck and thanks for talking to me.'

He nodded.

Eve let the interview play round her head as she left the teashop. Smith had been about to say something when she asked for his fondest memory, but then abruptly changed his mind. And what did he know about Verity's parents? Why had he paused before claiming she hadn't mentioned them much?

She glanced at her watch. She still had half an hour before Jade Piper was due, but nerves already tickled her stomach. As she walked alongside the village green, her senses were on high alert. She had a weird feeling that sent the back of her neck prickling.

She looked round. Was someone watching her? But she could only see Mrs Crocket, on her way to clean the church hall, and a couple of other locals. She shook the feeling off and went back to filtering Pete Smith's words.

It was only when she crossed over to reach Haunted Lane that the uneasy sensation struck again.

And this time when she looked round, she found Jade Piper was standing right behind her.

She was early, and unless Robin was too, Eve would be tackling her without backup.

CHAPTER TWENTY-FOUR

'You found my sister's grave.' Jade Piper's voice was shaking. 'What kind of an obituary writer are you that you go poking into my background, and tracking down where my family's buried, for God's sake?'

Eve's mouth went dry and she felt the heat rush up her neck. She'd been sure the gardener at the graveyard would give her away, but dealing with the repercussions still left her reeling. 'I could tell there was more to your relationship with Verity than met the eye. A few people seemed surprised you'd chosen her as Wide Blue Yonder's ambassador. She was a very strong figure,' she swallowed, 'but from what Kim Carmichael told me, her attitude didn't fit with your charity's ethos. I wanted to understand what drew you together.'

'You were suspicious of me! Just like the police! And I thought you were on my side, ready to help me raise Wide Blue Yonder's profile through your article. I liked you!' She shook her head. 'Why am I always so wrong about people?'

This was awful. Jade was in tears, and Eve had liked her too. 'Let's go inside and talk about this.'

The charity manager was shaking with distress and anger. 'You want to go inside with me, even though you think I'm a murderer?'

The need to be careful had gone from her head. She could hear Gus barking just inside Elizabeth's Cottage.

'I don't think you're a murderer.' Was that true? If she was this distraught, her feelings ran high. And a sudden spur of the moment act, thrusting Verity out of the window, could fit with that. What about Cora? If she'd tried to blackmail Jade, Eve could imagine Jade killing her to keep her secret. If she was arrested she'd have to give up her work, and Eve sensed she'd kill to avoid that if nothing else.

'I felt emotional when you told me about Wide Blue Yonder's work,' Eve said, trying to speak slowly, despite the adrenaline rushing round her body. 'What you do is amazing. But I could see there were things you weren't admitting about Verity, and it's her story I'm trying to tell. I almost wondered if you wanted me to question your relationship; it was you that put me onto Verity's mentee, and it was her story that set me thinking.'

Jade was crying, her shoulders heaving, as Eve unlocked the cottage and held the door open for her. Gus rushed up to them, jumping at Eve, but retreated, his expressive dark eyes anxious as Jade stepped over the threshold.

'Can I get you a coffee? Or a glass of water?' It was cool in the shadows of Elizabeth's Cottage, but Jade still looked flushed, and it was another earth-crackingly hot day outside.

'Water.' Her voice still shook.

'Take a seat and I'll bring it to you.' In the kitchen she unlocked the back door as she'd promised Robin, hoping he'd arrive early himself. Other than that she'd just keep her wits about her and not get cornered. She couldn't have left Jade sobbing in the lane.

Eve took out the bottle with the swing-top stopper from the fridge and poured water for each of them. She felt a wave of heat rush over her and added ice for good measure. It ought to help them both cool down.

She set the water on the coffee table between the two matching couches in the living room and sat down opposite Jade.

She was slumped forward, her eyes and cheeks red. 'It's true. I wanted you to understand Verity's real nature, but it was so personal, to track down my sister's grave.'

She was right, of course. 'I know. I'm sorry. There was a man there, tending the plots. Did he mention I'd been?'

Jade took a sip of her water, making the ice chink against the side of the glass, and nodded. 'Not many people visit.' She took a gulp of air – trying to hold back more tears, Eve guessed. 'My father never comes and my mother's dead. I'm really the only person who goes to see her.'

Eve nodded.

'His description was clear, and after your call, I was convinced it must have been you.' She shrugged and suddenly her look was angry again. 'What else should I expect from a journalist?'

It wasn't the kind of criticism she normally had to face. If it had been a standard obit, she'd have been curious about Jade's story, but she wouldn't have pushed. This was different.

'I'm interviewing the friends, colleagues and relatives of a murder victim, Jade. When I became convinced you were hiding something about your relationship with Verity, yes, I did want to know what that was. Partly because I can't get to the heart of her character without putting the hours in, but partly because I'm likely to come face to face with a killer. I'd prefer to work out who that person is than have them take me by surprise.' She wished she could look over her shoulder. Any hint that Robin was already in her garden would make her feel safer.

Jade pushed her thick brown hair out of her face, revealing red-rimmed eyes.

'Verity was in your room when she fell,' Eve went on, taking a sip of water to ease her dry mouth. 'And now I understand she rescued Ruby from drowning. You never told me that, so there's something I'm not getting here. If you'd like to explain, I'm a good listener.'

The charity manager raised the condensation-covered glass Eve had given her to her cheek and held it there for a moment. It was just what Eve had wanted to do when she'd visited the woman at the community centre earlier that week.

'I suppose Pete Smith gave you the standard version of events: they did everything they could, followed safety guidelines, full course of antibiotics et cetera, et cetera.' Her voice was wooden now.

'Pretty much word for word. What do you mean about "standard version of events"?'

'It was what they told the press, after he and Verity "saved" Ruby when she so nearly drowned. And I believed them at the time. They were still out in Egypt, but I sent flowers, thanking them for saving her life.'

So she'd contacted them, back then. 'But they didn't realise who you were, when you approached Verity to be an ambassador for Wide Blue Yonder?'

She shook her head. 'I just put, "All my love and gratitude, Ruby's sister" on the card. I was glad of that later.'

'So what changed the way you felt about them? Was it something Ruby said?'

Jade's eyes were full of tears. 'No, but that's the point. You have to understand that before she left for that trip, Ruby told me everything. We were so close. But when she came home, she turned in on herself. It was horrible. She wouldn't speak to me about anything that mattered.'

'I suppose if she was ill—'

'I thought that at first. The doctors said patients with pneumonia sometimes get depressed. But it was so extreme. I started to wonder what had really happened out there. And each time I probed, asked if Verity had been disappointed with her or treated her badly, she'd shake her head and start to cry. I found this video.' She called up a web page on her phone and clicked play, turning the screen so Eve could see it.

It was an interview with Verity. She was sitting on a couch in a studio, talking to the presenter.

'If you panic when you're underwater, you've got no business cave diving,' she said. 'You're a danger to yourself, but also to your team. You have to recognise that and move on.' Her tone was blunt. 'It bugs the hell out of me when people don't know themselves well enough and put lives in jeopardy.'

The tears that had been running down Jade's cheeks dripped onto her top.

Eve looked at the date. 'But she can't have been referring to Ruby here.' The film was seven years old.

'I know, but that's not the point. You can see what she was like. Maybe Ruby failed in some way and then watched that. She'd have felt like nothing – hopeless. And when I asked one of the doctors on her ward about her state of mind, he said she might be worse because the infection had taken hold before she was sent to hospital.'

'You think they prioritised the expedition over her well-being?'

Jade nodded slowly. 'I asked Ruby about the timing of the rescue, and piecing that together with the course of antibiotics she had and when she was taken to hospital, I realised there were needless delays.' She paced towards the inglenook fireplace, grinding her knuckles into her eyes. Gus moved closer to Eve and put his head by her knee. She ruffled his fur to give him some reassurance, her eyes on Jade.

'Ruby was ill for months afterwards and whatever I said, she wouldn't tell me what had happened. I think they made her feel too ashamed.'

Eve got up to pass her a box of tissues. 'Wouldn't it have been Pete's responsibility to get her home if she wasn't well enough to carry on?'

'Verity was the expedition leader. She wasn't the sort to brook any dissent. And I'll bet it was she who broke Ruby's spirit. Pete's very affable, but Verity always said what she thought.' She blew her nose. 'It was ironic. I'd been desperate for Ruby to pursue some other career. Divers who do that type of deep, dangerous exploration don't tend to last long. But she'd set her heart on it. Our father had rubbished the idea and that made her all the more determined.' She gasped a sob again. 'I'd encouraged her to take anything he said and let it drive her forward. It was her and me against the world. But I didn't realise that she'd pick something so risky. And then at last, in the hospital, I sensed she'd lost hope and that she'd never dive again. I'd got what I wanted, but it was awful.'

She put her glass down on the windowsill and stared out, her expression fierce, as though she was trying to keep control. 'For all I know it was Verity who knocked Ruby's mouthpiece out. Anger makes people clumsy.'

Eve put a hand on her shoulder, watching her tears fall. 'I'm so sorry. But if Ruby wouldn't talk to you, isn't it hard to know what really happened?'

'Why else would she cry when I asked if they'd mistreated her? And how could they justify delaying her treatment?'

Whatever the truth, Eve's heart ached for Jade. But her sorrow and anger didn't make her innocent. Why had she tried to get close to Verity, if not to make her pay?

'I wonder if she was onto you,' Eve said carefully. 'Maybe she and Pete had discovered your connection to Ruby and wondered if you had some way of damaging them.'

'Meaning you think I killed her?' She was facing Eve head on again now.

She could have, if Jade had some form of revenge planned that depended on keeping her relationship to Ruby secret. As soon as her cover was blown, her chance might have been lost.

Jade was shaking her head now: sharp, quick movements. 'That was never my intention. Never.'

'So what was your plan?'

The woman put her head in her hands. Her voice was a whisper. 'I didn't know. I just needed to watch her; to catch her out being cruel. To prove what she was like in some way. Unmask her.' She raised her eyes again. 'And I saw the news about Cora Seagrave's murder today. Why would I kill *her*?'

But there was an obvious answer to that, if Cora had noticed something that convinced her Jade was guilty. The woman might have lied about her movements, for instance – or the timing of them. Then maybe Cora had confronted Jade on her trip to London. Eve imagined relaying everything the charity manager had said to Palmer. It made Jade sound obsessed. She could well understand that – extreme grief and so many unanswered questions needed an outlet. But the DI would be sure she was guilty. For Eve, it was still something that needed proving.

'What happened to Ruby consumed me,' Jade said, looking at the floor for a moment, her eyes heavy and puffy. 'I split up from my husband. He couldn't stand it any more.' Eve remembered the image she'd seen on the JustGiving page. 'But although I was heart-broken about that, I couldn't be with him if he didn't understand.

'Ruby never recovered from what she went through. She wasn't properly right from the pneumonia for months, and never herself again. All those years I spent bolstering her up when my father made her feel like nothing were pointless. She couldn't concentrate, or sleep; it was like she'd been brainwashed. When she walked out in front of that car and was killed, she was still like a zombie. The cave diving trip might not have ended her life instantly, but it did in the end.'

After Jade left, Eve sat on one of the couches and stared into space for several minutes, with Gus at her side. The woman's pain was gut-wrenching. She'd drawn conclusions based on guesses and instinct, but the lack of facts wasn't relevant. Her conviction and the depth of her sorrow were what counted. Eve could believe she'd killed Verity in a moment of madness, and that she might have killed Cora too, out of desperation.

At last, Eve shook herself, got up and texted Robin to explain she was safe, and that Jade had been and gone.

His reply came back instantly.

I know. I've been outside all along. Told you you wouldn't see me!

CHAPTER TWENTY-FIVE

Eve sat opposite Viv in the Cross Keys that evening. It had taken a good hour to get over Jade Piper's visit. At last she'd written up her notes to shelve her thoughts, taken a cool shower and come out to meet her friend. Now they were sitting at a table having ordered their food. The oppressive heat had given way to a thunderstorm, and through the window, the near-indigo sky was streaked with lightning.

Moira Squires had come over to their table as soon as they'd sat down. She'd wanted to update them, now she'd heard Mrs Walker's account of finding Cora's body. Her gossip raised new questions in Eve's mind, as did Viv's odd expression while the storekeeper talked.

'Are you all right?' she asked, once they'd been left in peace.

'Fine. Why?'

'You just had an odd look on your face while Moira was talking.'

Viv bit her lip. 'Did I? I thought I'd kept my face normal.'

'How d'you mean, kept your face normal?'

'Pelvic floor,' Viv said. 'My doctor said I should pick something that happens regularly to remind me to do my exercises. Moira buttonholing me is one of my cues. But I thought I could do them without changing my expression.'

'Not entirely. And isn't it hard to concentrate on what she's saying at the same time?'

'What? You concentrate on what Moira says?'

Eve batted her with a menu. 'She's a valuable source of information.'

Viv swigged her Sauvignon Blanc. 'Fair enough. Did she mention anything fresh?'

'Just one oddity. As you'd expect, Cora was dressed in her swimsuit when Mrs Walker found her, but the other gear she'd taken to the pool – a towelling robe, some flip-flops and a small bag – had all been thrown into the water.'

Viv frowned. 'That's strange.'

Jo Falconer arrived with the food they'd ordered. As usual, Eve was conscious of Gus, who'd already been cowering by her ankles, thanks to the thunder. He moved nearer still now.

'The chicken and Parma ham?'

Eve raised her hand and the meal landed in front of her. It came with buttered new potatoes and green beans in mustard sauce, and smelled divine. 'Wonderful, thank you.'

Jo gave her a gracious smile. 'And one crab linguine with cherry tomatoes.'

Viv beamed for all she was worth. 'Smells delish!'

'Nasty business with Cora Seagrave.' Jo folded her arms, her weight on one hip. 'We've had more press in, needless to say.' For a second her eye lit on a man and woman sitting at a corner table, glued to their phone screens. 'How's the obituary going?'

Eve frowned. 'Lots of work to do still.'

'Well, that food will give you strength. Good luck.'

As she left, Gus eased off Eve's feet and Viv raised an eyebrow. 'Anyone would think you weren't already being well fed at Monty's! I'm glad you finished off those shortbreads, by the way. I still can't believe Pete Smith didn't take a single one.'

'I know. You'd think he was a fitness-conscious professional diver or something!'

Viv pulled a face. 'Was your talk with him useful?'

Eve took a deep breath. 'It added another layer of impressions over everything I've found out so far. It was Jade's visit afterwards that really threw me.'

Viv leaned forward. 'What happened?'

A sustaining sip of her Pinot Grigio was called for. She took one, and a mouthful of food, then explained what the woman had said.

'Oh my goodness.' Viv twirled her linguine round her fork as Eve ate another restorative mouthful of her chicken. 'So you were right that Jade had an ulterior motive for recruiting Verity then.'

'Yes, and whatever the facts, the situation is tragic.'

'I can see why it's left you upset.'

'I feel terrible for Jade – for what she's had to suffer. But if she'd been nursing such hatred for Verity, justified or not, I could see her having committed murder, crossing that line when the balance of her mind was disturbed.'

Eve had thought Viv would protest, after championing Jade so hard, but her friend sat back in her chair and finished her mouthful, frown lines creasing her brow. She looked down into her wine, then nodded. 'I really liked her when we met, but I do see your point. What about Cora though? That was no spur of the moment act. And why wait several days before killing her?'

Eve explained, using what Robin had said to frame her rationale. It was handy that she knew independently that the Seagraves had travelled to London just before Cora died. 'The timing's interesting. The London trip might be unrelated, but Cora did go off on her own to run some errands, I gather. If Jade's guilty, maybe Cora somehow worked that out. Perhaps a minor detail gave her away – something Cora only realised was significant later. She might have hitched a lift so she could visit Jade in person, or deliver a note, asking for money in exchange for silence. Either way, Jade could have driven up to Suffolk to kill her.'

Viv shivered. 'I guess it's possible.'

Gus pottered out from under the table. The thunder had been quiet for a few minutes now, and his eyes were on Hetty, who had also appeared from some dark corner and was now by one of the pub's front windows. Gus glanced at Eve for a moment and she nodded. 'Go on then!' He scampered forward towards his playmate.

'Pete Smith's based down in London as well, isn't he?' Viv said.

'He is, and he could have killed Verity too, if she was intent on ending their love affair – assuming that's what it was. It might just be because I spoke with them both today, but suddenly Verity's outside contacts' motives seem to rival Rupert's.'

'And as you said, they both bear a passing resemblance to family members, so although Tilly Cotton seems to be protecting someone, that doesn't rule them out.'

'Exactly. And I went back to Seagrave Hall today, to a press conference the police organised. I had the chance to look up at the windows again in strong sunlight and it's true: it's really hard to distinguish details inside. Tilly was probably aware of the tensions at the hall, so she'd be predisposed to worry Rupert or Cora might be guilty, even if all she saw was a shadowy figure.'

Eve sighed. 'I don't know what to do.' She'd been stuck on the question ever since Jade had left her house. 'If I tell Palmer what I've found out, that'll be it for Jade. From what I hear, he's already convinced she's guilty, and he doesn't want it to be one of the family. He'd do anything to avoid offending the local gentry.'

At that moment she looked up to see Jo watching them and applied herself to her chicken. It was mouth-watering, but her chest felt heavy inside. 'I don't think I should say anything,' she said at last.

Viv looked shocked.

'I know. But the only verifiable information I have is that Jade's sister was on one of Verity's expeditions. The rest is just hearsay, and I doubt Jade would repeat what she told me to the police.'

Her friend chewed her lip. 'I see what you mean. So you'll just leave it at that?'

'What?' Eve put down her wine glass. 'No, of course not. I'm still uneasy about it, but I need something concrete. Jade says she was out of the hall in time to see Pete Smith failing to revive Verity. If anyone saw her appear later than that, say, then it would show she was lying to point the finger at someone else. It's that kind of detail that I need.'

Viv ate a mouthful of her crab-topped pasta. 'So, you're focused on Jade and Pete Smith now. What about the others?'

'I've been wondering about Sir Percival. There was some nasty speculation going on at the press conference about how he might have tried it on with Verity, then killed her when she objected, to stop her talking.' She shuddered.

'Then he or Belinda could have killed Cora, if she found out he'd done it,' Viv put in. 'My money would be on Belinda for Cora's murder. She strikes me as ruthless.'

Eve felt much the same about the woman, and Robin had pointed out that she had no alibi for the night before, except for her husband. 'It's a possibility. I honestly couldn't see Percival killing Cora. He looked heartbroken at the press conference and by all accounts he was genuinely fond of her. But now I've had the chance to think it through, I don't believe the overall scenario makes sense. Percival's renowned as a lech.' Even the journalists outside the hall had known that. And Jim Thackeray implied that Rupert and Verity talked openly about Percival's flirting with Verity specifically. 'I just don't think he'd kill to cover his tracks, because it wouldn't be a shock to anyone. It's horrible, but I get the impression he's used to behaving that way without proper repercussions.'

What century were they living in, that he could carry on unchallenged?

Eve turned her mind back to the possibility of the Seagraves senior, working as a pair. 'If Percival and Belinda discovered either woman's plans for the estate it might have angered them. But I couldn't see them killing over it. They'd have appealed to Rupert first, and they clearly didn't. As far as he knows, they're still unaware of the proposals.'

'That sounds logical.' Viv sipped her wine.

'Then Ivy Cotton's an outside candidate.'

Her friend's eyes widened.

'I know. I don't really believe it either, especially not now Cora's dead too.' She couldn't imagine the worried-looking woman beating her unconscious. 'But Rupert's still very much on my list.' Eve explained how Pete Smith had shown up at the press conference.

'That explains it. I was wondering how you'd managed to track him down at last.'

'It was weird, watching them hijack the police's media session. Pete told me it was Belinda Seagrave who invited him. I wouldn't be surprised if she talked Rupert into funding the China dive too.'

Viv raised an eyebrow.

'Maybe the rumours about Pete and Verity having an affair got out beyond the family. Cora gossiped to me, after all, and the press were asking about their relationship. It gave Rupert a strong motive for murder. Perhaps Belinda felt the best way to quash the speculation was to show Rupert didn't give the rumours any credence. Funding an expedition with Pete Smith in a senior role would be a way of doing that.'

'Good thought. How did Rupert seem when Smith turned up to speak to the press?'

'Uncontrolled and emotional. He probably can't get Cora's accusations out of his head, whether or not he killed Verity because of them. And now maybe he's shot the messenger by killing Cora. He looked despairing and bewildered at the press conference. It would fit with disbelief and horror at his own actions.'

'And yet Palmer's basically ignoring him as a suspect.' Viv sipped her wine.

'I know. And I've hit a block with him, too. He has a very strong motive, but I can't see how to move forward with proving his guilt, unless he slips up or Tilly's got hard facts and decides to talk.' She sat back in her seat and took a deep breath. 'I think the only route forward is to keep going with the other suspects. If I find proof that eliminates Jade or Pete Smith, I can hand that to the police. Hopefully it would force Palmer to challenge Rupert.'

'You think he might crack if the police question him?'

Eve remembered the man's emotional outbursts and his lost look. 'It's possible. He's close to the edge.' She'd wondered about confronting him herself. She had a feeling it might not take much for the truth to come tumbling out, but that same lack of control would make her position desperately vulnerable. For a second she pictured Rupert battering Cora's head with a heavy object – a hammer perhaps. It would have been sickening. If Rupert had done that, he'd be perfectly capable of killing Eve in cold blood.

'Do you think Belinda reckons he's guilty, or is she guarding against him being wrongfully accused?'

Eve ate a mouthful of chicken, green beans and mustard sauce. 'She certainly didn't want him to talk to me the day I went over to fetch our stuff back from the hall. I'd say she's not sure, but she thinks it's possible. And Tilly Cotton might be in the same boat.'

Viv nodded.

Gus pottered back over to their table, and Eve bent to make a fuss of him. 'The way Cora's belongings were thrown into the pool makes me wonder. It sounds like the act of someone with a personal grudge, whatever their motive for killing her.'

It fitted with Rupert as murderer, if he was furious with Cora for the accusations she'd made against Verity. She shook her head. Within the course of her conversation with Viv, she was back to the theory of a Seagrave killer. She knew Rupert had the required strength of feeling for Cora's murder.

Yet she'd come into the pub convinced that Pete Smith and Jade Piper were strong candidates too. Each time she followed a line of argument it changed the direction of her thoughts. She needed something more. Flip-flopping like this left her feeling rudderless.

She considered the interviewees she'd yet to track down: Verity's childhood friend and her parents. Neither seemed likely to hold the key to the puzzle of her murder, but they were both crucial to the story of her life. And knowing her through and through might just unlock something.

The following day she'd take matters into her own hands.

CHAPTER TWENTY-SIX

Friday morning dawned clear and bright and the cheerful chirping song of a linnet reached Eve through her open bedroom window. She lay for a moment appreciating the cool of her thick-walled room. The place made her feel cocooned; its beams reached over her bed like protective arms. But the sense of peace didn't last. Her mind was fizzing with thoughts of the day ahead.

Her attempts to reach Verity Nye's fellow divers had paid off. She'd come home the night before to an email from a man who'd hired her right at the start of her career. Thanks to an immediate phone conversation, she had an appointment to meet him in London later that day. She'd claimed she'd be in the capital anyway, which was a lie, but she knew she'd get way more out of him if they talked face to face. Part-time job or not, she'd go bankrupt if she put this much effort into every job, but this was no ordinary obituary.

But there were still the chunks of missing knowledge she'd identified the night before to tackle too. Eve's sense of Verity's childhood was sketchy at best. It was clear neither her parents nor the schoolfriend she'd managed to track down wanted to talk. The messages she'd left had been met with a wall of silence and that said something in itself. There were secrets to unearth.

She pottered downstairs and through to the kitchen to refresh Gus's drinking bowl and give him his food.

'I'm going to have to push,' she said to the dachshund, as water cascaded from the tap, catching the light from the kitchen window. 'I can't imagine what her parents are going through right now, but it doesn't seem right to submit my copy without speaking with them, even if it's only to double-check they don't want to contribute.' She set his drink down. Gus was looking at her with his head on one side. 'I know,' she spooned out his food, 'you think I'm joining forces with the gutter press. But honestly, Gus, how can I tell Verity's story properly if I miss out her childhood? If they turn me away, I won't take it any further. At least I'll know I've done everything I can.'

She'd checked Verity's father's church website again. He was leading a Bible study group at eleven thirty that morning. She could intercept him on his way out. One sentence was all she'd need.

'And I'll stop by the gift store her friend runs, too, just to size up the situation.'

Gus's look didn't alter, but maybe he was just impatient for his breakfast. When she set it down he focused on that instead, and left Eve to feel faintly guilty on her own.

An hour later, after she and Gus had walked down the estuary, she set off for Dunwich, where the childhood friend, Stacy Riley, had her store.

It was an atmospheric village on the coast, with an eerie history. It had once been the capital of the Kingdom of the East Angles, with a port to rival London, but relentless North Sea storm surges had tugged the land away. The harbour had been taken and most of the town. Legend had it that you could hear the sound of the drowned church bells, ringing under the waves.

The place now was small but beautiful, and Dunwich Heath, which ran down to the sea, drew in birdwatchers and ramblers.

Eve walked past the village's inn – the Ship – and a number of tearooms until she found Stacy's store. Through the bay window she could see two women sitting on stools behind a counter, chatting. One of them might be Stacy; she looked the right age. Eve didn't stop – she didn't want them to see her staring – but as she walked by she took note of the situation. She'd go in, claim she'd been passing, and see if she could get a handle on Verity's early life. She retraced her steps, noting the items in the window. They were all sea-themed: from anchor earrings and port-and-starboard lanterns, to an enormous glass light that looked like a fishing float.

After a moment she walked through the store's open door, which was held wide by a heavy old ship's bell.

Inside, the place was intriguing: dressers stood, their drawers part-open, giving tantalising glimpses of extra wares inside. There'd be lots to discover if she had the time to go digging.

The two women who faced her looked alike, with long oval faces and straight hair. The younger one had hers hennaed and wore lots of silver rings on her fingers.

'Hello.' Eve walked straight up to the counter. 'My name's Eve Mallow. I'm writing about the life of the diver, Verity Nye, and I understand the owner here, Stacy Riley, went to school with her. I left a phone message, to see if it might be possible to ask more about Verity's childhood, but I imagine things are really busy during the vacation period.' The store was empty. 'I thought I'd stop by in person, as I was in the area.'

As soon as she'd introduced herself, Eve had detected a very slight reaction from the women. It was weird. They hadn't even looked at each other, but she sensed a subtle shift in their posture. Was it that they'd moved slightly closer together? A defensive reflex?

A gentle draught blew through the store from somewhere beyond the counter.

'I'm afraid Stacy's away at the moment,' the older woman said. 'I imagine you'll need to submit your article before she's back. I'm sorry.'

There was a finality about her words.

Eve took out a business card from her bag and handed it over. 'No problem; maybe you could give her this just in case. Thanks anyway.'

She exited the store, her mind working. Mother and daughter? Was the woman with the hennaed hair Stacy? She might be making something from nothing, but she didn't think so.

The breeze that had drifted through the store filled her head.

They must have a window or a door open at the back. Before she could think about what she was doing, with Gus's judgemental gaze in her mind's eye, she slipped down a passageway at the side of the store. It was wrong, and she knew it. But what was going on? If it provided a clue to Verity's murder, it had to be worth pushing the boundaries. She silenced her mobile.

Her heart was thudding in her chest. There was a side gate off the passageway, wooden with an iron latch. Opening it would make a noise, but if the two women were alone in the store, and still minding the counter, they shouldn't hear her.

She had to decide then and there. If she wanted to find out what they said in response to her visit, delay wouldn't do. Gently, she lifted the latch and pushed on the gate. It was catching on something the other side. She leaned against it a little harder and it opened, revealing an overgrown buddleia that had been partially blocking the way. She glanced left. Through a window she could see a kitchenette where the staff must make drinks, and ahead of her was an open back door. If either of them came through for a cup of tea, they'd see her immediately. She edged towards the door and stood in the store's back lobby, listening, a creeping sense of shame and discomfort flooding through her. What did she think she was doing?

'I could have spoken to her.' The younger woman? Eve thought so. She was talking through tears.

'Not if it upsets you. But, love, it's time to let this go. It wasn't your fault you and Verity drifted apart.'

'It was! I was a pathetic coward.' The younger woman's words rang out; there was real anguish there.

'Don't say that.'

'Pete was so much better than me—'

'That boy!'

What? Pete? Not the same Pete, surely? It was a common enough name, but Eve felt pins and needles break out over her body.

'Pete was never better than you,' the woman went on.

'What do you mean?'

'I overheard him, talking with his friends once. They were bad-mouthing Verity and he was joining in when she wasn't there to listen. He was always out for himself, that one; sucking up to curry favour.'

'That just makes it worse. We both let her down!'

'But Stacy,' the older woman said, 'it was her dad who was to blame. Who follows a religion that forbids children from having fun? From seeing friends and letting their hair down? It was cruel. And her mum was almost as bad.'

'But Mum, you don't know—'

'What?'

'One night, Verity asked me to cover for her.' Her voice quavered.

'Yes?' Her mom's tone was gentle.

'She'd been seeing this guy, and you know what her parents' rules were like. She had to keep it secret. I agreed to say she'd slept over at our place if her dad asked.'

There was a pause. 'You gave her away?'

Eve heard Stacy gulp. 'Her dad came to find me when I was alone on the beach. He put his hands on my shoulders, looked me in the eye and asked if she'd really been at our house. He said he'd know if I was lying and that I'd end up in hell.' There was a pause. 'It was crazy, but I was like a rabbit in headlights. I felt like he would know, whatever I said. And I told him the truth. I couldn't even stand up to him asking the question I'd known was coming.'

'Oh love. You were young.'

A pause. 'There's more. He wanted me to tell him who she'd been with, how long it had been going on. The works. He said he'd tell you and Dad what a shameless little liar I was if I didn't tell.' Her voice shuddered. 'I told him the lot, just to avoid being yelled at and grounded.' Her voice dropped, so Eve had to strain to hear her words. 'Even though I knew her punishment would be so much worse.'

There was a moment's silence.

'I remember her parents withdrew her from school that year,' her mom said at last. 'But I didn't know why.'

'Me. That's why. She was virtually a prisoner after that.'

Once again there was a pause. Was her mom shocked? Struggling to find words of comfort? 'At least they let her come back to do her exams.'

'It must have been hell for Verity. We never spoke again.'

'Oh, love. Let it go. Come here. Let me find you a tissue.'

Eve had heard enough. She retreated through the side gate, shutting it after her. She felt awful for intruding on the woman's grief, but as she walked smartly back towards the lane, she couldn't regret it.

It shone a light onto Verity's past. And could the pair possibly have been referring to Pete Smith? Might he, Stacy and Verity have been childhood friends? *That boy*, the older woman had said.

What was going on?

CHAPTER TWENTY-SEVEN

Eve googled Pete Smith from her car.

He'd been to the same school as Verity. They were both mentioned in a press release about a youth diving team. There was no photograph, but common name or not, it was too much of a coincidence when you put the diving connection into the mix. Why the heck hadn't he mentioned that when she'd interviewed him? Was he worried people would think she'd hired him out of nepotism? But why? It made total sense for her to team up with an old friend if he had the right skills.

She wasn't sure how long she'd sat there for, pondering the implications of her discovery. At last she found her car keys, ready to drive to her next appointment, but as she put them in the ignition, Stacy Riley emerged from the gift store.

Eve glanced at her watch. She had an hour before she needed to be in Stoningham to catch Verity's father. Without giving herself time to think, she got out of her Mini and followed the woman down the road. She was clutching a tissue. Maybe her mother had sent her home to recover herself. When they were a distance from the store, Eve called her name. It felt like a low trick.

Stacy looked round instantly and flushed. 'You knew it was me all along.'

'I guessed.' That much was true. She couldn't bring herself to admit she'd listened in to her and her mom's conversation. 'I'm sorry my visit upset you. I'm finding it hard to get anyone to talk to me about Verity's childhood, and it feels wrong not to cover that period of her life in my article.'

The young woman blew her nose. 'No, I'm sorry. She had a rotten childhood, and I… I made it a thousand times worse. Even though she was my best friend. Until I let her down. I can't… I don't want to—'

Eve stepped forward. 'I understand.' It was all she could do not to blush after eavesdropping. 'But I wonder if I could ask you about Pete Smith?'

She watched as Stacy's expression flooded with relief. 'Oh, I see.'

'I gather he, you and Verity were at school together? If there are any fond memories you have that I could include for colour, that would be great. My readers will be curious about a childhood friend who joined Verity's dive team.' And Eve would be more than interested to get the details, under the circumstances. 'You could email me your thoughts if that would be easier? They're on my card.'

Stacy nodded. 'Thanks.'

'Pete Smith's a good-looking guy. I suspect my friends and I would have fought over him if he'd been in our friendship group.' Would Stacy take the bait and comment on Pete and Verity's relationship as they'd grown up?

'I never really saw him that way. We'd known each other since nursery.'

Darn. That didn't tell her enough. She'd have to try again. 'Do you know if Pete and Verity were in regular contact between leaving school and working together on the dive team?'

Stacy frowned, and for a moment her look was far away. 'No, they weren't. We all went our separate ways. As a matter of fact, Pete contacted me to ask if I'd put him back in touch with Verity. He clearly hadn't noticed we'd… grown apart too. I don't know why he imagined I'd have her number. Maybe he was more wrapped up in himself than I'd realised.'

Eve thought of the conversation she'd overheard and Stacy's mother's words about the medic's selfishness.

But what stayed with her, as she drove inland, towards Stoningham, was the news that it was Pete who'd made the effort to track Verity down after being out of contact. He'd told Eve he'd approached the diver when a friend of a friend mentioned she was after a medic. Another lie. It seemed that both Jade and Pete had their own reasons for latching on to the dead woman. Once again, the suspects outside the Seagrave family held her attention.

Stacy was interesting too. How much had her betrayal affected Verity, the woman who'd advised her mentee never to rely on anyone else, because it made you weaker and left you vulnerable? Her friends must have been crucial to her, if her dad was such a hard man.

Her pulse quickened at the thought as she found Verity's home village; she'd have to face him in a moment. The church he helped run was at the far end of the settlement, down a narrow cul-de-sac. It was a modern, squat red-brick building, with a small car park. Someone had opened the windows and she exited her car to the sound of a carrying voice, quoting the Bible.

The church website had no photographs of the staff, only names. Would she be able to guess which of the attendees was Mr Nye? At last, the participants started to appear through double glass doors in dribs and drabs, clutching books and notepads. The women wore plain long-sleeved blouses and skirts that reached their calves. Eve suddenly felt conspicuous, even though she was in three-quarter length cotton trousers and a T-shirt. Hardly outrageous.

The last people to appear were a couple who looked around sixty. The woman walked slightly behind the man, her head bent. He glanced over his shoulder at her, and suddenly she wondered if she'd found both Verity's parents.

'Mr and Mrs Nye?'

The man was large and unsmiling, with a head of thick grey hair. 'What do you want?'

The woman looked down at her feet.

'My name's Eve Mallow. I'm so very sorry for the loss of your daughter. You might have got my email. I'm writing her obituary and I wanted to speak with you before I submit my copy. I thought you might have something to add.'

Mr Nye stopped abruptly as his Bible class carried on their way to their cars, or up the road on foot. Eve waited.

'Miss Mallow, Verity has been dead to us for a long time now. If you don't understand that writing about her... her... exploits, simply continues her own obsession with self-aggrandisement, then I am afraid you too may be lost.'

His eyes bore into Eve's and she imagined Stacy, alone with him on the beach, his hands on her shoulders.

'We've had Rupert Seagrave visiting too,' he went on, without blinking, 'coming here, after forgiveness. Thinking he can simply express regret and receive absolution. Words are easily said. Actions require a lifetime of commitment.'

'He wanted forgiveness?'

Nye nodded. 'That's not what he said. Like you, he offered condolences. Hollow sentiments. But I know the signs of a guilty conscience. He was wringing his hands. It might be he has blood on them. But if so, Verity was as much at fault for walking into his orbit.'

Unbelievable.

'She knew our views. Please leave us now.'

'But could I just ask—'

Mr Nye turned away, and his wife followed suit, though only after a long look at Eve over her shoulder. She wanted to say more, Eve was sure.

At that moment, one of the women who'd been at the class reappeared from her car, clutching a book of essays.

'This is the collection I mentioned, Pastor Nye.'

He walked over to examine the book, and Mrs Nye turned quickly towards Eve. 'Rupert wanted to know about Verity's past,' she said quietly. 'Her youth. I had the impression something had made him question his opinion of her before she died.' Her eyes were hollow, her expression utterly bleak. 'Maybe he killed her.' Her voice was just a whisper now. 'But we're not to go to the police. God's judgement is all that matters.'

Eve felt she wouldn't have spoken out if her mind was easy on that score.

CHAPTER TWENTY-EIGHT

Eve returned to Saxford and walked Gus with Mrs Nye's words circling in her head. She'd already concluded Rupert was on a knife edge: uncertain about who to trust, Cora or Verity. But going to Verity's parents for more background on which to base his judgement showed desperation – a man who'd become obsessed and unbalanced. Suddenly, Eve could see him killing Cora whatever he'd concluded: either for being right, and rubbing his nose in the fact, down in London, or for being wrong, and igniting the most destructive jealousy in him.

She found it hard to get his image out of her head. She closed her eyes for a moment. She'd just have to stick to her plan and follow up the leads she'd uncovered that morning. If she managed to eliminate the other suspects, she'd turn the police's spotlight on Rupert. And with each secret she unravelled, the chances of finding something unexpected to prove his guilt increased. The thought of DS Boles working away behind the scenes was a comfort too. He was a much better detective than Palmer; he'd likely been investigating Rupert quietly from the beginning. He might find useful clues.

So, after Gus's walk, she sat down to lunch and indulged in a Google-fest with renewed determination.

'I still feel bad about my methods, but I'm definitely further on than I was,' she said to the dachshund as he pottered up to her in the dining room.

She scrolled through page after page featuring Pete Smith and Verity Nye. The results tied in with Stacy's suggestion that they'd temporarily lost touch after school. She found no websites mentioning them both again until Pete joined Verity's dive team. After that there were plenty of photographs for Eve to view. She was testing a theory. It didn't sound as though Verity and Pete had been romantically involved when they were at school. Stacy had talked to her mother about Pete being better than her, as though she was comparing herself to him in the same role – that of a friend. And during her teenage years Verity had been involved with the other guy Stacy had mentioned – the one she'd been seeing secretly. Of course, a platonic childhood friendship could have turned into something more. But after all these years?

A photo in a celebrity gossip magazine taken just a month earlier showed Verity and Pete at some high-class party. They each held glasses of champagne, and a waiter stood to one side with a plate of canapés. The medic had a blonde woman on his arm, but there was no hint of jealousy or disquiet in his colleague's expression. All three of them were laughing, sharing a joke. In every picture Eve found they looked close, but not like lovers.

But if she was right, what the heck had they been discussing in the marquee? Pete had wanted to talk; he'd told Verity 'We can still make this work'. But she'd been angry and said of course they couldn't. How could he not see that?

And why had Pete Smith smelled of Verity's perfume? None of the images showed them embracing, the way friends sometimes did.

It was almost time to leave for Monty's when she found a picture that made her pause. Holding her breath, she read the details.

'Okay, Gus,' she said, shutting down her laptop and getting ready to leave the cottage. 'This one might mean something.'

Eve filled Viv in on the latest developments while she made a batch of summer berry drizzle cakes. It was a fresh recipe for the teashop that season, and the first time Viv had entrusted something new to Eve. During Viv's demo, Eve had written herself meticulous step-by-step instructions to make sure she didn't miss any of the stages. Out of the corner of her eye she could see Viv looking askance at her approach. She was preparing miniature lemon and elderflower cakes with the air of someone who could do it in their sleep. Eve didn't care. She had a job to do and she was going to make sure it worked.

When Eve admitted she'd sneaked round the back of Stacy Riley's store, Viv's expression changed.

'I can't believe you did that! I love it when you break the rules! It makes you seem human.'

'Flatterer.'

'So, you think the affair between Pete and Verity's looking less likely?'

'It seems that way. I started to wonder when I reviewed what Stacy had said, but it was the photos I looked at over lunch that really convinced me. I don't have proof, but I do have a theory for why he smelled of her perfume.'

Viv gave her a sidelong glance. 'Excellent. What did you find?'

'A publicity photo for the upcoming dive they're doing. They've got their arms around each other in the shot. It's cheesy rather than romantic. I'd guess the photographer wanted to show them off as a champion team. Their heads are close together and they're holding up a cup they were awarded last year. They're definitely close enough for her perfume to have rubbed off on him. You know what the expensive stuff's like.' Ian had bought a bottle she didn't like once; she'd worn it to please him and it had taken days to get rid of the smell. 'The key thing is, the picture was published online the day they came up to Suffolk. Looks like it was taken that morning, before they set off. And Pete was posing in a stylish leather jacket. Even if he'd had time, he wouldn't have been able to sling it in the washing machine.'

'Blimey.'

Eve nodded. It was a horrible thought. Cora might never have dripped poison into Rupert's ear if it hadn't been for that photo shoot. She'd been playing with fire, and maybe Verity had been the immediate casualty. The question of how Cora had been close enough to Pete to smell the perfume remained.

'I'm increasingly sure Verity and Pete weren't hiding an affair.' She frowned. 'So I need to fathom out what was going on when I heard them in the marquee. She was telling him not to follow someone around – that he was being too obvious. And then he said something like "We can still make it work". He wanted to talk to her for longer but she rebuffed him pretty thoroughly.'

'Could it be something to do with Cora, if she was the woman he was following? If Pete was coming on to her, it might explain why she smelled Verity's perfume on him. Perhaps it was all to do with a plot they were hatching to stop her hotel plans?'

Eve shrugged. 'I just don't know. Maybe. I've managed to get hold of another cave diver who knew Verity well. I'm going down to London to meet him this evening. Angie says she'll look in on Gus.' She glanced over her shoulder at Viv for a second as the last of her flour went through her sieve. 'The guy will be a great addition to my obituary interviewees, but maybe he'll know more about the dynamics between Verity and Pete too. I just need a way to access the right information. Whatever the truth, Pete's been dishonest with me. He deliberately kept back the fact that he's known Verity since childhood, and he was certainly angry with her, the day she died.' She'd been wrong about the reason, but it didn't alter how desperate Smith had sounded inside the marquee.

CHAPTER TWENTY-NINE

Eve was sitting opposite the cave diver, Liam Edwards, on a decked jetty outside the Mayflower pub in Rotherhithe, looking down at the River Thames. Liam had pointed out the 1620 mooring point of the Pilgrim Fathers' *Mayflower* ship, but now they were sitting over their drinks – a Punk IPA for him and a St Clements for her. She'd come by train but her car was at the station in Suffolk, and besides, she needed to concentrate. She had her notebook in front of her and peered at her interviewee. Dark hair tinged with grey, ash-coloured stubble, square jaw and broad shoulders. He was ruddy-looking – from years outdoors, she guessed. He probably spent weeks on end in countries much sunnier than Britain.

He grinned and she could see sorrow mixed with fondness in his eyes. 'So you want to know what Verity was like to dive with?'

'And how you first came into contact. That would be great.'

He nodded his large head. 'She was recommended to me when she was starting out. A friend of mine had helped train her. Said she was level-headed, driven, and one hundred per cent unflappable. I was after a team member for a dive – someone else took sick and dropped out at the last minute – so I took a chance on her.'

'And how did it work out?' She could see the memory amused him, from his expression.

'She was a character. I only ever had to pull rank when we were up on dry land. She questioned why we hadn't gone further and argued vehemently for us to go down again and take the next step. I put my foot down, and she struggled with that. Couldn't wait to be in charge. But though she hated me for putting the brakes on – and I mean properly hated, for a week at least – it didn't make a difference where it counted, underwater. If she'd put a foot wrong in that area she'd have been out on her ear.'

'Did you dive together again?'

He shook his head. 'We remained friends but my regular team member was back on his feet for the next trip, and it was a bit more relaxed, working with him. But you get that. People who are destined to be in command of expeditions have to be sure of their ground, and she was. She just about managed to button up her desire to take control while she was gaining her stripes. After that, so long as your judgement's sound, then being a forceful leader's a good thing in my book. You have to listen to your team, of course, and be ready to admit it if you're wrong, but you also have to make split-second life or death decisions without flinching. Shrinking violets need not apply.'

Eve nodded. So she'd have needed both Pete Smith and Ruby Fox to accept her as their chief out in Egypt then.

'Did you ever meet Verity's medic, Pete Smith?'

'I did, as a matter of fact.' His eyes were on hers, his brow slightly furrowed. 'Odd sort of bloke. Very affable, but one time he, Verity and I were walking to a pub here in London and he marched straight past an accident in the street. A cyclist had come off his bike.'

Eve frowned. 'You mean he didn't try to help?'

Edwards shook his head. 'A gaggle of people were already standing round, but none of them was doing first aid, and the ambulance only arrived after we'd walked by.' He sat back in his chair. 'It made me wonder about his sense of priorities. In my book if you're a medic you step in, even if it's not convenient.' His eyes met Eve's. 'Why do you ask about him?'

How could she put it so that she'd encourage him to share confidences, rather than shut down? 'I wasn't quite sure how to take what he said about Verity.'

Liam Edwards let his gaze drift out over the River Thames, where an evening sightseeing cruiser was motoring past. 'That's interesting.' He turned back to Eve and sipped his beer. 'I hadn't thought about Pete in a while, but Verity messaged me the day before she died on the subject of expedition medics.'

Eve held her pen tightly. 'Really?'

He nodded. 'She... well, she said she thought she'd have to find a replacement for Pete for the China dive. Asked if I could recommend anyone. It made me wonder if I'd been right about him all along. She asked me to keep the matter to myself. I got the impression she hadn't told Pete yet.' He took a swig of his ale. 'It's been on my mind. If he'd somehow found out...' She watched his broad chest rise and fall under his navy T-shirt. 'But then that other woman was killed, and I came to the conclusion it must be some kind of family thing.' He shook his head. 'I felt sorry for Verity. I don't think the clan she was marrying into liked her much. But she wouldn't have taken any notice. Not her style.'

When Eve arrived home, she found a gift box from Monty's on her doorstep. Viv had written 'I'm impressed! on the lid, where the greeting ought to go, and just for a second Eve was distracted from her thoughts about Verity.

With Gus scampering round her ankles (it seemed he had missed her after all), Eve shuffled through to the kitchen and lifted the lid. The box contained two of the summer berry drizzle cakes she'd baked that afternoon. They'd been too hot to try when she'd left the teashop. She stowed one in the fridge, and put the second on a plate, feeling slightly nervous.

A moment later, she sat on one of her couches, in the glow of a standard lamp. Gus settled himself by her feet as she took a hesitant bite to assess her handiwork. After a second mouthful the tension went out of her shoulders. The cake tasted *almost* like something Viv might have produced. It was a good balance of sweet and tart, wonderfully moist, with the fruit evenly distributed. The sugar-coated berries on top tingled her palate. The effect dispelled any tiredness after her journey home. She finished the cake in short order. 'Why didn't Pete Smith go and help the cyclist Liam Edwards mentioned?' she said aloud, putting her plate on the coffee table. Gus opened half an eye. 'I can't believe he looked away because he was desperate to get to the pub.'

It was so stuffy in the cottage that she felt she couldn't think. She went to open the casement window which looked out onto the garden, and sounds of the evening drifted in: the churring of a nightjar and the distant hoot of an owl.

She padded round, opening more windows, but was only part way through the job when she paused again.

What if... In a moment she'd abandoned her mission and set off to find her laptop. Gus pottered off to his bed in the kitchen and she bent to stroke him absently as he went by.

Why had Verity wanted to replace Pete? If it wasn't down to an affair gone sour, some professional deficiency looked likely.

Within a minute she was sitting on the couch again, her bare feet tucked up under her, googling. Pete didn't appear on any of the usual career sites she found. It took ages to check, trawling through all the other Peter Smiths. Using LinkedIn was hopeless: there were nearly ten thousand results for that name. Adding the word diver to the search whittled it down to a handful, none of which was him. Try as she might, she couldn't source details of where he'd trained. She stretched, went to make herself a coffee, then settled down again.

Eventually, she found a list of medical schools in the UK and began the laborious task of googling each one of them, together with Pete's name in quotes. As with LinkedIn, there were a daunting number to check. She was a third of the way down the alphabetical list when she got a hit.

It wasn't anything official; the result led to the gossip section of a student magazine. The headline read: *The three musketeers don't just cheat on their partners*

Eve read on.

And so the university med school waves goodbye to Joe Deverell, Alex Murray and Pete Smith, always known as party lads who'd do anything for one another but who were otherwise one hundred per cent unreliable. Caught out in so many ways, boys! So long. x

There was a small, rather pixilated photograph next to the snippet, of three lads with pints in their hands, gurning at the camera.

Unclear though the image was, Eve was sure the left-hand guy was Verity's Pete Smith. He'd had brown hair back then…

Eve scanned the other hits for Pete and that medical school. Just below the first link, she found a PDF detailing official proceedings at the institution.

The three students had been thrown out for cheating in their first-year exams.

Eve sat back on the couch and let out a long breath. No wonder Smith hadn't wanted to talk to the press, to have them delving into his past, finding out where he'd trained. She'd talked him into a conversation focused on Verity, but only by hinting she'd give him an easy ride, while making him look more open. And it explained him walking past the cyclist who'd come off their bike. If the injuries had been complex, he'd probably have lacked the skills to help. Verity and Liam Edwards would have been on to him in an instant.

And then she remembered Jade saying he'd looked incompetent when he'd attempted to resuscitate Verity. But even people with basic first-aid training knew that drill. Eve's hairs lifted. He hadn't wanted her to survive and his mismanagement of the situation had been deliberate. Surely that had to be more likely.

She thought back to the conversation she'd heard between him and Verity in the marquee. The hurt and anger in her tone. He'd wanted to talk. ('We can still make this work!') And she'd rebuffed him. ('We've talked already. Of course we can't "make this work". How can you not see that?')

She'd only recently found out he was unqualified.

Their partnership had been strong for a long time, and Pete said it could still work under these new circumstances. Verity had almost wept with frustration at his lack of understanding. And once again she'd been let down. Eve was sure she'd never leaned on Pete, but she guessed she'd treated him as a respected equal, and even that level of trust had made her vulnerable.

When had she found out? The day before she died, prompting her to contact Liam Edwards to look for a new medic? Then that day or the next she must have confronted Pete.

Eve felt hot and cold all over. He'd clearly hoped they'd carry on as before, but of course Verity couldn't allow that. And if she'd lived, she'd certainly have replaced him. People would have asked questions, even if she didn't broadcast the reason why. Any nosy journalist or colleague might have found the same information Eve had. His career and reputation would have been over. She thought of his book contract and glamorous lifestyle – he'd had a lot to lose. He was lucky he had such a common name, or his old medical school might have noticed him in the press. Even showing his face was a risk, but he'd have only been in classes for nine months. And he'd gone blond; an extra precaution? It seemed likely.

And now, Verity was dead and he was down to take part in the China dive with no one any the wiser. Eve thought of Jade Piper's sister. Had his negligence led to her decline, and indirectly to her death?

A moment later, she was back at her laptop. And five minutes after that, she had her answer. Pneumonia wasn't uncommon in cases of near drowning. Pete said Ruby's illness had caught him off guard, but it shouldn't have. The advice she found online said antibiotics should be given without delay to anyone who developed a cough in those circumstances. But Pete wouldn't have known that. Okay, he'd treated her eventually, but probably only after her symptoms had become severe. The delay that Jade had identified.

She needed to do something to stop him. But if you took part in an expedition and lied about your qualifications, could the police act? It was just a private venture. Maybe it depended on the claims he'd made. At the very least he must have defrauded his insurance company, she guessed, by claiming to be something he wasn't.

And what about Cora? Could she have discovered the truth about him too? If Verity had asked Pete to make up to her, to distract her from lobbying Rupert about the hotel plan, maybe she found out she'd been duped. She could have dug for something to use in revenge.

Eve couldn't sleep on the information, even if Palmer said she'd gone 'beyond her brief'. The discovery strengthened Pete Smith's motive for murder, and the thought of him operating on another expedition was awful too. She sent an email to the police case coordinator before she went to bed, stating what she'd discovered.

CHAPTER THIRTY

Eve woke on Saturday feeling groggy. Pete Smith had filled her dreams. He shouldn't be out with expeditions where friends and relatives like Jade Piper would certainly take it for granted he was qualified. She'd feel a lot better if his history was public.

She finished her morning coffee, then wrote an email to Robin Yardley, explaining what she'd found out since they'd last talked. She'd just cleared away her cup when there was a knock at the door of Elizabeth's Cottage. Leaving it in the sink, she followed Gus, who'd propelled himself to the front of the house as though he was on springs.

When she opened up it took her a moment to rally her thoughts. Ivy Cotton, the housekeeper at Seagrave Hall, was standing on the doorstep holding a punnet of strawberries.

Her pinched, worried-yet-kindly look reminded Eve of the last time she'd seen her.

'I brought you these,' she said, holding out the fruit in front of her. 'I was wondering if I could have a quick word. I came over to the village to get my shopping. Though I don't mean to...'

Eve pulled herself together. 'Of course. Thank you so much for the strawberries, and do come in. Would you like a cup of tea or coffee? We could sit at the table in the garden.'

'You mustn't trouble on my account.'

Eve ushered her through and assured her she'd been about to put the kettle on anyway, even though it was a fib. A couple of minutes later they were sitting outside. Gus was pottering round the lawn, with the occasional glance in their direction.

'How can I help?'

The woman looked down into her drink for a moment. 'I just – well, it's none of my business, but I just wanted to ask you, what with everything that's going on, to please be kind to the family. In your article I mean. I've heard all sorts of rumours flying round and I – oh, I don't know. I just know for all their ups and downs and squabbles, none of them would have hurt a hair on Cora's head. And as for the idea that Rupert might have pushed his lady out of the window! It's crazy. But everyone seems to be worried about it.' She closed her eyes for a moment. 'I've known him since he was a baby and he wouldn't do it. Take it from me.'

Eve could see Mrs Cotton was on the verge of tears. The woman fished in her bag for a packet of tissues.

'Don't worry. I never include hearsay and speculation in my obituaries. And I'll be focusing on Verity, not the family.'

Ivy Cotton didn't look convinced. 'It's all getting out of hand.' She leaned forward, her voice a whisper now. 'Even Tilly thinks Rupert did it. I overheard her talking to him. I didn't mean to. I was by one of the stalls just after Verity's fall, and I thought she'd seen me. When I realised she hadn't it was too late.'

'What did you overhear?'

She hesitated a moment, but then her words came out in a rush. 'She was advising Rupert to say he was in the woods when it all happened. That he'd gone for a smoke.' She put her hand over her mouth and started to cry. 'I don't know what I'm doing. You're the first person I've told. But I've no one to confide in. I know what you're going to say. I should have told the police.' She must have read Eve's expression. 'But I couldn't.' She pressed the tissue to her eyes. 'Tilly would get into trouble for convincing him to lie, and they'd wonder why he did.'

They would indeed. 'Why would he?'

'I don't know!'

But Eve had a feeling she knew more than she was saying. Maybe he'd been in the hall when Verity fell. And Rupert had told Eve the lie about being in the woods too, when she'd first interviewed him. How many of the household knew more about his movements than the police?

'Sir Percival's been so good to me,' Ivy Cotton said. 'He – well, you might have heard on the village grapevine, but he sent my other half packing when he mistreated me, no ifs nor buts. I was scared when he let Walter go, I don't mind admitting.' She sipped her tea. 'I thought he'd want our cottage for a new estate manager, but he made temporary arrangements, then trained Tilly up for the role as soon as she was old enough. It's not everyone who'd want a young woman doing that job. But he looks after his staff.' She took a deep breath. 'You might have heard that he didn't approve of Rupert and Verity's relationship at first, but please disregard that. He's a stickler for people keeping to their proper stations in life. Once he and Verity got to know each other he came round.'

Despite Eve's efforts, Ivy was clearly still convinced the family was central to the obituary. They were important of course, especially for Eve's investigation, but Sir Percival's precise attitude to Verity before they'd first met wouldn't form part of her article. It made her wonder what he'd thought when Rupert dated Tilly though. The daughter of his housekeeper. If he was a stickler for upholding class boundaries, she imagined he'd have disapproved. Might he have intervened? It sounded as though Tilly had ended the relationship rather suddenly, from Simon's description. But on reflection it seemed unlikely. It didn't sound as though Tilly had been upset by the break-up. Simon said she'd moved straight on to another boyfriend; if Percival had warned her off, Eve couldn't see cheerful compliance being the result. She guessed the pair had split up naturally, before he'd felt the need to interfere.

Ivy Cotton put down her empty cup, picked up her bag and stood up.

'Thank you for talking to me.'

As Eve walked round to the lane with her, the woman's brow creased again. 'You will take into account what I said, won't you?'

'I'll only tell the truth about Verity's life as I find it, supported by the evidence I come across.'

But rather than reassuring Ivy Cotton, her words seemed to cause the woman's frown to deepen.

CHAPTER THIRTY-ONE

Late in the afternoon Eve gathered Gus up for a walk. They made for the shade of Blind Eye Wood. She loved the tranquillity there, and it was best of all in summer, when the sun shone through the branches, making patterns on the ground.

Gus dashed busily ahead on his extendable leash as they walked down Love Lane, with the Cross Keys on their left and the village green on their right. A family was emerging from Moira's store with ice creams, joining others already sitting on the grass, reading books and playing ball. A normal Saturday in summer – yet Cora had only died two days earlier.

As they entered the woods, Eve bent to let Gus off his leash and he dashed ahead, bounding over the fallen twigs and leaf matter that formed the wood's floor. For a moment, everything seemed still, then small details came into focus. Eve could hear the fluting call of a blackcap warbler somewhere close by and after a moment she spotted a tiny treecreeper, scuttling along a branch, exploring crevices in the bark for food.

'You lied to me, you hypocrite!'

The voice came from behind her, making her jump and causing the treecreeper to fly from its perch.

Pete Smith was there in the wood. He towered over her, fists clenched, knuckles white. Eve's legs quivered under her, her breath catching in her throat.

Was this the man who'd killed Rupert Seagrave's fiancée and his cousin? A vision of him filled her mind, holding a hammer high above Cora's head, ready to strike. Ruthless, reckless, and determined, with so much to lose…

Her tongue seemed to stick to the roof of her mouth, and it was a moment before she managed to speak. 'What are you doing here?' The words came out in a croaky whisper.

'I decided to pay you a visit.' His voice was tight, barely controlled. 'The police called me this morning. I've just come out of a voluntary interview with them. It's been a long day.'

They'd taken her email seriously, but still he'd walked free.

'I parked my car by the village green and saw you and the dog walk by. I thought I'd follow you, since I've come all this way. I guess it's you I've to thank for the hours I've just spent at the police station.'

He couldn't know it was she who'd given away his secret. Even Palmer wouldn't release her name.

'What makes you think it was me?' Her mouth was still too dry for her to speak easily.

He gave a hollow laugh. 'I googled you after we spoke. You've written about murder victims before, and helped the police with their enquiries. You weren't honest when you talked me into an interview. You wanted to see if you could fit me up for murder. When the police called, I remembered you asking how Verity recruited me. I hesitated and I saw you pick up on it.'

Eve thought back to their conversation. 'You told me a friend of a friend let you know she was looking for a medic. And that you were up against some competition, but you clicked. No wonder. I know you were at school together now – and that you sought her out. You needed to work for someone who trusted you implicitly. She didn't even ask to check your professional certificates.' Stacy Riley's mom said Pete had always been out for himself. She'd been spot on.

'She was right to put her faith in me!' His eyes were dark. 'I'm perfectly competent and I'm a bloody good diver.'

'You must have lied to her. Surely she asked about your experience – out of interest and friendship if nothing else.' She emphasised the word friendship and got a dismissive little shrug in response. Who knew what stories he'd come up with? 'What's the charge for what you did?' She wanted to focus his mind; he seemed totally unconscious of why his wrongdoing mattered.

'Fraud by misrepresentation. They've bailed me pending further investigation.'

But what about the murder? Why hadn't they held him under suspicion for that? Maybe there wasn't enough evidence.

Gus appeared in a clearing and looked in their direction. His tail had been wagging but now it went still; he couldn't work the situation out.

Eve saw Smith's chest rise and fall under his white cotton shirt. Gus appeared at her side. Through the corner of her eye she glimpsed him looking at her anxiously, but she didn't want to lose focus on the medic.

'How did you find me out?' His arms were all muscle. He'd be strong, just like Verity had been. His diving would ensure it.

Eve darted her gaze round the wood, this way and that. She mustn't give in to panic. It was a sunny Saturday afternoon. Surely someone was around. 'It's there on the internet – what you did at med school. People are bound to look when you're caught up in two murders.'

He blinked. 'What the hell do you mean? I was at the hall when Verity died, but I was miles away when Cora Seagrave was killed. I didn't even see the news until yesterday. Did you say something to the police about her too?' He stepped forward, breathing fast. 'They asked enough questions about her death.'

'No, I didn't.' She decided to take a chance. 'But she visited you, down in London, the day she died. What about?'

She shrank back in case he lashed out, but his reaction wasn't what she'd expected. He was still furious, she could see that, but his body language changed. Confusion seemed to be pulling some of the force out of him. 'The police asked the same thing. What do you mean? Why the hell would Cora visit me? We hardly knew each other.'

She hesitated a moment. 'Something she said made me think you were close.' She was staring into his eyes, looking for the truth, but all she saw was anger and bewilderment. Either he didn't know what she was talking about or he was a very good actor.

'What did she say, exactly?'

Eve went for it. 'That she smelled Verity's perfume on you; it suggested she'd been close enough to detect it.'

His frown deepened. 'I don't understand.' He stopped suddenly. 'Why was Cora commenting on it? Did she suggest Verity and I were having an affair?'

At last she nodded.

'This is getting crazy. We weren't sleeping together; let's get that out of the way. And she smelled the perfume on me…' Suddenly his eyes widened. 'We did a photo shoot the day we came up to the hall. The camera guy got us draped over each other and I was conscious of Verity's scent. It was heavy; cloying in the heat. I took the jacket I wore for the shoot to Seagrave Hall but I didn't wear it. It was oppressively hot the entire time I was there. I slung it on the coat stand when I arrived and picked it up on my way out.' He shook his head slowly. 'Cora must have smelled the perfume when she hung up a jacket or something. She came for dinner on Thursday evening, and she'd have walked back to her cottage after midnight.' Suddenly the anger was back in his eyes. 'Who else did she tell? It could be what got Verity killed! If Rupert believed her—'

She bit her lip. He *looked* genuine, and if he really believed Rupert might have pushed her out of the window, he was in the clear. But what if he was acting? Eve's chest still felt tight.

'It wasn't necessarily him.' If his reaction was for real, she didn't want Smith dashing to the hall, hellbent on revenge. 'The whole family situation is complicated.'

'You're telling me. I wish I'd never set eyes on any of them. Or you. But I'd been thinking Jade Piper might be guilty.'

You might be spot on... 'I overheard you and Verity discussing someone you were keeping tabs on, the day she was killed. She said you were being too obvious about it. I'd thought it might be Cora. But it was Jade?'

For a moment he didn't move, but at last he nodded.

So Pete and Verity's scheme to keep Cora and Rupert apart had been a figment of Eve's imagination.

'I know Jade is Ruby Fox's sister,' Eve said, watching the medic's eyes again.

He flinched, but his sigh was resigned. 'We only discovered two days before we came to Suffolk. It was one of those coincidences that brought it to light. Someone from Jade and Ruby's home village is friends with someone who once worked for Verity. We didn't understand why Jade had kept her relationship to Ruby secret, but we knew there must be a problem. Verity had an odd feeling about her from the start. Jade was really determined to get her as Wide Blue Yonder's ambassador, but she was never warm towards her.'

Eve's mind was back on the conversation she'd overheard from outside the marquee. 'So when you told Verity it was necessary to keep tabs on Jade, to protect both your interests...'

'Verity had just found out the truth about me dropping out of med school.'

'Dropping out' was stretching a point. He didn't mention the cheating.

'The moment we discovered Jade was Ruby Fox's sister, I knew she must have an agenda. And my lack of proper paperwork makes me vulnerable. I got so tense. It was that which put Verity onto me.

She could see how worried I was and it made her look for reasons. I guess she found the same records you did.'

'So she told you it was over. You'd never work together again.'

His eyes were like slits. 'After all those years of supporting her; running things her way, keeping the team safe.'

'But you didn't. Ruby believed she was travelling to Egypt with proper medical backup. Jade must have thought so too. And Verity had no idea you'd been thrown out of med school for cheating. What you did was unforgivable.'

Eve guessed Jade hadn't uncovered his secret; she laid the blame for Ruby's death squarely at Verity's door.

Smith drew himself up tall. 'I made one stupid mistake. Some friends had stolen copies of the papers and I was too weak not to look. Too scared of failure. But I'd studied. I could have passed on my own. I'm competent, and that's what counts, down in the caves: not bits of paper, but knowledge and reliability.'

'You didn't know pneumonia was common after near drowning. You were ill-informed. Your arrogance could have killed Ruby.'

His face darkened. 'But it didn't. We saved her.'

'You delayed her treatment and getting her to hospital.'

'You only had to look at her to see she wasn't fit to travel. I think she really might have died if we'd made the journey any earlier.'

'Because you'd let her get so ill. I expect you were desperate to keep her away from the hospital until you managed to stabilise her. What would they have said?'

He was shaking with anger. 'That's nonsense. I was in charge and I made the logical decision for Ruby's welfare. I saved her, and Jade was grateful at the time.' Eve remembered Jade had sent flowers. 'I don't know what the hell changed; why she tracked us down and wormed her way into our business.'

'Grief wore away at her after Ruby died. You know she was killed in a road traffic accident?'

He shrugged. 'That's not my fault.'

Eve took a deep breath. She wasn't going to get anywhere by trying to make Smith see sense. 'Verity was going to let you go. You sounded angry with her in the tent.'

'You thought I might have killed her in the hope of keeping my secret? Or out of fury that she was giving me the sack?'

She was silent. Seeing him appear to suspect Rupert had almost wiped him from her list of suspects. But he was manipulative; he could have been acting. She couldn't rule him out.

He shook his head. 'You're crazy. We'd been friends since school. And look at the facts. Her death marks the end of my career. Any other diver leading a team will ask to see my certificates. Even if you hadn't reported me, I'd never have completed the China dive Seagrave's so graciously paying for. I can't risk Verity's replacement checking up on me. I realised that as I drove home, the day of the press conference. I was planning to quietly drop out, with grief as an excuse. While she was still alive, there was a chance I could talk her round.'

His egotism was hard to believe. She felt anger and revulsion on Verity's behalf. If his fury at the idea of Rupert killing her was genuine, she bet it was because the murder had robbed him of his status and carefully constructed career, not because he'd lost a beloved friend.

'Do you think Verity went to Jade's room to try to find out how much she knew? Using the need to get the tent downstairs as an excuse?'

'It's possible. She didn't tell me her plan. She was furious with me but she wouldn't have thrown me to the wolves.'

Though that was certainly what he deserved, regardless of whether he was a killer. 'What did happen, out in Egypt?'

'It was just as I told you. Ruby panicked when she got trapped in a narrow channel between two caves. She flailed around and kicked up the silt so we couldn't see a thing. We managed to free her, but as we were getting her to the surface, she yanked her mouthpiece out. It took us a moment to get the backup regulator in. She'd taken in water and she almost drowned.'

'Why did she pull her mouthpiece out?'

'She said afterwards that she couldn't breathe – thought it was blocked. But we checked and there was no sign of a problem. It could have been her fear at work. Panic attacks can make you feel as though you're suffocating.'

'Wait. How did you get the antibiotics to treat Ruby if you're not qualified to write prescriptions?'

His look was bored. 'If you know who to approach with the right money it's easy enough.'

For all Eve knew they might have been substandard or cut with something. She doubted Smith would care.

He took a step towards her. 'The delay helped Ruby. She didn't *want* to go home. She was desperate to keep what had happened secret and determined not to make us cut the trip short. She hoped we'd keep her on for our next expedition, but we knew diving wasn't the career for her. Panicking like that is simply too hazardous. We sat her down and talked through our worries. There were other things she could have done.' He sounded irritable. 'She hardly spoke after that. And then her symptoms worsened, but she still didn't want to go. It was as though returning to normality represented the end of her dreams.'

Eve remembered Jade saying her father had belittled Ruby's plans of a diving career. She'd persisted, determined to fly in the face of his disapproval; she must have felt he'd won.

But her pleas to stay shouldn't have governed Pete's actions. It had been his job to insist she leave. He was using her emotions as an excuse; he'd acted for his own ends.

His eyes were on hers, as though he could read her thoughts. 'Diving was Verity's triumph, but it was also her weakness. She saw places no one else has ever seen, dared to do what few people do. It's hard to give that up, especially when you're part way through an expedition.' His eyes were on the middle distance.

He was shifting the blame onto his dead school friend. It had all been her fault, apparently. But if Verity had found diving addictive, so had he. He'd lied his way into a job at her side, not bothered to learn about the complications that might occur after an accident that must be typical in their field. And then not acted when he should have, blaming Ruby and Verity for his failings.

And at that moment, Eve thought again of what Jade Piper had said about Smith's efforts to resuscitate the diver. Even if he hadn't pushed her, she could imagine him making that awful split-second decision to let her die.

He was ruthless and addicted to the life he'd created for himself. With her dead, he might have been free to retire quietly, and enjoy his celebrity existence on the back of past glories, avoiding the awkward questions that would have come if she'd replaced him.

Eve was glad he'd have to face the music now, for the fraud at least.

She wondered if Palmer thought he'd killed Verity too. He'd be keen on him as a suspect, since he wasn't a Seagrave. Rightly or wrongly, Pete and Jade would probably swallow up the DI's time, to the exclusion of Rupert once again.

CHAPTER THIRTY-TWO

Eve had spent the first ten minutes after they'd returned from the woods just interacting with Gus: hugging, fussing and talking nonsense. He'd put up with her sentimentality nobly at first, but ultimately abandoned her for an exciting scuffling noise down at the bottom of the garden. It had taken a lot longer than that for the adrenaline of her encounter with Pete Smith to subside. She'd been elated at having escaped her run-in unharmed, but now, she felt low. The thought of Smith's deception weighed heavily on her mind. The chain of events leading up to the previous Friday seemed clearer now, but that didn't bring her any comfort. She was no further forward on the question that mattered: who had killed Verity and Cora? Rupert, with his hot-headed jealousy and despair; Jade, with her searing grief and desperation; or Pete Smith, who'd acted his way through years of his life, fooling everyone? How could she narrow down the options? For a second she thought of the crimes she'd heard about where no one was ever found guilty. How could she rest if that happened in this case?

It was a relief when Viv invited her to the Cross Keys for an evening meal and a debrief. They were working their way down chilled glasses of Sauvignon Blanc and dishes of tagliatelle, topped with rainbow chard, vine tomatoes and Parma ham. The humidity in the air had built into the evening, but had now broken into a heavy summer downpour.

'So it was chance that led Pete and Verity to discover Jade's relationship to Ruby?' Viv said.

'That's right.' Eve sipped her drink. 'And then guilt led Pete to panic; his paranoid behaviour made Verity suspicious and her tenacity led her to the same web page I found.' Once again, Eve felt a bond with the diver – imagined her scanning the same information, felt the rush of heat she must have experienced when she realised the truth. That terrible sense of betrayal. 'I think that's one line of falling dominoes that could have led to Verity's death.' She paused a moment, rationalising her thoughts. 'I'd come to the conclusion that Smith might be innocent when we were face to face.' Eve explained the look of shock and anger in his eyes when he'd seemed to suspect Rupert of Verity's murder. 'But now I'm not so sure.' She was used to judging people for her articles and the medic was just the sort to lie convincingly: confident and amoral. 'Smith claims he wouldn't have killed her because his career died with her; no one else would have employed him without checking his qualifications. But in reality, it's clear his professional diving days were over anyway. He'd never have talked Verity into keeping him on, and when she replaced him, the gossip and rumours would have started. Whatever he says, he had a very strong motive for murder.'

'So he's right up there with the others?'

Eve sipped her wine while she considered the question. 'My gut instinct tells me he's less likely than Jade or Rupert. He seemed genuinely confused when I suggested Cora might have been to see him, which puts the theory of her blackmailing him in doubt.'

'So that gives you a bit of a steer.' Viv wound some tagliatelle round her fork.

'But I might have missed something, and I'm still stuck with both Jade and Rupert as strong possibilities.'

'Equally likely?'

Eve sighed. 'Rupert still comes top for me. He was influenced by a separate chain reaction in the run-up to Verity's death: the chance photo shoot, meaning her scent ended up on Pete's jacket, which was detected by Cora Seagrave, on the lookout for ammunition to smash Rupert and Verity's relationship apart.'

'Yes.' Viv finished a mouthful. 'Her sniping must have pushed all his buttons. I can well believe he's guilty.' She gave Eve a look. 'It's harder to imagine Jade as the killer.'

Eve shook her head. 'You didn't see her when she came to visit. What happened to her sister sent her emotions spiralling out of control. Clinging on to her charity work is all that's holding her together, I think. And if Cora knew she was guilty that final reason for her continued existence was under threat. Darn it!' She put down her wine glass. 'It's just so frustrating. I feel like a bee trapped in a jar. The way ahead looks clear, but each direction I turn I hit a barrier.' She sighed. 'I need proof. I'm just going to have to keep digging for all I'm worth and hope something slots into place. I've still got fundamental questions about Verity, and if I don't know her properly that's going to damage my chances of working out who killed her.'

Had she really loved her fiancé, or had she been marrying for money? Diving had steered her life, yet the vicar hadn't questioned her fondness for Rupert, and he was a perceptive man. And Verity hadn't struck her as the sort to make that kind of compromise. Eve had always felt surprised at the idea she'd have an affair with Pete Smith and her feelings had been justified. But hunches weren't enough. If there had been a practical side to her decision to marry, had she felt guilty about it? Conflicted? After all, she'd been so independent – in favour of a person standing on their own two feet. It was clear Rupert had been prepared to sell land, which might have helped fund her adventures, but had she wanted that?

Her reflections pulled her up short. She must have shifted in her chair and Gus stirred at her feet. 'I've just thought. If Verity *wasn't* relying on Rupert to fund her dive in China, she must have made alternative plans. She wasn't the sort to leave anything to chance.' Pete Smith would probably know if she'd approached other sponsors, but he was hardly likely to help her now.

'I'll google as soon as I get home. Verity was featured in celebrity magazines all the time. If she's been photographed drinking with any millionaires lately it might provide a clue.' She'd need to check who'd sponsored her past dives too, in case she'd approached them again.

'Great idea,' Viv said. 'Blimey, I bet DI Palmer isn't looking into all these—'

Her words were interrupted by a commotion in the entrance to the Cross Keys. Gus looked up and barked, which he hardly ever did when they were in the pub. Hetty was standing too, on high alert.

A weather-beaten man wearing a long dark raincoat entered the pub, looking over his shoulder at a younger guy behind him. They were mismatched, Mr Rough followed by Mr Smooth, who wore an open-necked white shirt and chinos, and carried a smart black umbrella, which dripped onto the floor.

Jo had been on her way out from behind the bar to deliver food to another set of customers. Eve watched her eyes fall on the men and open wide for a second before they narrowed. She recognised at least one of them, Eve guessed, and wasn't pleased to have them in her pub.

The rugged guy – who must be around sixty or so – had a roguish grin and ought to have been attractive, but there was something mean in his eyes. He looked faintly familiar, even to Eve. The younger guy followed him closely, an eager smile on his lips.

'Walter.' Jo nodded at the first man as she skirted past with her plates of food.

'Ain't seen you in ages, Jojo,' the guy said. 'Just as generous in your welcome as ever, I see.'

She didn't reply. The men were at the bar now, and Eve looked questioningly at Viv, who frowned and gave a tiny shrug.

Matt and Toby Falconer were both on the bar this evening, but Matt walked away as the men approached. Toby's expression told Eve he'd like to have done the same.

'Walter. How've you been keeping?'

The man gave a rough laugh. 'How'd you think? After the way I was treated, it hasn't been easy. This gentleman's buying.'

The presentable guy stepped forward.

'Mine's a double whisky.' The man called Walter grinned. Eve had the impression he'd been drinking already.

'And a tonic water for me,' the second guy said.

Viv raised her eyebrows. The whole pub seemed to have gone quiet and the tension in the air rubbed off on Eve as she devoted herself to her food. Why did the name Walter sound familiar?

A moment later, the pair took a table not far from theirs. In any case, it wasn't hard to hear their conversation. Walter's voice was raised. He'd definitely drunk too much.

'Oh, yes,' he said, 'there's a lot I could tell you.'

Maybe the presentable guy was a journalist. But Walter? She ran through all the information she'd gathered recently.

The man she assumed was a hack put a restraining hand on Walter's arm. He probably wanted to signal that he should quieten down. If the guy was after a story, he wouldn't want Walter to tell it to the whole pub.

But the double whisky had been a mistake.

'They got rid of me quick enough when they thought I was in the way. Same with Cora, I guarantee it. Cuckoo in the nest, that one. And the rich, they get away with murder, don't they? The police will brush it all under the carpet.'

'Please, Mr Cotton!' his companion said in hushed tones.

Of course, he was Ivy Cotton's husband. The man who'd been sacked by Sir Percival when Sylvia had pointed out the bruises Ivy had been trying to hide under her make-up. Poor woman. And now here he was again. Was he looking to get his revenge on the family and make a fast buck by selling his story to the papers at the same time?

No wonder the Falconers hated the sight of him. Jo was approaching their table now.

'Carry on like that and you'll get yourself sued *and* thrown out of this pub!' she said to Walter Cotton.

He leaned back in his seat. 'Ah, you're a darlin', Jojo. Always were, with that sweet tongue of yours.' He held up his hands as Matt came out from behind the bar. 'All right, all right. I'm not making trouble.' He turned to the journalist, who had shrunk back in his chair and was avoiding everyone's eyes. 'I should talk to my old woman, Ivy. The family don't count us as human. That means they forget when we're there, listening in. A housekeeper gets to know a lot, and although loyalty goes a long way, I'll bet I can get her to talk. She probably knows a thing or two. Nice and close to *some* members of the family she was—'

At that moment, Matt and Toby – and in fact the journalist, who appeared to think he'd bitten off more than he could chew – escorted Walter Cotton from the pub.

Toby met Eve's anxious eyes on his way back in. 'Don't worry,' he said. 'I'm going to call Ivy right now – and Sir Percival too, just to warn them Walter's back in town. We'll all look out for her.'

Back at home, Eve sat on one of the couches in the living room, her mind full of Walter Cotton's words.

Now, she faced up to the thoughts rushing round her head. 'Heck, Gus.'

He looked up at her questioningly.

'I think it's fairly clear what Walter was implying about Ivy at the pub.' *Nice and close to* some *members of the family she was...*

'I mean, we all know Sir Percival's a "giddy old goat".' Could Ivy Cotton have had an affair with him? Tilly said how good he'd always been to them. And he'd thrown Walter Cotton out, quick sharp. It was the right thing to do, but had there been an element of self-interest too? He might not approve of the classes mixing, but the marriage of his son and heir was a very different matter to a secret dalliance of his own. Eve had a feeling men like him made up their own rules.

She felt a creeping sensation shiver its way down her spine. 'What if Tilly is Sir Percival's child and not Walter Cotton's?' She'd have a claim to the hall. Eve thought back to what she knew about Cora's murder. Robin said Ivy had gone home early that night, because she felt unwell. Tilly had been at the hall, but Ivy could have been anywhere. Eve had entertained the idea of the housekeeper as the guilty party before, of course, but only as an outside possibility. If Ivy and Percival had been lovers, it put a whole new spin on things. And as she'd concluded previously, Ivy being responsible would sure as heck explain why Tilly had kept quiet about what she'd seen the day Verity died. If she knew her own mother was guilty, she'd definitely clam up, while suffering with her secret knowledge.

'It can't be true!' Gus looked startled at her vehemence. 'I could just about imagine her pushing Verity in a moment of complete madness, but Cora?' The idea of the kindly, anxious housekeeper beating the woman she'd known from a child, then leaving her to drown, seemed impossible. But she made herself consider it. 'What if Ivy's resentment built up? Maybe she heard Rupert and Verity talking about selling the land around the hall, and felt powerless to stop them breaking up the estate. She might have felt Tilly had just as much right to it as Rupert. And then she could have killed Cora in desperation, if she believed she was about to talk Rupert into developing the hall into a hotel. In framing Rupert she'd have played her final card. There'd be no one left to run the estate but Tilly.'

Maybe she hoped her daughter might inherit the place eventually. Perhaps she could challenge Sir Percival's will when he died, armed with a positive paternity test.

Ivy had spent much of her visit that morning protesting Rupert's innocence. She'd seemed terribly concerned, but the effect had been to highlight the lies he'd told.

Eve lay in her bed that night, staring sleeplessly at the ceiling. Surely it couldn't be true.

CHAPTER THIRTY-THREE

Eve felt exhausted on Sunday morning. In the end, she'd resigned herself to wakefulness the night before and got up in the small hours to do the research she'd planned. She'd gathered details of Verity Nye's past sponsors, and wealthy individuals she'd associated with recently. With a list of people the diver might have approached to fund the China expedition, she'd whizzed off a few emails, making tentative enquiries. Her role was useful; she could ask if they'd seen Verity recently, which would invite them to reply with some context. There was no need to demand delicate details on things like sponsorship straight off.

She'd managed a couple of hours' sleep afterwards before rising early and walking Gus on the heath. Back at Elizabeth's Cottage, she was deep in thought when her mobile rang, making her jump and Gus leap up. Robin Yardley's name was on the screen, which unnerved her. He wasn't in the habit of ringing.

'Robin?'

'*I've just heard from my contact. Percival Seagrave's been killed in a hit-and-run, out along the lane that leads from the hall to the coast.*'

She felt the strength drain out of her at the news. 'When?'

'*This morning. He walks that way every day, apparently, so assuming this isn't some horrific coincidence, it looks like our murderer knows his habits.*'

Eve's body was covered in goose bumps. This narrowed the field all right, but not in the way she'd wanted or anticipated. It had to be someone from the Seagrave camp after all. Killing Cora was one thing – Eve could still see Pete or Jade being involved – but the hit-and-run meant being on the spot in the early morning, ready to take a chance if conditions were right. Because once again, it was an uncertain way of killing someone, just as Verity's fall had been. Had the murderer acted on the spur of the moment, losing control after seeing Sir Percival leave the hall grounds in the usual way?

Who was responsible? Could Percival have worked out that Ivy Cotton had a motive for killing Tilly's rivals, if Eve's guess about the estate manager's parentage was correct? If he'd accused Ivy, she might have panicked and rushed to eliminate the threat. Or had he been killed by his own son? 'Do you know if Rupert's still at the hall?' Her mind flitted to the suggestion that Percival had made a pass at Verity. *A giddy old goat…* Maybe Rupert was striking out at anyone who'd threatened their relationship – remorse making him look for others he could blame. Or perhaps his father knew he was guilty, and had been wavering about how to handle it. Everyone said how fond he'd been of Cora.

'*Yes, he's still there, I gather.*'

'Was Percival killed outright?'

'*No. They reckon the driver knocked him down, then reversed up.*'

She could hear the shudder in his voice. 'How awful.' Surely Ivy wouldn't have done that. It was so utterly brutal.

'*It's a lonely road but it was still a risk. It goes without saying, but whoever's doing this is way out of control. I'll call or text when I get any new information. Eve?*'

'Yes?'

'*I'm heading out of Saxford. I've got business that means I need to be in London.*'

She failed to fill the pause. She was wondering what he was up to, and about the phone call she'd heard him take in her garden. What was so private?

'*But I'll keep you up to date,*' he went on. '*Don't take any risks.*'

'I won't.'

She meant what she said. She'd walked into danger before; she wasn't about to do anything stupid. But five minutes later, when Belinda Seagrave called, she realised his instructions weren't as straightforward as she'd thought.

'I'm so sorry for your loss,' Eve said when she realised who it was. Lady Seagrave's tone hadn't altered at all. If anything she sounded harder and more controlled than ever. Eve had interviewed people who regarded it as very low to show their feelings and maybe that was the case with Belinda, but she wasn't sure.

'I'm not calling for your sympathy. I know your article will reflect on me and my family. After Percival's death it's imperative I talk to you here at the hall today. I have information to pass on, and a request to make.'

Eve wanted to know what Belinda might say, but she objected to being ordered about. Lady Seagrave might be used to people taking it, but she hadn't been brought up in the same old-world system and she wouldn't be bound by it.

'I'm afraid it's not convenient. Perhaps you could tell me what's on your mind over the phone?'

'I'm a doubly bereaved woman, and you're telling me you can't spare twenty minutes of your time? I wonder what Icon *magazine would think of your behaviour. After all, you're representing them. And the police? Detective Inspector Palmer warned me you'd overstepped the mark in the past.'*

This was pure blackmail. What could be so urgent? Maybe she'd heard about Walter Cotton's loose talk the night before. It would give her a motive for Sir Percival's murder if she thought he'd been unfaithful, though Eve couldn't imagine her being so uncontrolled.

There was a moment's silence.

If Eve wanted to know what was on her mind, now was the time. She guessed the police would still be around. It would keep her safe.

'Okay. I'll come right over.' She didn't want to risk waiting until the officers had gone again.

CHAPTER THIRTY-FOUR

As Eve approached Seagrave Hall she saw that DI Palmer was standing outside, next to a patrol car, talking to a pair of uniformed officers. She paused and reversed back into the lane. She could park a little further on, where she'd pulled up when she'd come to look round the estate.

Her decision took her closer to the scene of Percival Seagrave's death. Beyond the turning she needed, the lane was cordoned off, and Eve could see CSI vans and officers in white overalls beyond the barriers.

She parked and locked her car, then cut back towards the hall along one of the woodland paths.

By the time she reached the edge of the trees, Palmer and the officers he'd been talking to had moved on. She breathed a sigh of relief. She wanted them around, but not in her path; her conversations with the DI seldom ended well. He'd be all too keen to clip her wings.

A moment later, she was standing on the doorstep of the hall, looking up at the imposing building with its sombre windows.

It was Ivy Cotton who let her in. Eve tried to keep her expression even, hiding her suspicions. The moment their eyes met the woman burst out crying. She wiped furiously at her tears, and pulled a tissue from her dress pocket. 'I'm sorry. Excuse me.'

She seemed a lot more upset than Belinda Seagrave. But if she'd gone out and mown down her ex-lover, that would be a natural reaction. Still, Eve baulked at the idea. The person who'd committed these crimes was angry, brutal and ruthless. She just couldn't match that description with Ivy.

'Please don't apologise. You must all be in a state of shock, and it's devastating news. I'm so sorry to call at a time like this, but Lady Seagrave—'

'I know,' the woman said. 'She told me she'd called for you.' Mrs Cotton stood back to let her in, then escorted her down the reception hall.

'Did Lady Seagrave explain why she wanted to see me?' Eve was almost too tense to make conversation; her throat was dry.

Ivy took a deep breath. 'No. But I wonder…' She broke off, then restarted: 'I had a call from Toby Falconer at the pub last night. My Walter's back in town.' She darted Eve an anxious look and flushed. 'You might have heard.'

That news *could* have led Ivy to talk to Percival, if she'd thought a past affair was about to come out. And then maybe he'd realised the motives she had for killing Verity and Cora – and challenged her.

Eve tried to conjure up the scene but found it hard. 'I was at the Cross Keys yesterday evening too,' she said, after a moment.

The woman's hands flew to her face and she came to a standstill, part way down the hall. 'Toby was too polite to mention it, but I can imagine the sort of things Walter's been saying. He could never credit that Sir Percival and I had a proper, professional relationship. He wanted to sling mud, to make himself feel better and for me to look bad. But Sir Percival, God rest his soul, would never have crossed that line. And nor indeed would I. Walter was a bad husband, but I was never a bad wife.'

Her face was a deep pink. Eve could see the thought of the gossip was more than she could bear. Her gut instinct was firm; this wasn't a woman who'd have slept with her employer. She was too upstanding, and too dignified.

'I understand.' They started to walk on again. 'Has Lady Seagrave finished with the police for the time being?' Eve would hate Palmer to appear at the wrong moment.

'Yes, though they're coming back later,' Ivy said. 'They've gone off to the site where Sir Percival was… where he was… killed.' She took a shaky breath. 'I was over here, preparing their breakfast when it happened. I saw him head off, just as usual. I don't always work Sundays, but I had yesterday off, when I came to see you, so I was on today.'

Eve could still smell bacon, eggs and toast in the air. It was something fact-based to back up her feelings: how could Ivy have managed to produce breakfast if she'd been out killing her employer? She longed to ask if Rupert had been around, but knowing he'd been absent wouldn't prove anything. At that hour, he could claim he was still in bed or taking a shower.

'Rupert's car hasn't been moved, that I do know,' Ivy said, as though reading her mind. 'I saw it on the drive as I came in, and it was in the exact same position later. The police don't think it's been used this morning and there are no dents on it.' She shook her head.

It was clear those facts hadn't been enough to banish her worries about the man. Why was that?

They'd reached the door to the drawing room.

Belinda Seagrave stood up to greet her, then watched without speaking as Ivy Cotton retreated, closing the heavy panelled double doors behind her.

'I understand our ex-employee, Walter Cotton, is back in the village and out to make trouble. A friend called me last night, after hearing him make a spectacle of himself – in the village pub of all places. Do you know about this?'

'I was there.'

'My friend was under the impression he was with a journalist. With your position in the media, I want you to find out the man's name and put us in contact.' Eve opened her mouth to speak but Lady Seagrave cut across her. 'You owe it to me. You've insinuated your way into my household, and who knows what you'll write about my son's late fiancée. With the press involved, time is of the essence. Percival's death will be all over the tabloids and if they get hold of Cotton's nonsense, they'll have a field day. I want the journalist's name. You recognised him? Or you'll find out.'

'Lady Seagrave, I have no idea who he was or how I'd track him down.' She'd met people like Belinda before. They were used to getting everything they wanted and couldn't accept that some things were out of reach. 'Whoever he was, I'm sure he won't report old rumours and hearsay. You'd be able to take legal action.'

'And I would, without hesitation. The whole story is utterly ridiculous. Believe you me, I'm not a fool. If I'd ever seen the slightest indication that Percival was moving in Ivy's direction she would have followed Walter Cotton, out of her cottage and off the estate.'

No repercussions for Percival, Eve imagined.

'I'm aware my husband showed his appreciation for attractive women. Men do; it's their way.'

Eve bit her tongue.

'But he never went further.'

Looking into her eyes, Eve didn't doubt her. She was ruthless. She'd never have kept Ivy on if she'd suspected her, and she'd have been vigilant, Eve was sure. And on reflection, she couldn't imagine Sir Percival being any good at subterfuge.

Lady Seagrave's words crystallised Eve's thoughts on Ivy. Her character had always made an affair with Percival seem unlikely, let alone the murders.

'And what of Verity's obituary?' Lady Seagrave asked. 'What will you write about Rupert?'

'I'm afraid I haven't drafted it yet.' It was against Eve's rules to discuss the contents in advance with contacts of the deceased. She needed to tell the truth, not be influenced by people with an axe to grind. 'But my focus will be on Verity herself: her experiences, feelings and achievements.'

Despite Eve's reassurance, Belinda Seagrave's hands twisted in her lap. She glanced out of the window for a moment towards the front drive and Rupert's car. Like Ivy Cotton, her thoughts seemed focused on him. Yet the police didn't think his car had been involved in the hit-and-run. Surely that should reassure them?

It was only as she left the room that the realisation came to her.

Rupert wouldn't have had to use his own vehicle. When Tilly Cotton showed her round the estate, she'd pointed out the garage where he kept his collection of classic cars. There was no way he'd have tried to run his dad over in a proper vintage model, but she doubted Rupert would collect that sort. Something like a classic Jaguar from the seventies; that would probably match his aesthetic. What if he'd used one of those, and the police didn't yet know about his garage, deep in the woods? They'd discover its existence eventually, Eve guessed, but maybe not before Rupert had managed to get rid of the car.

Her palms felt sweaty. She wondered where he was now. As Ivy Cotton let her out onto the gravel driveway she looked for Palmer, or anyone from his team, but they'd vanished. She could go to the CSIs out in the road but they were focused on collecting evidence. She needed someone who was coordinating the effort.

As she retreated along the path that led back towards the woods and her car, she pulled her mobile from her bag. Glancing over her shoulder, the house looming large behind her, she called the police control room. They assured her they'd get a message to the right person on the ground. She presumed they meant Palmer. *The right person…* Well, at least she'd done her job. She doubted Belinda would have mentioned the garage, given her desire to protect her son.

Eve was just nearing her car, close to Tilly and Ivy Cotton's cottage, when she heard a noise deeper in the woods.

Voices. Or a man's voice.

She strained to hear more. Not just someone calling, but hasty footfalls on dry twigs, the pace quickening…

She dashed forwards. It was instinctive. Between the trees she could see Rupert Seagrave, hurrying more urgently as the figure in front of him increased their speed. He was hastening after Tilly Cotton, who was flushed and tearful. As Eve watched, she broke into a run, shouting at him to leave her alone.

'I won't,' Rupert yelled back. 'Not until you talk to me!'

Eve's legs felt like jelly. There was no time to get help. She couldn't call Robin – he was miles away in London, and he'd never have reached them in time in any case. Even the CSIs in the lane were too far away. Rupert was closing in on Tilly. Eve had always been afraid for her, wondered if she'd seen him push Verity, but she'd never been sure. There'd been multiple suspects and no proof. And now, a man who was clearly out of control was racing towards his quarry.

She started to dial 999, but it wouldn't be in time. If she stopped long enough to explain it could be too late. She followed, as quietly as she could. If Rupert lashed out, she'd have to distract him.

CHAPTER THIRTY-FIVE

'This is insane!' Rupert shouted as he ran, his voice shaking in time with his feet hitting the hard, dry ground.

Tilly looked as though she was flying, her blonde hair streaking out behind her. Eve guessed she spent her whole life rushing the length and breadth of the estate. Her fitness was paying off. She reached her cottage ahead of Rupert and flung her front door open. She must have left it unlocked. If not she'd never have managed to escape before he caught her. She ploughed inside and slammed the door shut against him.

'I didn't kill him! I didn't kill any of them!' He was hammering on her door with his fists. Desperate. Angry. 'Let me in. I just need to talk!'

With a glance over her shoulder, Eve started to edge backwards. If she reached a safe distance, she could call for help now that Tilly was locked inside her house. But as she reversed, Rupert slumped against the cottage door, gave it one last hammer with his fists, let out a howl like an animal and started to retreat himself.

Eve shrank behind a tree. He was so close to her, but his eyes were glazed. Maybe his mind was on his father's body, out in the lane, or the lies Cora had told about Verity, or the way he'd doubted the fiancée he'd loved with a passion.

She only realised she'd been holding her breath when she started to feel her chest go tight. She took a deep lungful of air and strained to see where Rupert was now. He'd reached the edge of the woods.

She glanced back at Tilly's cottage. Would she come to the door if Eve knocked gently, and showed her face? Then they could go straight to the team out in the lane, so she could tell what she knew at last. Eve remembered her reluctance to talk to the police last time she'd visited. She'd been convinced she was safe. That she wasn't in danger from the killer. But she probably hadn't guessed they'd strike again. And then Cora had died and still she'd said nothing. She hadn't been sure of the truth at that stage, Eve guessed. She'd still wanted to protect Rupert – couldn't really believe in her heart of hearts that he'd murder his cousin.

But now? Surely now was the time. Not one but two more deaths.

She had one more careful check to make sure Rupert had really gone, then walked over to the cottage and knocked lightly on the window.

'It's only me, Tilly,' she called softly. 'I saw what happened with Rupert. Do you want to talk about it?'

The woman's pale, tear-streaked face appeared at the window. For a moment she just stood there, but at last she disappeared from sight again, and a second later, Eve heard her unlocking the door.

The estate manager stood back to let her in. Her eyes were red-rimmed, her hands shaking. 'Are you sure he's gone?'

Eve stepped inside. 'Sure. He went off towards the house.'

Tilly caught her breath. 'Do you think my mum and Belinda are safe?'

'I think so. There are still lots of police around, and they're together.'

Tilly shut the door behind Eve and locked it. 'If he doesn't know you're here I bet he'll be back.'

'I won't leave you. But Tilly, we need to talk to the police now, and tell them what you know.' What exactly was that? Eve wondered. Were her fears still a strong suspicion, or did she have proof?

The woman put her hands over her face. 'It's just so hard! We've always been like siblings.'

Except when you dated, Eve thought.

'I know it's weak of me, but I kept hoping the police would find proof of their own, so I wouldn't be the one to betray him.'

Eve took a deep breath. 'I can understand that.' She thought of Rupert's garage full of classic cars – perhaps containing the one that killed his father. 'And maybe they would, in time.' They might even do it that day. 'But there are three people dead now, Tilly. It's too dangerous to wait. Whatever you know, or think you know, it's best to just lay it all before them, and let them take it forward.'

Tilly put a hand over her mouth.

'Are you okay? Do you want to sit down?'

'I just feel a bit sick.'

'I'm not surprised. Maybe take some deep breaths.' She tried to damp down her impatience to get outside and sound the alarm. Rupert had no reason to go and attack his mother or Ivy Cotton, and a fourth murder when the place was crawling with police would be crazy. He hadn't persisted with his attempts to get at Tilly. 'Do you want me to get you some water? Or a coffee, to steady your nerves? You can take some time and then we can go out to the CSIs. They'll know who you should speak with. I'll be with you; I can tell them what I saw.'

Tilly sank into a chair. 'Okay. Thanks. A coffee would be good.'

Eve went into the kitchen at the rear of the cottage. It was tiny, but beautifully well kept. The taps gleamed, and the butler sink was spotless. Someone had oiled the wooden worktop regularly so that it was unmarked by the water that must splash onto it every day.

Eve found a coffee pot, added water to the bottom chamber and grounds to the top one, then lit the gas under it. Her heart was still pounding unnaturally hard. Adrenaline from the sight of Rupert chasing Tilly, combined with the fight ahead. Tilly had to go to the police now, and Eve needed to make sure she did.

She adjusted the gas and glanced around the kitchen. All the Cottons' cooking equipment and ingredients must be stowed away in the cupboards. A wicker basket in one corner held incoming mail. The top item was a letter. She wasn't meaning to pry, but one word caught her eye as she waited for the coffee to brew.

Vineyard.

Eve remembered Simon saying how innovative Tilly was as an estate manager. She'd asked him if he knew anything about the wine-making industry. He hadn't been able to help, but he'd been confident she'd find the information elsewhere.

It looked like he'd been right.

The coffee was bubbling now. Eve hunted in the hand-crafted wooden kitchen units for cups and saucers and grabbed the sugar container from the counter too. Even if Tilly didn't normally take it, she might be glad of some, under the circumstances.

As she fetched milk from the fridge, and put everything on a tray, ready for when the coffee finished brewing, she thought again of the letter about the vineyard.

It set a tiny, nagging feeling going in her brain. Something jarred, but what? There was a growing unease, deep in her chest. What was she reacting to? Memories of her last visit to the cottage filtered through her mind.

Tilly had had magazines on the table that day, conspicuously open at the jobs pages. She'd rushed to tidy them away, but then admitted she was looking for another role. She said she'd never intended to stay at Seagrave Hall long-term.

And yet…

Eve stepped quietly over to the post basket again and glanced at the date on the letter about vineyards. It had been written five days earlier. Looking more closely, Eve saw it was from a consultant who could provide the right expertise on developing a wine-making business at Seagrave Hall. The letter included terms and conditions. Legal stuff.

It wasn't a response to an initial enquiry. Tilly had everything she'd need to seek approval for the project from Belinda – and until that morning from Sir Percival, who'd applauded her work as estate manager.

Maybe she'd been on the point of putting the case for the development when Verity was murdered. That – and her suspicions about Rupert – could have triggered a sudden decision to leave her job.

Except she'd told Eve she'd been planning to move on for a while. She'd said Rupert marrying Verity seemed like the perfect time to go. The couple could hire a new manager of their choosing and she wouldn't feel too guilty for abandoning them. She'd implied she was looking forward to gaining her freedom.

But the letter about the vineyard told Eve otherwise.

As the coffee bubbled on, the hairs on the back of her neck rose. Had Tilly left the magazines out for her to find on purpose? And gone on to highlight her apparent intentions for the future, in case Eve had been too restrained to sneak a look at the pages she'd been reading?

What did it mean?

CHAPTER THIRTY-SIX

The more Eve thought about it, the more certain she became. Tilly's job hunt had been for show. It was the only solution that fitted the facts. Her mind fogged at the urgency she felt. She had to work this out, and quickly.

She adjusted the gas. She needed the coffee to take more time. If the job hunting had been a fiction – to make her seem more detached from the hall – what else had been staged, and why?

It came to her in an instant, and as realisation swept over her it felt like someone trickling iced water down her back.

She could have acted seeing Verity fall.

There was nothing to say she'd really been looking up at the window just as the diver pitched forwards.

She thought back to the scene. At first there'd been silence. Just the shock of what had happened. Then everyone had talked at once – confusion, clamour, people rushing forward from all directions, staring at the place where Verity lay. It was a while before Dylan Walker called out that Verity had been pushed.

Time enough for Tilly to get downstairs, slip out of one of the hall's many doors, round behind the zombie-like crowd, and overhear what the boy shouted.

Eve imagined her thought processes. She'd been seen! What the heck could she do? No wonder she'd looked so scared. And then she'd acted her part – so well! Made it look as though she'd witnessed the whole thing, and that something had worried her. When asked, she'd said, with a tremor, that she'd seen nothing – but she'd chosen her words carefully. (*No. No, I don't think so. Verity filled the window.*) She'd meant everyone to think she might be lying. And she really had been, but not in the way they'd thought.

Eve tried to remember what Robin had said about her supposed whereabouts at the time of the fall. Hazily, it came back to her. She'd told the police she'd been sorting out a loose stake, to stop a tent collapsing. Claiming she'd been crouching down was a good option. She'd have been below people's eye level; it wouldn't seem odd if no one remembered seeing her. But if she'd been focused on a loose stake, why would she have been looking up at the window? Her story didn't hold water.

Eve's icy chill gave way to a rush of heat. She tried to keep her breathing steady, but she already felt dizzy. She needed to focus – to check the facts.

It was all right. Tilly had an alibi for Cora's murder. Eve must be wrong about her.

But as she wrestled with the fact, she wondered what it really amounted to. Tilly had spoken with the Seagraves senior when she'd arrived at the hall that evening, then disappeared into her office to make phone calls. Belinda and Percival said they'd heard her talking when they went to the lavatory, close to her room.

On reflection, wasn't that just a little bit convenient? What kind of business calls had to be made during the evening? What if Tilly had set up a recording of her voice or something? The Seagraves were unlikely to interrupt her if they could hear she was mid-conversation. Maybe she'd locked her door to be on the safe side, then climbed out of the window. Her office faced the woods directly…

It was possible. Horribly possible.

Other small details fell into place: the way she and Tilly had 'stumbled' on Belinda Seagrave advising Rupert not to talk to Eve, for instance, when Tilly had taken her into the hall to find him. It had convinced Eve that Belinda either thought or knew her son was guilty. But it must have been Tilly who'd told Lady Seagrave that Eve was there, and why. She'd raised the alarm, set up the cameo, then left Eve to make assumptions.

And then Ivy had let on that she'd heard Tilly advising Rupert to lie about where he was when Verity was killed. She remembered Ivy's words. *I overheard her talking to him. I didn't mean to. I was by one of the stalls just after Verity's fall, and I thought she'd seen me.* Tilly had seen her mother all right. And deliberately left another false clue. It made Rupert look guilty, and Tilly look protective. It seemed she'd tried to frame him from the start.

With a crawling sensation down her back, Eve wondered if even the chase minutes earlier had been a set-up. Everything had been quiet as she'd walked back to her car. The footfalls and shouting had begun suddenly, when she was close by. Tilly probably knew Eve had been summoned; it was the kind of news her mother would share. Had she been talking to Rupert about his father – expressing her sympathy maybe – when Eve approached? It would have been easy enough to engineer the scene after that. Tilly could have hurled accusations at him suddenly, acted scared and let him do the rest.

She thought of Rupert's words. *This is insane.* And the way he'd protested his innocence.

But if all this was true, why delay going to the police to report him? The answer came instantly, as she framed the question. Tilly wanted to plant seeds of doubt in everyone's minds, but not to stick the knife in directly. It was too unsubtle. Rupert knew he was innocent, and that it was Tilly who'd advised him to lie, despite that fact. And now she'd acted scared around him, her actions coming out of the blue. As it was, he'd probably write that off as a result of the emotionally charged atmosphere of distrust at the hall. But if she reported him, he might start to question her motives. And once he did that, the estate manager was seriously vulnerable. Refusing to betray him was a good way of putting Rupert off the scent.

What about Tilly's motivation? She'd lived in the cottage at Seagrave Hall since she was small. It was her home, just as much as it was Rupert's and Cora's. Eve thought of the day she'd shown her round the estate. Her love for the place was clear. She remembered the way she'd patted the wall in the attic, almost as though the hall was a living thing. And she had big plans to turn the estate around, while preserving it as a grand family home.

Both Verity's proposal, to sell off swathes of estate land, and Cora's to rent it all out, would make her meaningful work redundant and leave her plans in ruins. And she could easily have overheard them discussing their ideas, or had them reported back by Ivy, who was busy at the hall, day in, day out.

Framing Rupert also fitted. He'd told Eve the status quo wasn't an option with the estate; if Tilly didn't want him taking control when he turned thirty, she'd needed to move quickly.

But there was more to this. Something she wasn't getting. Why had she killed Sir Percival? She'd seemed fond of him and vice versa. He'd probably have been Tilly's best route to getting the vineyard plans approved too. He'd likely have given her a free hand if Rupert ended up in jail.

It didn't make sense. She must be wrong.

But somewhere deep inside, she felt a thrill of pure terror. Her gut told her she was in danger.

The coffee had stopped bubbling. Tilly would notice the quiet. Eve had no idea how long she'd been. She needed to act fast.

She went to transfer the coffee to the tray, but her hands were shaking so much she spilled some of the liquid. This was no good. She had to stay calm. Tilly mustn't spot her anxiety. If only she could text to raise the alarm, but her phone was in her bag in the other room.

She scanned the kitchen desperately, looking for something to help her escape. She had no pockets in her dress – nowhere to hide a weapon.

There was a kitchen timer. Was there any way that she could… She heard footfalls coming towards the room and acted in an instant, not knowing how things might play out.

A second later she met Tilly in the doorway.

'Did you find everything you need?' She seemed calmer now.

'Yes thanks!' Eve's voice sounded falsely bright. The cups on the tray rattled in their saucers as she manoeuvred into the living room, towards the table. She tried to smile, but Tilly's eyes were on her, and in them there was a tiny, knowing flicker.

CHAPTER THIRTY-SEVEN

Eve set the tray on the table in the living room, trying to seem normal. Tilly's gaze never left hers.

'Milk?'

'No thank you.'

She must work out her options. If only she could keep calm… She snatched a look at the door, but the sight sent her heart rate into overdrive. It was bolted now, the key missing.

In a second she realised her bag had disappeared too.

Tilly's eyes were still on her. 'You took so long, I went to see if you were okay. You can watch people through the gap between the door and the frame. You were staring at the post basket. You seemed so preoccupied. And then you looked scared and you turned down the gas. After that, I came back through here and got ready. I couldn't be sure you'd guessed, but I wasn't going to take any chances. When I saw your hands shaking, I knew I'd made the right call.'

'It's not too late, Tilly.' But Eve knew she didn't sound convincing. Three people were dead. It was way too late. 'If you let me go, it could affect your sentence.'

But Tilly shook her head. 'I don't know where Rupert is, but I'll bet you suspected him. Others do too – my mum for one. Even Belinda's worried. She knows he was in the hall when Verity died and that he lied to the police. Assuming he's not sitting quietly with Belinda in the drawing room at the hall – and I doubt he is – I can probably pin your death on him. It's a chance I'll have to take. I can still make this work, even if it's not the future I'd anticipated.'

Eve tried to make sense of her words, but it was impossible to switch off her panic. Think – she must think. Where did Sir Percival fit in? If she could find some answers it might shock Tilly into talking – and more talk meant more time. It was something she desperately needed.

Tilly stood up and reached into a cabinet at her side, without taking her eyes off Eve. She drew out a shotgun. 'There are advantages to living on a rural estate.'

Eve swallowed. 'The police will hear if you use that.'

'I haven't seen any officers in the woods. They've been up at the house and down in the lane.'

'That means they'll come here next.'

She shook her head. 'I'm not stupid enough to kill you here unless you make me.' She glanced at the gun. 'This is just to make sure you drink your medicine.' She stuck her free hand into her dungarees pocket and drew out a pill box. 'Four of these should do it.' She dropped them into Eve's coffee.

How long had she got? She didn't even know if she'd set the kitchen timer correctly. She'd been so scared back there. If it came to it, should she risk trying to break a window to escape? It would be crazily reckless for Tilly to fire a gun when the police were around.

'Why did you kill Sir Percival?'

Tilly's grasp tightened on her weapon. 'I hated him!'

'I thought – I thought you got on okay.' But maybe he'd worked out she was guilty… just like her.

'Oh yes, he was so supportive!' Tilly's eyes were full of fury. 'Booting Walter out, giving me the estate manager's job when I was barely out of school uniform. Ma liked him so much she even called me after his mother. Isn't that sweet?'

And until now, Tilly had seemed to love Percival too – despite his questionable behaviour on occasion. Why hadn't she been angry when he put his arm round her at the fete? Was his behaviour so habitual that she'd stopped noticing? She'd been there so long. Like part of the family. She said she thought of Rupert as a sibling – now, at least, though they'd once been in a relationship…

Tilly's expression was bitter. 'Time for you to drink up.'

But Eve was shaking as a wave of realisation washed over her. The rumours about her mother and Percival didn't have to be true. It was what Tilly believed that mattered. 'Oh my goodness… You thought Sir Percival was your father.'

'Stop it!' She shrieked the words out. 'I can't bear to see your pity. Drink your drink!'

Eve dared to lean forward. 'You thought your mom had had an affair – that that was why Percival kicked your dad out. And why he promoted you so young. You didn't mind him hugging you. You thought he was being fatherly. And your mom accidentally fed into your fantasy. But she called you after his mother because she liked and respected Percival, not because you were his child.' She'd seen Matilda's photo at Sylvia and Daphne's house, but she'd never made the connection. Of course, it shortened to Tilly.

The woman's eyes were wild. 'I first heard the rumour about Ma and Percival when I started to date Rupert. One of the villagers made some snide comment when they saw us together at the pub. I thought it was just spite – based on imaginative local gossip – but then Percival spotted us kissing by the stables and took me aside. He said our relationship was "unwise under the circumstances". I put two and two together: we were half-siblings. Percival put a hand on my arm and said: "You do understand, don't you?"' Tilly's knuckles were white. 'So I ended the relationship, but I didn't want to betray Percival's trust by explaining why. For ages Rupert wouldn't leave me alone – endlessly asking why I wouldn't see him. He was so weak and needy. I came to hate him. And then at last he took up with Verity, and they were set to ruin my family's estate. If they didn't, then Cora would. I was convinced Percival would stop them if he could – for my sake – but I was worried he didn't know what they were up to. I only knew because of what Ma had overheard. Percival would have had no way of keeping control once Rupert hit thirty.

'It was when I saw Verity, leaning out of the window, struggling with the tent, that I realised I could solve the problem. It was a split-second decision to kill her. It had to be. But once I'd taken that first step, all my other moves fell into place.

'With Cora out of the way as well, and Rupert imprisoned for two murders, it would be logical for Percival to name me as his heir instead. I was sure he'd want to. I needed to wait for a suitable chance to kill Cora: a time when Rupert had no alibi. In the end my hand was forced. The pair of them came back from London chatting. It was clear they'd made up, and it was essential Cora died before that got out. I wanted everyone to think Rupert had been full of hate for her on the day she was killed. But luckily, he was tired after the trip down south. As it happened, he went to bed early, so even his parents couldn't vouch for him.' She seemed to feel no guilt.

'How could you kill three innocent people?'

'Innocent? Cora and Verity were like vermin, set to destroy an old and precious thing they'd no right to. I knew I could turn the estate around if I had control, but Rupert was blinded by love and guilt into going along with their wishes. It was my job to exterminate them – wipe out the threat they posed.'

'And what about Sir Percival?'

Tilly's face was chalk-white. 'I always thought I was his favourite child. That was how he acted. I was convinced he'd acknowledge me once his other dependents were out of the picture.'

'How did you find out he wasn't your dad?'

Tilly flinched. 'He was up early this morning, petting one of the horses at the stables, and I saw him there. I knew he hadn't been sleeping well since Cora died and I wanted to comfort him. I might have killed her, but I didn't like watching him suffer. I was tender, and he hugged me. And then I called him Dad. It seemed like the right time.' Her eyes were wide. 'He pulled away as though he'd been stung and asked me what the hell I was talking about. I couldn't believe the look of horror on his face. He didn't care a rap for me. I was a servant. He took advantage of my affection – felt it was my duty to give it.' She took a shuddering breath. 'It was then that I understood why he'd split me and Rupert up. I was simply too common for his son. Good enough to flirt with, easy on the eye, but not *Seagrave* material.'

Eve remembered Ivy saying he hadn't approved of Verity at first, because of her lowly background. If she hadn't been famous, maybe she'd have been warned off too.

Tilly thumped her hand on the table. 'I was so angry. I'll be delighted to see Rupert convicted of the murders and I'm not sorry I killed any of them. They didn't deserve control over a place like Seagrave. It's precious and they played with it. Percival with his extravagant spending, Verity with her proposed sell-off, Cora with her stupid hotel—'

The kitchen timer rang out, loud and sudden in the other room.

In that split second, Tilly recoiled. Eve knew it was her only chance. She threw her hot coffee in the woman's face, then lunged for the flimsy-looking window. There was no way she could break down the door.

She thought of Tilly behind her, momentarily blinded, the gun by her side. What if she fired?

She launched herself onto a chest of drawers under the window. The glass was leaded – the panes far too small to climb through. She shoved desperately at the catch but it wouldn't open. A small pin locked it in place.

Tilly hadn't risked a shot, but she was behind her, pulling her legs, dragging her back into the room. Eve grabbed a metal vase from a bookcase next to the chest of drawers and swung it behind her. As Tilly yelped with pain and loosened her grip, Eve smashed the vase forward, pummelling the leaded panes for all she was worth.

Tilly was pulling at her legs again. Eve grasped the locked catch and dragged herself forward, smashing the glass once more.

Suddenly, in the distance, she could see movement. Police – going in the direction of Rupert's garage. Responding to the call she'd made a short while earlier. She rammed the vase against the window again. This time, the leaded structure came away from the window frame.

'Help!'

DS Boles – the detective Robin Yardley knew – had heard something. His face turned for a second in the direction of the cottage.

'Help!'

Palmer was looking now, a tetchy expression on his face. And then suddenly they were all running. Eve kicked out behind her. She was wearing low heels, but she'd summoned more strength now, knowing she only had to hang on a minute longer.

'It's over, Tilly!' She kicked once again. 'It's over.'

CHAPTER THIRTY-EIGHT

It was Monday morning at Monty's and another fine day. Viv's son Sam had propped the front and back doors open, and a gentle breeze stirred the mild air. Eve was meant to be working a shift, but after spending the previous day escaping a triple murderer, then being grilled by the police, Viv had ripped up her weekly schedule. Sam, Kirsty and Angie had come to the rescue.

'Just don't almost get murdered in the autumn, will you?' Viv said. 'Sam and Kirsty will have started uni by then.'

Eve produced the required eye roll. 'I'll try to remember.'

Sam arrived at their table, which overlooked the lush green back lawn and the River Sax. 'Here we are.'

They'd ordered exquisite miniature citrus and honey cakes, decorated with cream-cheese icing, edible flowers and orange zest. (Viv normally recommended her chocolate intense selection in the aftermath of near-death experiences. 'But if you're going to make a habit of it, we need some variety and in this heat, fruit makes sense. Fresh flavours for a fresh start.') Sam put them on the table, along with a pot of Darjeeling.

'So,' Viv said, after they'd thanked him, 'how are you feeling?'

'Weird. Dumb. I don't know. I was so convinced that it was Rupert. He seemed to have motives for all three murders.'

'You couldn't possibly know Tilly thought she was his half-sister.'

'All the clues were there, if I'd looked. And that was just a detail. The key thing was her passion for the hall, really. It was her childhood home. Poor Ivy.' The appalling truth of what she must be going through was all-engulfing. 'And she's on her own now.'

Viv reached out a hand and squeezed Eve's. 'There's no denying it's appalling, but she's not on her own. Moira has the details.'

'Of course she does.' Eve had ceased to be surprised by the extent of the storekeeper's information gathering.

'She got the latest from Molly Walker. Apparently Ivy's younger sister's turned up from Norwich. She'll be there every step of the way. Once the trial's over she wants Ivy to go back home with her. She runs a bed and breakfast, I gather, so if she goes, they'll be there for each other and Ivy will have the business to focus on. It's small comfort, but it's something.'

Strong support and a new mission. Viv was right; it might help her through what had happened.

'I wonder what Rupert will do with the hall. All the memories associated with it…'

'Moira says—'

'She can't know that! All this only happened yesterday!'

Viv laughed. 'No, I know. But apparently Rupert's told Ivy she can stay on at Seagrave Hall if she prefers.'

Eve was pleased. She bet Belinda wouldn't have made that offer after what Tilly had done, but maybe her son was finally pulling free of her, making his own decisions. A process he'd started with his engagement to Verity. He'd wavered after her death, full of confusion and grief, but it sounded as though his independence was reasserting itself now. 'He'll have to make changes to the hall to save it,' she said. 'He told me that much.'

Viv nodded. 'It'll be interesting to see what he does.'

'Maybe I'll find out his plans. I want to visit him as soon as possible. He might still think Verity was unfaithful to him. And that Cora lied about smelling Verity's scent on Pete Smith's jacket. At least I can reassure him that his fiancée loved him, and that Cora was genuinely mistaken, however low her motives were.'

'It's good to think of him getting some closure.' Viv sipped her tea. 'So what's next for you? Have you written the obituary yet?'

'I'm a bit behindhand, what with one thing and another.'

Viv tutted. 'Slacker.'

'It wasn't just the murders that held me up. I hadn't fathomed Verity out, but I had an interesting answerphone message when I got back from the police station yesterday.'

Viv raised her eyebrows.

'It was in response to an email I sent to her previous sponsors and wealthy contacts, to see if any of them had heard from her recently. A guy called Monty Farquhar responded.'

'Seriously? What a name! And you called him back?'

'Of course.'

'You never let up, do you? You must have been exhausted by that stage.'

'But I was curious – I'd never have slept if I'd left it until morning. It turns out Verity had been in discussions with him about the China dive for a couple of months. He was on for backing it; they were just sorting out the details. My guess is the thought of Rupert underwriting her adventures hadn't even crossed her mind; she was used to operating solo. It's something else I'll be able to tell him when I visit.'

Eve enjoyed jigsaw puzzles. She got a thrill putting in the final piece. Talking to Monty Farquhar had been like that, but a hundred-fold better. Everything made sense. All Verity's observable actions fitted with the judgements Eve had made about her character. She knew what she was going to write now.

'So you're sorted then,' Viv said.

'Pretty much.' She still had a few questions for Robin Yardley, but she couldn't tell Viv that.

CHAPTER THIRTY-NINE

Robin was back in Saxford and had invited Eve over once she was free. Viv shooed her away from the teashop, so she walked across the village green and down Dark Lane to see him. She was more than keen to hear any reports he had from Greg Boles, but his trip to London was also on her mind – that and the phone call he'd taken in her back garden. What was going on? Were things on the move for him? Could he be thinking of leaving Saxford? An odd sinking feeling dragged at her chest.

He opened the door, which led straight into his low-beamed kitchen, calm, cool and shady in the heat of the summer's day. She stepped over the threshold as he stood back.

'Coffee? Or something iced?'

'Something iced sounds great, thanks.'

He closed the door after her and went to the fridge, fetching some of the still lemonade she liked. He half-filled two tall glasses with ice, then poured the chilled drink on top and added slices of lemon.

'I didn't have you down as a lemonade man.'

A very slight smile crossed his lips. 'I've seen it at Moira's before, then I noticed you bought some when I last came to garden for you.' He handed her a glass.

Had he got it in specially? 'Thank you.'

'How are you?'

She shrugged. 'I felt like the biggest jerk yesterday. Once I'd stopped feeling terrified, that is. You told me who had alibis for Verity's murder. Tilly wasn't one of them; she'd just tried to provide herself with one and I fell for it, big time. I can't believe the clues I missed. Viv's brother told me about Tilly's plans for the future of the estate. It was clear she was in it for the long haul, but I still didn't question it when she claimed she was looking for a new job. And she asked me if I was sure I'd seen nothing when Verity fell. She had such a scared look in her eye. I thought she was afraid Rupert was guilty, and I might know it. But she was checking where she stood.' She shook her head.

'Having Belinda and Percival swear she was in her office when Cora was killed muddied the waters.'

'How did she fake the calls they overheard? Had she left a recording playing in her office?'

'Not quite. She hadn't much time to prepare, I guess, so her solution was more immediate. She created a new Skype account on her phone, then launched a call to her office PC before climbing out of her window. After that she proceeded to perform a one-sided conversation which was broadcast into the room. Reception around the hall happens to be good, which she knew, of course. And it meant she could keep an eye on what was going on, back in her office. If she'd heard a knock she could even have responded, and asked her visitor to come back when she'd finished her call.' He was very still for a moment. 'She's not making any secret of what she did. My contact says she seems proud of herself. Apparently, she muted the call for long enough to sneak up on Cora and attack her, then started broadcasting again as she watched her drown.'

'That's horrific. What was the murder weapon – do the police know?'

He nodded. 'They think they do: one of the mallets she used the day the fete was set up. They need to look for trace evidence and cross-check it with Cora's injuries, but it's clear Tilly tried to hide it. It was wrapped in cloth at the bottom of her filing cabinet, underneath veterinary records for the horses.'

'So after she'd waited to check Cora was dead, she went back to her office again?'

Robin nodded. 'She climbed back in through the unlatched window.' Their eyes met. 'It wasn't a coincidence that Ivy Cotton went home early that evening, feeling unwell. Tilly gave her something. She wanted her home and asleep, to avoid any chance of being disturbed. Their cottage is close to the pool.'

Eve shuddered. 'That's so ruthless, but I can believe it.' After all, she'd thrown Cora's belongings into the pool after her. A reckless act when she must have been in a hurry. It spoke of passion and hatred. 'She talked about getting rid of Cora and Verity as being like ridding the estate of vermin.'

'My mate says he has to walk outside each time they finish a session. She makes his skin crawl.'

They sipped their drinks in silence for a moment. 'Has he passed on any other details?' Eve said at last.

'Some. It helps that Tilly Cotton's told them so much. It sounds as though her fury and bitterness mean she's letting rip.'

'I can imagine that.' Eve reviewed the details she still wanted to clarify. 'What about the day of the fete? I remember her offering to help Verity bring the tent down, but she said she could cope on her own. And then, I suppose, in true estate-manager mode, Tilly decided she should follow her up anyway, in case she found the thing heavier than she'd thought. She was overseeing the whole event; she took her job seriously and minded about her work. As far as she was concerned, she was better placed to look after the hall than anyone.'

Robin nodded. 'That's the story she's telling. Verity had a head start, and by the time Tilly went looking for her, to check she was okay, she was already back down from the attic. Tilly says she was about to call out to her when she saw her enter Jade Piper's room. She was curious, so she walked down the corridor and peered round the door. Verity was glancing round the room, apparently.'

'That figures. You've probably heard about Pete Smith's guilty secret?'

Robin nodded. 'My mate said you uncovered it. Nice work.'

She felt a blush come to her cheeks. 'Thanks. So, given Pete wasn't qualified, he was getting seriously worried Jade would find him out. He was so paranoid Verity spotted there was something wrong, got suspicious and did some digging herself. That was when she found out he'd lied to her.'

Robin nodded. 'It sounds like she was scanning Jade's room to see if she could get a clue as to what she knew. Pete was the one who lied, but if it had come out, it would have affected her future too.'

Eve sighed. 'Yes. She should have checked his paperwork, but they were such old friends she didn't think she needed to.'

'From what Tilly Cotton says, she probably went into Jade's room on a whim. It doesn't sound like she did a proper search; maybe she regretted her spontaneous plan as soon as she was there. Either way, she still decided to throw the tent out of the window. Maybe she heard movement out on the landing and that forced her hand. It was her excuse for being there if she got caught, and Cora had suggested the method in everyone's hearing.'

And it would have been Tilly's footsteps that Verity heard. If she hadn't followed Verity upstairs, the diver might never have been in such a risky position. It was terrible to think of the way things had played out. Sometimes your future really did turn on a dime. Eve pictured the scene. 'Then Tilly, who'd genuinely gone up to help, saw her chance, presumably. She'd been viewing her world through a distorted lens. She felt if she got rid of Verity she'd save the estate.' Eve imagined the woman standing there, absolutely quiet now, watching the diver open the window. And Verity, busily acting out her reason for being there, unaware that the person she'd heard on the landing was now just feet behind her. She shivered.

'That all sounds right. And the police reckon that's when she put her sunglasses on. It was a precaution, just in case she was seen. She might have tucked her hair out of the way too – but the police have no way of confirming that.'

Eve remembered Dylan Walker's description. *Big shiny black eyes.*

'She claims she was wearing the sunglasses when she went inside, but who wears shades indoors, when they've just come in from the glare of a summer's day?'

'She's trying to suggest she didn't pause to think before pushing Verity? Will it make a difference?'

Robin sighed and lifted his shoulders. 'Very little, I'd say, especially given the other killings.'

'How did Percival's murder work?'

Robin took a swig of his drink. 'Although you got the wrong person, she *did* use one of the classic cars from Rupert's collection to kill him. She knew where Rupert kept the keys. As the estate manager, she had the run of every inch of Seagrave land. One of the cars had clearly been in a collision and the tyre marks matched those on the road. She'd wiped the steering wheel, but after she'd been caught red-handed preparing to kill you, she gave up trying to frame Rupert. She was so angry about Sir Percival that it all came rushing out.'

'Why the heck did he walk out in the lane, rather than through the woods?'

'It's a good question. Maybe the village grapevine might provide an answer to that one.'

Eve made a mental note to see if Moira Squires knew. There was a chance someone would have supplied her with the information. 'So how was London?'

He cocked his head, his blue-grey eyes on hers. 'You overheard that phone call at Elizabeth's Cottage, didn't you?'

She didn't want him to think she was nosy, but he was too intelligent not to spot the signs, so she nodded.

He half rose to reach a newspaper that sat on a pine dresser to one side of the table, next to the chimney breast.

DI Robert Kelly missing, the headline read.

DI responsible for lifting lid on high-profile police corruption has not been seen since Wednesday.

The paper was around eleven years old. 'That's you?'

He nodded. 'I'm like you. Once I suspected there was something amiss in my local team, I couldn't leave it alone. But that made me a lot of enemies, from my corrupt colleagues in the force to their criminal contacts. I had a girlfriend back then. She started to get threats.' *Back then?* 'And I couldn't get the evidence I needed to shut the operation down. It was like trying to cut the mould out of a block of Stilton. I'd find one main channel and think the job was done, only to discover another patch.'

'So you left to start afresh?'

He nodded. 'It was affecting people I minded about, so I decided I had to. But I'm still involved. I'm in contact with anti-corruption officers, helping covertly with research. I couldn't turn my back on it. And once in a while they want me in person – at a meeting, or to look at a line-up of suspects. It's a long while back now, but I saw things that mean I can still be useful.'

'It must have been hard – to walk out of your life.'

'I don't have much family.'

'But the girl…'

'We were never meant to last.'

She sat back in her seat. 'You worked with Greg Boles?'

A flicker of a smile crossed Robin's lips. 'I should have guessed you'd have discovered his name. You tried to find out about me by looking into his past?'

This wasn't good. Eve felt the colour rush to her cheeks.

'I'd be disappointed if you hadn't.' There was laughter in his eyes. 'No. Greg and I were never on the same team. He's married to my cousin.'

'Oh!' It was weird somehow, to think of Robin in a family context. She'd always seen him as a loner.

'And Jim Thackeray?' She'd often wondered why the vicar knew more about Robin than other people.

'He officiated at Greg's wedding. When I arrived in Saxford, Greg asked if he could tell Jim my history. He knew he'd be discreet, and he'd help me settle in. People trust me because he does.'

It made Eve think of the twins' teasing.

'Do you still think you're in danger from the criminals your colleagues worked with?'

He shrugged. 'I don't think they'd bother trying to trace me. But if I used my real name, and it became obvious where I was, or someone spotted me, and mentioned me to a contact in this neck of the woods? I don't know. The name change was necessary to start with, and now I'm stuck with it. And I love gardening.'

'You do a wonderful job.'

He gave a mock bow from where he sat. 'Thank you.' Then his eyes turned serious. 'I'm sorry I wasn't there when you ran into trouble with Tilly Cotton.'

'Well, even though you multi-task, you're not actually a police officer any more, and you were off doing something important.'

'Yes. But I wish I'd been there.' His eyes were on hers.

'Goodness, you look very cheerful, Eve!' Moira put her hands on her curvaceous hips. 'I thought you'd be in an awful state after yesterday. And what a thing to have happened! Poor Ivy Cotton!'

Eve had decided to drop into the village store on her way home, in case there were any extra details to pick up.

'Now, you must tell me—' Moira's lipsticked lips moved at double-quick time.

'Actually, Moira, I was wondering what *you* could tell *me*,' Eve said quickly. 'You've probably heard all the news on the grapevine. The police weren't at all chatty when they interviewed me.'

The storekeeper leaned forward and beamed. She might be disappointed not to get more details from Eve, but passing on gossip would be the next best thing. 'Well, of course I'll help if I can.'

'It's just a tiny thing, but it's been bugging me. I know Sir Percival was killed walking down the lane towards the sea. And I gather he uses that route every day. But why would he do that, when he could walk through the woods, on his own land?'

A smug smile spread across Moira's lips. *She knows! How on earth?* Eve hadn't had much hope of an answer.

'Ah well, of course, lots of people have been going over the facts since it happened,' she said.

She'd still worked fast. Maybe she'd scoured the village for news.

'A little bird told me he used to walk through the woods every day, but his wife objected. There was some gossip about him using that route so he could "pass the time of day" with that monster Tilly. And I must confess, I'd seen him being a little… overfamiliar with her, shall we say?' She shook her head and smiled.

Eve closed her eyes for a moment and thought of the dead man. Tilly's actions had certainly been monstrous, but that didn't make Percival's behaviour acceptable. He'd abused his position and seeing Moira laugh it off left her feeling mad at the world. But things were changing – slowly.

'Anyway,' Moira went on, 'I don't suppose there was anything more to it, but when Belinda Seagrave makes her feelings known on a topic, people tend to take action. And of course, Percival was already in her bad books after spending money on that racehorse. I ask you! So I imagine he did what he could to keep her sweet.'

'Ah! That makes sense. Thanks, Moira. I'll just take the milk then, if I may?'

Within five minutes she was home (a triumph!). An hour later she was checking her submission for *Icon* magazine, as Gus pottered round the dining room table, peering up at her with pleading eyes.

'Two minutes! Promise!'

VERITY PRUDENCE NYE, ADVENTURER, EXPLORER AND CHARITY AMBASSADOR

Verity Nye, known for her technically demanding and boundary-pushing cave dives worldwide, has died at the age of thirty-two. A woman has been arrested for her murder.

Nye was brought up in a strongly religious household, with puritanical values, and quickly found herself at odds with her father's outlook on life. What he saw as self-aggrandisement, she saw as using the skills she'd been given to explore some of the most inhospitable places on earth and extend human knowledge. Her bravery and independence meant she broke free rather than buckling. Those qualities also led her to conquer the challenges involved in her chosen field, from raising all her own funding to managing life-or-death emergencies underwater.

Her upbringing instilled a fierce self-sufficiency, and a belief that leaning on others made both individuals weaker. Yet when someone won her trust, she put her faith in them, on occasion too completely. At the end of her life, she discovered the betrayal of her colleague, Pete Smith, who took the post of medic on her team fraudulently. However, her trust in her fiancé, Rupert, appears well-founded. They were very much in love, and he gave her the space she needed, while providing an anchor when she was on home ground.

Nye's career necessitated quick, rational thinking. She didn't shy away from speaking her mind, even when it might cause hurt. Though she saved the life of her team member, Ruby Fox, in an act of heroic bravery during a dive in Egypt, it seems Fox never got over her failure to stay calm when things went wrong. It's possible that Nye's uncompromising attitude played a part in that, though no one can know for sure. Practicalities were more important to her than diplomacy. That said, she was always true to her beliefs, honest about her feelings and touched the lives of many people with her inspiring achievements.

Eve still wasn't happy with the opening. She'd give it another go before she sent it off. At least Kim Carmichael had come back already, to approve the section where she was mentioned.

Eve needed to contact Jade Piper too, to update her before the details she'd uncovered went public. After all Eve's research, she could believe Verity might have lost her temper with Ruby immediately after her accident, but she couldn't imagine her being deliberately cruel following that first rush of anger. She'd tell Jade that, for what it was worth. Her evidence was the way Verity had treated Tilly Cotton and Jade herself. She'd been irritated with each of them but tried to make up for her short temper within moments. But it was still probable her sharp words had affected Ruby. The girl had been in a vulnerable state and it sounded as though she'd been bitterly disappointed that she'd panicked. The pneumonia couldn't have helped either; her delayed treatment had probably made a difference. Eve laid that at Pete Smith's door.

The police would try him for fraud, but maybe Jade would take action against him too. If she did, Eve had no doubt she'd plough any proceeds back into Wide Blue Yonder. The memory of her class of girls, out on the deck overlooking the sea, came back to Eve. She'd felt their strength.

'Walk, Gus?'

Her beloved dachshund leaped about excitedly and then rolled over.

'All the treats at once, right?' She crouched down to tickle his tummy. 'C'mon then.' She stood once more. 'Let's go!'

A LETTER FROM CLARE

Thank you so much for reading *Mystery at Seagrave Hall*. I do hope you had as much fun working on the clues as I did! If you'd like to keep up to date with all of my latest releases, you can sign up at the following link. Your email address will never be shared, and you can unsubscribe at any time.

www.bookouture.com/clare-chase

I got the idea for *Mystery at Seagrave Hall* when imagining the tensions that might erupt if a proud old family with an inflated sense of its own worth was challenged by the arrival of a newcomer with very different ideas. I find families and the way the class system endures in pockets of society fascinating. This book allowed me to explore both.

If you have time, I'd love it if you were able to write a review of *Mystery at Seagrave Hall*. Feedback is really valuable, and it also makes a huge difference in helping new readers discover my books for the first time. Alternatively, if you'd like to contact me personally, you can reach me via my website, Facebook page, Twitter or Instagram. It's always great to hear from readers.

Again, thank you so much for deciding to spend some time reading *Mystery at Seagrave Hall*. I'm looking forward to sharing my next book with you very soon.

With all best wishes,
Clare x

@ClareChaseAuthor

@ClareChase_

www.clarechase.com

ACKNOWLEDGEMENTS

My best love and thanks as always to Charlie, George and Ros for the pre-submission proofreading, encouragement, and cheerleading. And the same too, to Mum and Dad, Phil and Jenny, David and Pat, Warty, Andrea, Jen, the Westfield gang, Margaret, Shelly, Mark, my Andrewes relations and a whole band of family and friends.

And then, crucially, huge thanks to my brilliant editor Ruth Tross for her clear-sighted clever ideas and enthusiastic help. I'm also more than grateful to Noelle Holten, for her superhuman promo work. Sending thanks too, to Peta Nightingale, Kim Nash, Alexandra Holmes, Fraser, Liz and everyone involved in editing, book production and sales at Bookouture. I can't imagine being published and promoted by a better or nicer team.

Thanks to the fabulous Bookouture authors and other writer mates for their friendship. And a massive thank you, too, to the hard-working and generous book bloggers and reviewers who take the time to pass on their thoughts about my work. It makes a huge difference.

And finally, thanks to you, the reader, for buying or borrowing this book!